PRAISE FOR DAVE EDLUND

"**Edlund is right at home with his bestselling brethren**, Brad Thor and Brad Taylor."
–Jon Land, *USA Today* bestselling author of the *Caitlin Strong* series

"**compulsively readable**"
–*Publisher's Weekly*
Praise for *Lethal Savage*

"**a near-perfect international thriller**"
–*Foreword Reviews*
Praise for *Guarding Savage*

"**required reading** for any thriller aficionado"
–Steve Berry, *New York Times* bestselling author,
Praise for *Hunting Savage*

"**Crackling action**"
–*Kirkus Reviews*
Praise for *Deadly Savage*

JUDGMENT *at* ALCATRAZ

a Danya Biton novel

JUDGMENT *at* ALCATRAZ

a Danya Biton novel

DAVE EDLUND

Durham, NC

Judgment at Alcatraz (a Danya Biton novel)
Dave Edlund
www.petersavagenovels.com
dedlund@lightmessages.com

Published 2021, by Light Messages
www.lightmessages.com
Durham, NC 27713
SAN: 920-9298

Paperback ISBN: 978-1-61153-384-2
Ebook ISBN: 978-1-61153-385-9
Library of Congress Control Number: 2020950845

To my brothers Tom and Jac…
thank you for a lifetime of friendship
and fond memories.
I love you guys..

ACKNOWLEDGEMENTS

WHO WOULD HAVE KNOWN that my first exposure to the thriller genre around 1979 would have had an impact on my life that is still being felt? The book was *Raise the Titanic!* by Clive Cussler, and it ignited within me a passion for the genre. I suppose it was inevitable that one day I would begin writing, and my inspiration is readily traced back to the Grand Master. Sadly, Mr. Cussler passed on February 24, 2020 in Scottsdale, Arizona. Thank you, Mr. Cussler, for your gifts of story to all readers, but in particular to me and the wonderful path of discovery it has led me down—a journey that is far from over.

Writing and publishing a book is not a solo endeavor, far from it. From research to the process of assembling the publication-ready copy, a lot of people with a wide range of skills are engaged, and their contributions are invaluable.

Let's begin with the research. As much as I enjoy suspending belief when I read thrillers, there has to be (in my opinion) a strong element of factual grounding. In *Judgment at Alcatraz*, my long-time friend and explosives expert, Judd Holiday, advised on the shock sensitivity properties of various types of dynamite. Mr. Holiday has 17 years of experience as a bomb tech at the Energetic Materials Research and Testing Center at New Mexico Tech (sounds like the kind of job I would enjoy), and the scenes herein involving explosives have passed his scrutiny. Thank you, Judd, for sharing your expertise.

I am very fortunate to have Light Messages Publishing in my corner, as they have produced and published the Peter Savage series and now are backing me as we venture into this new series. Words cannot express my deep level of gratitude to the entire team, and most especially to my editor, Elizabeth, who never ceases to amaze me at her uncanny ability to catch what at first appears to be the tiniest of details, when in fact it is a big deal. Thank you, Elizabeth, as your skill, experience, and attention to detail makes these stories much better. And thank you to Betty and Wally, who handle more of the business routine at Light Messages, for always being responsive and professional, as well as executing the details of book publishing while making it look easy.

Since this is the first full-length novel featuring Danya Biton (pronounced *bit - on*) as the protagonist, there were many thoughtful discussions with the Light Messages team concerning a suitable title. After narrowing the options down to three, we ran a short poll on Twitter and Facebook. As the Fates would have it, it was a fan of my Peter Savage series who boldly rejected the candidate titles we put forth and came up with her own suggestion. This concept won unanimous support from the publishing team and now graces the cover. Thank you, Mona Stephens for your great idea!

I also wish to acknowledge and thank my talented daughter, Mackenzie, for the cover design and artwork.

As much as I love reading and writing thrillers, these stories are for you, the reader. Although Danya made her debut in *Hunting Savage*, and later appeared in *Lethal Savage* and the short story *Deadly Atonement*, my hope is to build a series on her adventures. If you enjoy *Judgment at Alcatraz*, please let me know. Posting a review (Amazon or Goodreads) is also great. Send messages to me through the contacts page on my web site www.DaveEdlund.com, or email me at dedlund@lightmessages.com.

Cheers

—DE

AUTHOR'S NOTE

THREE QUARTERS OF A CENTURY HAS PASSED since the Nuclear Genie was unleashed with twin mushroom clouds over Hiroshima and Nagasaki. Although not forgotten, that horror has faded with successive generations. Peaceful applications of nuclear power followed in the decades after the end of WWII, along with the inevitable accidents—perhaps most noteworthy being the disasters at Three Mile Island, Chernobyl, and Fukashima. And so, with time, nuclear power plants have fallen from favor.

Although there is still debate about where and how to store radioactive waste from the remaining operational nuclear power plants, the topic is no longer the headline grabber it was in the 70s and early 80s. Even the clean-up of the Hanford Reservation in southeastern Washington—the site where plutonium was made during the Manhattan Project for the atomic bomb nicknamed 'Fat Man' and dropped on Nagasaki—has fallen into relative obscurity.

So maybe it should be no surprise that other nuclear threats are lingering in plain sight. Shocked? You should be.

I was… and am.

To be fair, this question is, in part, a trick question. The most prevalent radioactive isotopes are those used in medical procedures and industrial radiography (examining metal castings and forgings, and welded seams for structural integrity). One of the most common is cobalt-60. Cobalt, in its stable or non-radioactive isotopic form, is a metal used in products ranging from lithium batteries to stainless steels to super alloys that withstand high temperatures and stress—i.e., alloys used in aircraft engines. And most of the global supply of cobalt originates in the Democratic Republic of the Congo.

So, it should be no surprise that cobalt is prized as a recyclable metal. Which is the problem.

You see, slipping in a little cobalt-60 will earn a greater payment from the recycler, but those handling the reclaimed metal have no idea of the deadly material they are processing.

Since the early 80s, there have been several documented cases of cobalt-60 turning up in metal reclaiming centers. In some cases, the radioactive cobalt even made it into newly manufactured products. A particularly notorious case occurred in Taiwan. Between 1982 and 1984, reclaimed cobalt-60 was incorporated into newly manufactured rebar and used in the construction of more than two-hundred residential and other buildings in northern Taiwan and Taipei. The government never took action to condemn the buildings. More than seven-thousand people have been exposed, and most without their knowledge.

In 1983 a resident of Ciudad Juarez, Mexico, attempted to recycle about six-thousand pellets of cobalt-60. The metal so contaminated his truck that the truck was scrapped. In doing so, five-thousand metric tons of steel was contaminated. The contaminated steel was used to manufacture kitchen and restaurant table legs as well as rebar. The contaminated products were transported into the U.S. and Canada. After discovery of the incident, the Nuclear Regulatory Commission installed radiation monitors at all major crossings from Mexico into the U.S.

Other similar incidents with cobalt-60 occurred in China, Thailand, Turkey, India, and Italy, often resulting in fatalities.

In a bizarre case in 2013, a truck transporting a medical cobalt-60 source from a hospital in Tijuana was hijacked near Mexico City. Following a nationwide search, the truck was found abandoned, but the deadly cargo was missing. Fortunately, the cobalt-60 was later discovered in a nearby field. The fate of the thieves was never determined.

Every now and then medical isotopes go missing, either because of errors in record keeping or transgressions in handling the material. However, most radioactive elements used in treatment of cancer or in diagnostics, have relatively short half-lives (the aforementioned cobalt-60 being an exception). This means they quickly lose their lethality.

However, there is another peaceful and common use of radioactive isotopes that has escaped, for the most part, public scrutiny, and yet represents a clear and present danger. I am talking about Radioisotope Thermoelectric Generators—commonly called RTGs.

From the perspective of science and engineering, these are truly elegant machines with no moving parts. RTGs generate electric power from heat, making good use of the Seebeck Effect. The Seebeck Effect describes the production of an electric potential when the junction of two dissimilar metals is heated. Such a device is called a thermocouple, and a group of several thermocouples is called a thermopile. Thermocouples and thermopiles are ubiquitous, but most commonly you would encounter them in your gas water heater and kitchen oven.

If our goal is to generate electric power for a long time (such as a deep-space probe), the heat source is the trick. Decades ago, NASA determined that radioactive isotopes, which produce heat as a byproduct of the radioactive decay process, would make ideal heat sources lasting years, even decades.

Therein lies the danger as well as the potential harm. You see, satellites and deep-space probes are not the only applications requiring reliable electric power for a period of years with no maintenance. A prevalent terrestrial need is remote navigational beacons. And a very large number of such beacons have been deployed by Canada, the U.S., and the Soviet Union (now Russia) in the Arctic. RTGs have also been deployed in Eastern Europe to power remote telemetry stations.

Ordinarily, this would not be a problem at all—provided the machines were periodically attended to, and all units were tracked and disposed of appropriately at end of life.

Perhaps that would have been the case had the Soviet Union not fallen. The chaos of transitioning to a new government, causing social and economic insecurity, created an environment where details easily slipped notice and were forgotten.

RTGs of Soviet or Russian manufacture, using strontium-90 as the power source, are scattered across the far northern frontier and the former Soviet bloc nations of Eastern Europe. And these machines are not secured. Several have shown up in the most unexpected places, like the wilderness in Georgia, 50 km east of the village of Lia. There, in December of 2001, three woodcutters found two abandoned RTG cores. They were not marked as hazardous. The men had no idea what they'd found, but they appreciated the heat emanating from the devices and used them as heaters while they spent a cold night in the forest. Within hours all three men began to display symptoms of radiation poisoning—burns over their backs and hands, headache, dizziness, nausea, vomiting. One of the woodcutters ultimately died from radiation exposure.

Other incidents with RTG cores containing strontium-90 occurred in far northern Russia in 2003 and 2004.

Fortunately, plutonium as a power source has been relegated to deep space missions only, so there is no danger of it being available terrestrially. Still, strontium-90 is extremely dangerous. Chemically, strontium is very similar to calcium, and if ingested, strontium-90 localizes in bone where it irradiates the surrounding tissue. The knowledge that these RTGs are scattered about, unguarded and unaccounted for, is truly frightening.

This is the Nuclear Genie that lives on in the shadows. A vengeful and spiteful genie, ready to bring death upon the unsuspecting.

—DE

June 2020

PROLOGUE

Northern Nevada
Seven months ago

LEWIS BLACKHAWK, A PROUD SHOSHONE, stood tall in the midday sun. He wore dark sunglasses and a wide-brimmed Stetson, the headband discolored from sweat. His weathered face bore the wrinkles of age, but his mind was sharp, and he had the energy of a man twenty years younger. His fingers were adorned with gold rings, while he sported a Rolex Oyster.

He'd made a fortune parlaying earnings from gambling into huge returns on the stock market. And his wealth was the reason he was here in the desert.

Although it was fall, the temperature was already approaching ninety degrees, and it wasn't even noon yet. The elder man looked like he was baking in an oven. A cooling breeze would have been welcomed, but the air was still—ideal, they said, for the forthcoming demonstration.

Despite the heat, Lewis wore black jeans and a turquoise long-sleeved shirt. He removed a water bottle from a cooler and pressed the cold container against his neck before downing the contents in one long swig.

Standing beside him, in a sleeveless cotton shirt and a grease-smudged ball cap, was Leonard Cloud. His hair, the color of raven feathers, was braided into a ponytail that extended to the middle of his back. His skin was bronzed and tight, not yet showing the cumulative effects of a life of sun exposure.

He squinted his brown eyes as he searched the horizon.

“Looks clear. I don’t see any vehicles.”

He didn’t expect to encounter anyone. The land was desolate for miles in every direction, too poor even to graze cattle. But the isolation and clear field of view were ideal for the demonstration he had prepared.

Lewis wiped his brow with his sleeve. “You call yourselves the Indigenous Peoples Movement, is that right?”

Leonard nodded. “That’s right.”

“Catchy, but why not just work with the American Indian Movement? I mean, they’ve been around for a long time. Had a lot of press back in the 70s and 80s. The organization is well-funded, based on what I hear. Why do you need my support to start a new organization?”

It was a fair question, one Leonard had been expecting.

With a wry smile he replied, “The AIM has become too mainstream. They prefer to lobby various congressmen from time to time, producing catchy sound bites to drum up more donations. They refuse to embrace new directives, and they won’t admit that the same old process is doomed to fail, as it always has.”

Lewis squinted and cast an appraising gaze at Leonard.

“And you’re telling me, you know how to effect real change, when everyone else has failed?”

“I’m not just telling you. I know. I’m going to show you.”

Lewis drew in a breath and exhaled. “Okay. Let’s get on with it.”

Leonard smiled. Unlike Lewis, he was acclimated to the desert heat.

The men were standing between two pickup trucks, separated by about fifty yards. In the cargo bed of each vehicle sat a young man holding a radio controller. Lewis had seen this type of controller before. It was used to fly drones, especially the helicopter drones that were popular with hobbyists.

With a swirl of dust, two quadcopters, each nearly three feet in diameter, rose from the desert and climbed to a stationary hover.

Lewis estimated they were twenty or so feet high. The electric buzz sounded like a beehive, only much louder.

Three gunmen, each armed with an AR-style semiauto rifle, were positioned ten yards in front of Lewis and Leonard. Another hundred yards beyond the shooters was a line of orange flags on ten-foot poles. On Leonard's command, the drones flew over the shooters and soon passed over the line of orange flags.

The rules were simple—shoot down the drones, but only once they had crossed over the line of flags. Each pilot was to fly his quadcopter at constant altitude along the row of flags, and they could not return the drones until given the order by Leonard. Each of the riflemen had three thirty-round magazines—ninety bullets each, 270 rounds total. Once all the ammunition was spent, the drones would be recalled—if they were still operational.

As encouragement for the drone pilots and gunmen to do their best, Leonard offered a $500 cash reward to any shooter who dropped one of the drones. The same reward was offered to each pilot if they could return their aircraft safely.

The air lit up with the crack of rifle fire. Lewis jumped at the sound of the first rifle shot, and clasped his hands over his ears. Bullets streamed at the drones. The pilots moved their quadcopters back and forth—fast, slow, sometimes coming to a dead stop, only to race left or right. It was a one-dimensional game. A handicap to the drones, which were not allowed to use either altitude or distance from the shooters to evade the attack. Even so, no hits were registered.

Each gunmen chewed through their first magazine, exhibiting over-confidence, and firing for volume rather than carefully aiming. On the second magazine, they slowed the rate of fire, taking more time to aim. But still no hits.

With the third and last magazine, each rifleman was deliberate. Aim, shoot. Aim, shoot. It took more time for them to empty their last mags than it took for the first two mags combined.

After the last shot and magazines were ejected, both drones flew back to the pickup trucks and landed. Wasn't so much as a nick on either of the remotely piloted aircraft.

Lewis Blackhawk shook his head, a big grin plastered across his face.

“That was certainly definitive,” he said. “I’m convinced those flying machines are dammed hard to hit. But they’re small. What can one or two achieve?”

“Not just a couple,” Leonard said, “but a swarm of drones. All loaded with some of the deadliest shit known to man.”

“A swarm. Like a swarm of bees, huh? And you’re telling me they’ll do more than just deliver a sting, right?”

Leonard nodded, his teeth clenched, eyes narrow slits. Lewis worked his jaw and locked eyes with Leonard.

After an uncomfortably long moment, he said, “I suppose if you have a whole bunch of those little airplanes, a few just might get through whatever defenses the police and national guard throw up.”

“They’re called drones, not airplanes,” Leonard said.

“Sure, sure. Whatever. You know what I’m talking about.”

“And just to be clear on what I’m talking about, you said you would fund this mission if I proved the drones were impossible to shoot down.”

“Yes, sir. How much do you need to bankroll your operation?”

Leonard rubbed his chin as he ran through the mental arithmetic.

“We need at least eight drones with special modifications to carry and dispense the payload. And the radio controllers will need to be modified, too. Plus, a boat. No, two boats. And weapons—”

Lewis reached to his back pocket and pulled out a leather checkbook adorned with silver studs.

“Just give me a number.”

Now it was Leonard’s turn to grin as he shared a six-figure total large enough to ensure a more-than-adequate contingency fund.

While he looked on, Lewis signed the check and then handed it over. But he held firm as Leonard placed his fingers on the paper. Leonard raised his brow.

“This is a bunch of money. I want your assurances that you will succeed.”

Leonard straightened. “It’s a tax write-off. A generous donation to the Indigenous Peoples Movement."

"That's beside the point. It's all money. And if you want me to invest in your operation, then I want your guarantee of success."

"We cannot fail. The government will have no choice but to accept our demands."

"So you say. Many others before you have been equally confident, and yet the United States Government has never accepted the demands of our people. What makes you so confident you're any different?"

"Because if they don't, we will rain death and destruction on their major population centers. The very poisons made by the white man in his never-ending quest for more powerful weapons—poisons that have been carelessly discarded, and are now polluting our ancestral homelands—will be used to turn the San Francisco Bay Area into a radioactive wasteland. Other cities will follow, until they submit to our demands."

Lewis released his grip on the check, the corners of his mouth curling in a broad grin.

"That's what I want to hear. Now make it happen."

CHAPTER 1

Northern Idaho
May 13

THE LITHE FIGURE GLIDED through the conifer forest with soundless steps, her body tense and senses alert. She had honed to perfection the skills of an accomplished hunter…but her prey was not of the four-legged variety.

The steep slopes and lose scree made for treacherous footing. Combined with the over four-thousand-foot elevation, the passing was difficult, as evidenced by the all-too-frequent grunts and curses of her companions whenever their feet slid out beneath them. Bic Turner and his nephew, Eddie Turner, were city slickers, rarely venturing away from asphalt and concrete. Neither man owned a decent pair of hiking boots, and their low-cut sneakers often failed to bite into the soil. They'd be lucky to complete this journey without at least one sprained ankle.

In his early forties, and carrying a bulging belly that added at least forty pounds to his short frame, Bic was a practicing gunsmith and owned a successful business in Portland, Oregon. He had learned his craft over twelve years in the Army, and considered AR-style semiautomatic rifles his specialty. Wearing thick glasses in black frames, and with short black hair and a tiny mustache, his appearance was nerdish.

The physical exertion of the hike was taking its toll on Bic, his round face dappled with sweat, and his pudgy cheeks flushed pink despite the cool spring temperatures and overcast sky. He did not like the idea of making the exchange at a remote location in the wilderness, close to the Canadian border. He'd suggested they complete the transaction at his shop, offering to open the store after hours, maybe on a Sunday or late at night. The buyer had refused, claiming it would be too risky—too easy for law enforcement to stake out the exchange if they got a tip.

"People always talk," the buyer had said.

Despite his better judgment, Bic relented—he really wanted the cash.

Accompanied by a string of eight pack mules Eddie had rented from an outfitting and guide service just outside Bonners Ferry, they had been on the trail since sunrise. Bic and Eddie were at the head of the pack string, while the woman remained off the trail and well to the side where she could keep an eye on the pack animals, as well as watch for any threat—not that Bic or Eddie expected any trouble. That was her job. She had been hired to worry, and to be prepared in case trouble was encountered. And their cargo was of the type likely to attract trouble. Like vultures to carrion.

Clad in layers of camouflage, she carried a custom-made, scoped, bolt-action Nosler M48 rifle with ease. The barrel was long and fluted, and fitted with a muzzle break to reduce felt recoil. If it had been fall, she could have passed for any civilian hunter except for two things. First, she wasn't wearing any hunter-orange garments. The neon allowed easy visibility, even at considerable distance and through foliage.

Second was the weaponry she carried. Strapped to the side of her daypack was a Colt M4 Carbine. Purchased with cash at a gun show in Reno, the semiautomatic civilian version of the standard military assault rifle she had extensively trained with, had become increasingly difficult to find after Colt stopped selling to the public. The camouflage coloration of the stock, action, and barrel allowed the weapon to disappear against the similar pattern of her pack and clothing.

But perhaps the oddest accoutrement she carried was a combat tomahawk secured in a sheath at the small of her back. A wicked and nearly indestructible weapon, the steel handle was forged to the head—a razor-sharp blade opposite a hardened steel spike.

Preferring to stay in the shadows of the evergreens whenever possible, she scanned from side to side with her dark brown eyes, searching for signs of movement or anything out of the ordinary. She was an attractive woman with tanned skin, a high forehead, and long and thin face. Her chestnut hair was gathered up in a ponytail that fell just below her shoulders. Even so, natural waves appeared where the hair crossed over her scalp. Standing at five-foot-five, her muscles were toned from regular workouts, although her loose clothing concealed all evidence of her physical condition. Unlike Bic and Eddie, she moved with agile grace as she glided across the forest duff.

She paused beside the gray bark of a mature pine and peered down the steep slope to observe the pair trudging onward. Each man had an AR-style rifle, assembled by Bic, dangling from a shoulder. They kept their heads down, focused on the trail, oblivious to anything beyond their fifteen-foot field of view. The surefooted mules plodded behind them, stopping whenever one of the men slipped and fell. As fatigue set in, it was taking longer for them to rise back to their feet.

She moved down to the trail and raised her hand to signal a stop.

"Something wrong?" Bic said, between deep breaths.

"No," Danya replied. "Take a break. Five minutes. I'll hold the reins for the pack animals."

Bic and Eddie ambled to a decaying log laying in the shade of several large conifers. They both drained water bottles and threw the empties to the side.

Eddie was a couple inches taller, at least ten years younger than his uncle, and not as heavy, but still overweight by twenty-five pounds. His skin was pasty, and his face dotted with pimples. But otherwise, his facial features carried a distinctive family resemblance. His hair, parted down the middle, covered the top half of his ears in a style that fell out of fashion by the early 80s.

Danya had been introduced to Bic through a mutual contact—an Internet associate who lurked on the fringes of lawful conduct. To his credit, Bic was smart enough to know he was treading into dangerous territory—an understatement, given the business transaction he planned to consummate.

His nephew was the only person under his employ, and Eddie had zero military training. Not encouraging, since Bic was a gunsmith and had never served in combat. Understanding the magnitude of the risk, Bic needed an expert to provide security. The introduction was made through a secure chatroom connection, followed by a face-to-face meeting, and the deal was struck.

"Okay, guys," Danya said. "Time to get moving."

They rose and joined her on the trail.

"You still carrying that radio?" she said to Bic.

He nodded and patted his pocket. "Got it right here. But I haven't turned it on yet. Wanted to save the battery until we get to the meeting point."

"Good. It's okay to turn it on now, and keep it in your breast pocket. You'll *feel* as much as *hear* the sound. I'm going to be ahead of you, and if I see anything I don't like, I'll key the mic twice. If I give you that signal, the two of you stop and find the nearest cover within thirty yards. Stay there. I'll be back for you."

"Wouldn't it be easier just to talk over the radio?" Bic said.

"I'm not supposed to be here, right? It's only supposed to be you and Eddie delivering the weapons to the buyer. Now, if someone sees you standing next to Eddie and talking on a radio, what do you think they'll conclude?"

Bic frowned. "Guess I didn't think about that."

"That's what you hired me for. Now, we need to get moving."

"How much farther to the meeting point?" Eddie said.

She consulted her handheld GPS unit. It displayed a topographic map in sharp detail, with a red dot marking their destination. A dashed line connected the destination to their current location, and the distance was logged on the bottom of the screen—2.3 miles.

"Not far," she replied. "Should be there within an hour. Maybe sooner."

Bic glanced at his watch. "We're way ahead of schedule."

"Not really. We need to arrive well before the buyer is expected. I'll need time to scout the area and set up a defensive perimeter."

"Why?" Eddie said. "We're selling, and they're buying. It should be simple."

"Should be, I agree. But what if they decide they like your merchandise *and* want to keep their money?"

"Oh, I get it. You think they might rip us off."

She looked at Eddie, amazed he could be so naïve.

"The thought crossed my mind," she said. "Which means it's crossed the mind of the buyer as well. Better to be prepared. There's no honor among thieves."

Eddie and Bic started walking, followed by the team of mules, while she hiked back up the slope to gain some elevation over the trail.

Her plan was simple. Arrive at the meeting location early, and scout the area. She'd set up tripwires connected to several homemade antipersonnel mines stashed inside her daypack. Finally, she would secure a sniper hide where she had good visibility and field of fire. From there, she could ensure the deal unfolded as planned.

During their face-to-face meeting, Bic had explained that the buyer was a radical paramilitary group that operated under the name Lawful Americans for Democracy, or LAD. They fancied themselves true patriots, and were signing up new recruits at a rapid pace. When Danya had asked, Bic said he didn't know how many members they had. Later, she did some research on the group. There were plenty of news accounts documenting their leaders advocating to overthrow the current two-party political system on the grounds that neither the Democrats nor the Republicans were truly working in the best interests of the United States and its citizens. But what she found most disturbing were the swastika armbands worn by the members.

A spokesman for LAD had tried to deflect suggestions that the group was a thinly disguised neo-Nazi organization by explaining that the Nazi party was universally misunderstood, and that it should be remembered for its nationalist platform that reinvigorated

Germany's economy following decades of economic depression which plagued the nation after the close of WWI. The Holocaust, he'd claimed, was exaggerated as a public relations campaign of the Allies against the legitimate German government. And the war—well, through the Treaty of Versailles, Germany had the right to re-arm and reclaim lands seized by the victorious Allied Forces.

"Dangerous propaganda," she muttered to herself.

The interest LAD had in Bic Turner turned out to be pragmatic—weapons. But not just any weapons. Believing they had a constitutional right to bear arms equivalent to any available to the US military, LAD was buying thirty select-fire M4 Carbines. Since firing M4 rifles on full-auto chewed through loads of bullets, LAD also ordered forty thousand rounds of ammunition. It took Eddie the better part of two weeks to load the rounds at his uncle's shop, and package them in water-tight storage boxes. To top it off, the neo-Nazi group also demanded at least 250 pounds of high explosives.

After months of searching, Bic finally turned up a deal on three hundred pounds of extra gelatin nitroglycerin dynamite. The seller of the dynamite claimed to have *acquired* it from a mining company in Wyoming.

Filling the weapons order took seven months, and a considerable outlay of cash to purchase the civilian rifles, which Bic modified, not to mention the ammunition components and explosives. He'd been able to convince LAD to front him seventy-five-grand to cover the upfront expenses.

Now, with the mules loaded with close to a ton of weaponry, ammunition, and explosives, he stood to make a nice profit. Enough to move his retirement up by at least ten years.

CHAPTER 2

THE RIDGE DANYA WAS FOLLOWING DIPPED down to a large meadow. She imagined this was a lake at one time. But now the water had mostly receded to a grass-covered plain. All that was left of the lake was a shallow pond ringed by a marsh.

As she descended, her path converged with the trail, and she joined Bic and Eddie.

She pointed forward. "Take the pack train to the edge of the cattails, and unload the merchandise. Stack the crates side by side on firm ground, and don't let the mules enter the marsh if the ground is too soft."

"How will we know if it's too soft?" Eddie said.

Once again she was taken aback by his simplistic thought process.

"Because they'll sink in the mud," Bic replied. "Go on, Eddie. I'll be there in a minute."

As Eddie led the pack mules away, Bic faced her.

"I hope you'll give my nephew some slack. He's a hard worker, and very conscientious. Just not too bright."

She nodded and gazed beyond Bic, toward the younger man following his uncle's orders.

"Does he understand what's going on?" she said.

"He knows we're meeting a group who will buy the rifles, ammunition, and explosives. And he knows he stands to make a good cut."

"Does he know how to use that rifle he's carrying?"

"Sure. He's done a lot of shooting at the range. Pretty good shot." Bic grinned.

"Really. At the range." Her tone oozed sarcasm. "So Eddie knows how to shoot, but does he know how to use that weapon as a tool?"

"Well…I…"

Truth be told, Bic didn't think of guns as tools, but as something merely to be used in sport shooting, or purely for entertainment.

"Yeah, I thought so. Tell me, does Eddie comprehend the risk?"

Bic pinched his eyebrows. "I'm not sure what you mean. You make it sound like we're trying to rip off the Mob. Or rob a bank. LAD has agreed to the price. If they want to renegotiate, well, that's why I hired you."

"Right. You should have told me."

"Told you what?"

Eddie had tied the mules off to bush willows, and was rubbing the nose of one. Looked like he was talking to the animal, but he was too far away for her to hear.

"Eddie is mentally challenged," she said, "and I'm not convinced he understands that we could find ourselves in a gunfight. Look at the way he's bonding with the mules."

Bic turned and watched as Eddie moved from one pack animal to the next, rubbing each nose and patting their necks.

"He has a way with animals. Always has. They seem to trust him."

"That's because they sense that he's not a threat. Don't you see? Humans are, by nature, predators. Animals sense this, and it puts them on guard, makes them warry. But Eddie's not that way. He's simple, pure. Do you think that will escape the notice of the people we're about to meet? They'll see Eddie for what he is, the weak link, and they will exploit that."

"What are you saying?"

"I'm saying you're an asshole. You should have fully briefed me. And because you didn't, you've placed your nephew, and this mission, at great risk."

"Just calm down." Bic raised his hands, palms toward her. "You work for me, remember? And I'm in charge here."

"Not anymore."

For a tense three seconds, the two just stared at each other.

Finally, Bic yielded. "All right. So now what? And why should we unpack the mules, anyway? It will take an hour for LAD to balance the loads and strap the cases back onto the animals."

"That's the point. They'll be occupied doing that while we get the hell out of the area." Danya closed the gap until she was inches away from Bic. "Look, I know you don't get it. So let me dumb it down for you. You're delivering thirty military-grade assault rifles to a bunch of neo-Nazis. Each rifle can fire fully automatic. You're also delivering a shit-load of ammunition and three hundred pounds of high-grade explosives. To top it all off, we're a long way from civilization. There won't be any cavalry to come to our rescue when this deal goes south."

"How can you be so certain they'll double-cross us?"

Danya furrowed her brow. "Are you for real? I just spelled it out for you."

Bic put his hands on his hips and paced in a circle.

"So you're convinced they'll take the weapons and keep the money."

"Duh. Do ya think?"

Bic glanced over his shoulder. Eddie was still absorbed with the mules. The younger man appeared completely at peace with the animals, and they with him.

"Tell me, then," Bic said. "Why did you agree to this job if you're so certain it's about to go bad?"

"I wanted a change of scenery. And I was tired of working for the drug cartels."

Bic's eyes were like saucers.

"What? I shared my résumé during our first meeting. You didn't think I made it up, did you?"

He shook his head. "Uh, no. Of course not."

"Yeah, right. Just make sure Eddie gets the crates off the mules, just like I said. Side by side. I've got work to do." She walked away.

"Hey! Where are you going?"

Without looking back Danya pointed to a rocky hill at the edge of the meadow.

"Up there."

CHAPTER 3

AFTER CONSULTING HER GPS, Danya recognized the hill—her destination—as a finger of the ridgeline running along the near side of the meadow. The far side of the meadow, across the marsh and pond, was more than two thousand yards distant. She climbed the slope at a measured pace to avoid overexertion. Once she reached her terminus, a jumble of boulders near the crest, she settled to a crouch and studied her view, which was unobstructed to her flanks, as well as across the opening to the opposite ridge.

It wasn't time to settle in yet, though. Although she had a commanding field of fire, she was vulnerable to approach from behind. But she had prepared for such contingencies.

Leaving the M48 rifle leaning against a boulder, she hustled around the top of the hill to avoid silhouetting her figure against the bright, but gray, sky. She still had the Colt M4 in her grip in case she encountered an advance LAD team. But it was the contents of her daypack that were important.

A game trail traced the top of the saddle connecting the hill to the major ridgeline. Beside the trail were scattered trees and a few rotting logs. Not surprising, wild animals followed the paths easiest traveled, and it was logical to expect that any bad guys in the area might also approach Danya's hide along those same trails.

She spotted a choke point formed where a waist-high log had broken across the well-trodden trail, yielding a narrow gap. The game trail passed through the gap rather than dropping down the steep sides of the saddle. It only took a couple minutes to run a thin tripwire—a translucent monofilament fishing line rather than steel wire—across the opening. With one end of the line secured to the half-rotten timber, she tied the other end off to a detonator on a homemade mine.

Danya had constructed the device using a combination of black powder and smokeless powder loaded into heavy-walled plastic pipe. She had taped nails around the outside of the pipe. Crude, but effective over short distances. Plus, the noise would provide valuable warning.

Turning her attention back to the rocky hill, she spied several other possible approaches and repeated the process of setting her antipersonnel mines in place with tripwires. After emptying her pack of all four explosive devices, confident an attack from the rear would not go undetected, she retreated to her sniper hide.

Once settled into a comfortable position behind a waist-high granitic ledge, she removed a spotting scope from her pack and splayed the short tripod. By swiveling the scope from side to side, she could glass the entire meadow. Finally, she used her laser rangefinder to measure off the distance to key landmarks—distinctive rocks, logs, or small trees at various locations. She recorded this information with pencil and paper she carried in a cargo pocket.

With the preparation done, she folded the pack and laid it on the rock ledge as a pad beneath the stock of her Nosler rifle.

Now, all she had to do was wait.

Bic and Eddie had unpacked the mules according to Danya's directions. They placed the six wooden crates containing the M4 assault rifles side by side, with the tops pried loose for inspection of the arms. They had also stacked the ammunition cases nearby. A third pile of crates held the extra gelatin nitroglycerin dynamite—an especially brisant and sensitive high-explosive frequently used to blast trenches.

Both men sat on a case of explosives, engaged in casual conversation. If they had any safety concerns, it wasn't evident in their body language. Not that sitting anywhere else within fifty yards of the dynamite would be any less lethal if the stuff went *boom*.

Even though they were more than four hundred yards away, Danya could clearly see both men through the high-powered optics. Eddie had one leg tucked against his chest, his shoeless foot resting on top of the case as he rubbed his ankle. For his part, Bic preferred to face the ground as he tossed pebbles at an imaginary target. Their weapons were leaning against a crate just beyond arm's reach. It would take a couple precious seconds to retrieve the rifles if needed—seconds they might not be afforded.

She shook her head in displeasure. They should have been alert, scanning 360 degrees for approach of the buyer. *Amateurs.*

She resumed scoping across the meadow, looking for motion. The LAD team was expected to arrive on foot. Bic had been told there would only be two men, but she seriously doubted that number. If she were planning this mission, she'd have at least four men. And more likely, six—all well-armed.

The overcast got thicker, and the clouds dropped lower, threatening to merge with the ground in a dense fog. If that happened, she wouldn't be able to see more than a hundred yards, and would have to abandon her position overlooking the merchandise below.

Bic and Eddie continued to behave as if this was a social outing rather than a high-dollar weapons transaction. No doubt in her mind that the LAD men would keep the money and take the weapons. Bic and his nephew were greenhorns—novices playing a dangerous game. Certainly, they would be outclassed and outnumbered by the neo-Nazi gang. And once the thugs had what they came for, they'd likely tie up the loose ends. *Dead men make lousy witnesses.*

But she was the wild card. And she was ready. No way in hell she was going to watch as a bunch of extremists walked away with the explosives and machine guns.

She had other plans.

Plans which even Bic was not privy to.

After returning her concentration to scanning across the vast meadow, a few scattered drops splashed on the rock ledge. After several minutes, the droplets ceased and the cloud cover, although low, failed to merge with terra firma to interfere with her glassing.

She looked at her watch. *Almost noon. Those guys ought to show up any time now, unless they're as inept as Bic and his nephew. Wishful thinking.*

As the view through the spotting scope reached the far left of the meadow, she saw it. Movement. Only one person at first, but soon she saw two more men, all dressed in civilian camouflage hunting gear. All carrying assault-style rifles. Not surprising. They were still a long way off—beyond the thousand-yard limit of her laser rangefinder. But they were moving on a trajectory that would lead them right to the crates of merchandise.

She nudged the spotting scope. Neither Bic nor Eddie had noticed the approach of the LAD men.

She frowned. *I hope Bic still has the radio on and is paying attention.*

She keyed the mic. Bic raised a hand to his shirt pocket, feeling the click as much as hearing the faint sound. He raised his gaze toward her. Although there was no way he could see her, she could read his features and movements through the magnification of the spotting scope.

Good boy, Bic. Maybe there's hope for you yet.

"I think we have company Eddie," Bic said. "Must be on the other side of the meadow."

"Huh?" The young man looked around, but couldn't see the approaching buyers, who were still hidden from view by the lush foliage of the wetland.

"Why don't you put your shoes on. I think I should greet our business partners."

While Eddie busied himself, Bic strode around the cattails and bush willows until he had cleared enough vegetation to see the approaching trio. He stopped and waved an arm above his head to draw their attention.

Without breaking stride, the three men advanced directly to within thirty yards of the gunsmith. Bic still had his rifle slung over his shoulder.

"Hello. I'm Bic Turner."

The three men stood apart from each other. Each had an assault rifle pointed toward Bic but not directly at him. The two men on either end wore day packs, but not the guy in the middle.

"Figured," the middle guy said. "You can call me Luther."

He was a big man with a shaved head and full beard. Tattoos were party visible on his neck, extending to the base of his ears. His arms and thighs bulged against the clothing, threatening to split the seams.

"Where's the merchandise?" Luther said.

"Follow me. Everything is stacked on the other side of the swamp. You can inspect the rifles if you want."

"Bet your ass we will. And the explosives?"

"It's all there. Everything."

"Then I guess you better lead on."

As Bic turned and marched off, Luther lifted his chin and nodded to the side. One of his accomplices crouched and darted in the opposite direction, around the marsh.

Bic was first to arrive at the cache of weapons and munitions, with Luther close behind.

"Here it is." Bic outstretched his arms to the side before turning around to face Luther. "Hey, where's the other guy?"

Luther glared at Eddie and sized him up.

"Who's he?"

"Don't worry. His name is Eddie. He works for me. I told the other guy—your boss, I think—that there would be two of us making the delivery."

Eddie looked down at his toes, refusing to meet Luther's gaze.

"Yeah, that's right," Luther said. "Anyone else here with you that you've failed to mention?"

Bic's heartbeat sped up. *Could he know about Danya? No. She's well-hidden. And besides, if he knew, he wouldn't be asking.*

He summoned his courage and shook his head.

"No, just the two of us. And the mules." He forced a smile, hoping his lie was convincing.

Luther turned his head to the side. "Karl, check out the merchandise."

Karl advanced first to the explosives. He opened two containers and examined the yellow sticks inside, each cradled in a foam slot for protection against shock. Seeing no sign of age, or liquid droplets on the exterior surfaces of the sticks—which could be nitroglycerin—he returned the tops.

"Looks good." Then he moved on to the cases of ammunition. "Are some of these rounds loaded in magazines?"

Bic nodded. "Just like your boss ordered. One hundred and twenty mags, each loaded with thirty rounds. They're in this case here." He slid the wood top aside.

Karl picked up two, selected at random. He pushed down on the top round with his thumb, happy with the spring tension. Then he moved to a crate of rifles.

"You modified these from civilian semiauto versions?"

"Yes, that's right." Bic said. "I'm a gunsmith. I specialize in AR models. Got my training in the Army."

"Is that supposed to impress me?" Karl scowled.

He looked like a man who didn't want to be where he was, doing what he was doing. Smaller than Luther by four inches and fifty pounds, Karl wore a ponytail, but the sides of his head were shaved, giving Bic the impression of a Viking warrior. Combined with his gruff demeanor, Bic decided he'd be on the losing end if he got in a fight with him.

"Sorry, man," Bic said. "Just answering your question."

"Well, then, Mister Gunsmith," Karl said. "Let's see if you do quality work, or if you are trying to pass off crap to us."

He pulled a rifle from the crate and rammed home one of the magazines. Pulled back the charging bolt to chamber a round. Moved the fire select switch from *safe* to *semi*. Shouldered the carbine and aimed the open iron sights at a distant rock.

He fired…three shots with three pulls of the trigger, and all the bullets struck home. Next, he nudged the lever to *full*. Still aiming at the same rock, he pulled back on the trigger and held it. A stream of bullets exited the muzzle, and in less than two seconds the magazine was empty.

Karl strode to Luther and handed over the carbine and the second full magazine. Then he took his position to the side and behind his team leader.

"I'm impressed," Luther said, while Bic and Eddie watched the showmanship. "Looks like you've converted a civilian semiauto weapon to a select fire, full-auto M4A1 Carbine."

"That's right," Bic said. "Just like spec ops use."

Luther nodded. "Just like we agreed. And now I suppose you want the money?"

Bic looked at Eddie, then back to Luther.

"That was the agreement. Three hundred grand."

"Yeah? Well, I've got a new offer. Sort of a take-it-or-leave-it offer."

Luther's lips curled up in a sinister grin.

CHAPTER 4

"WHAT DO YOU HAVE IN MIND?" Bic said.

His brain was reeling, and he slid his hand to the grip on the rifle, still hanging from his shoulder.

"Hmm." Luther sighed dramatically. "How about we take the weapons and keep the money."

"That's not the deal your boss and I struck."

"That's interesting. You see, the boss ain't here. So looks like you're dealing with me now."

"No, I did my job. Eddie and me. We delivered everything we agreed to."

Luther shrugged and wrinkled his brow.

"And as near as I can tell, you and…Eddie? Is that the kid's name?"

Bic nodded. "He's my nephew."

"Your nephew? So you run a family business?"

"Yeah, I suppose so. Look, a deal's a deal—"

"Until it ain't."

Bic slid the rifle from his shoulder and raised the weapon to his hip with surprising speed. The LAD team leader found himself looking into the business end of the gun barrel, from a close distance.

Karl had his rifle aimed at Bic, while Luther raised his hands, still holding the modified carbine in one hand.

"Everyone, just relax," Luther said, in a calm tone.

"Where's the money?" Bic said.

"Karl has it. All three hundred grand. Inside his pack."

"All I want is the money. That's what we agreed to. Tell Karl to put down his rifle and toss the pack over here."

Luther seemed to contemplate the request for a moment.

"No, I don't think so."

"Eddie?" Bic called, without taking his eyes off Luther and Karl. "You got your gun on these two?"

"Sure do. But you didn't say anything about shootin' no one."

"I was gonna let you two walk on out of here. Don't make me have to kill you." Luther sounded more confident than a man looking into the bore of a rifle had any right to.

"The first bullet goes through you, Luther." Bic tried to sound braver than he felt.

"Nah. You'll both be dead, and will have never seen it coming."

Bic looked from Luther to Karl, and back again.

"What are you talking about?"

"Did you forget already? Hey, Vic. Why don't you step out of the willows and properly introduce yourself."

The third LAD thug rose to his feet and emerged from the brush behind Eddie and Bic.

"Drop your guns, boys," Vic said.

"I'd do what he says." Luther smirked.

Slowly, Bic and Eddie lowered their weapons to the ground and raised their hands. Victor took one step forward, when his chest exploded in crimson mist. About a second later, the rifle report reverberated across the meadow. Luther and Karl spun in circles, trying to identify where the shooter was located, to no avail.

Blood and gore erupted from Karl's belly and back. He cried in agony for several long moments, before falling silent.

Luther slammed home the magazine in the M4 Carbine, and began firing full-auto bursts at the hillside where Danya was set up. The bullets impacted widely across the rock and gravel many yards below her location. She aimed again and slowly squeezed the trigger, sending a .30 caliber bullet at almost three times the speed of sound. Luther was dead even before the sound of the gunshot reached his lifeless body.

Bic and Eddie still stood ramrod straight, with their hands clasped over their heads. Within seconds, the three LAD men had been wiped out, and it had not yet registered to the uncle and nephew duo.

From her position behind the granite ledge, Danya reloaded her sporting rifle, having just fired the entire three rounds the magazine held. She knew all three expanding hunting bullets had struck home, center mass, and would be lethal. So the targets surrounding Bic and Eddie were dead, or soon would be. Still, something didn't seem right. Her senses were on high alert. Senses she'd learned to trust after years of field work in some of the most dangerous regions of the world.

Why would they only send three men?

She ran it over and over in her mind, and kept coming to the same answer.

They didn't.

A rumbling boom reverberated from the far side of the hill, and Danya knew one of the wires had been tripped, detonating the explosive device.

Leaving her bolt-action sniper rifle in place, she unlimbered her M4 Carbine and dashed up the hill. Just before the crest, she dropped to a crouch, and then a crawl. Somewhere down the back side were one or more adversaries.

As she cleared the lip, and the broken deadfall came into view, she saw a prone man writhing in agony. He pressed his hands against a leg, no doubt shredded by the nail shrapnel.

She moved her gaze from side to side, searching for movement. Nothing.

Could he be alone? No. There'd be at least two attackers.

After spying a decent-sized tree thirty yards down slope, she sprung to her feet and dashed down the gravel-covered incline, sliding every time her foot planted in the soft soil. Her reckless maneuver was rewarded with several gunshots fired at her, but none connected.

Without yielding forward momentum, she slid to her butt and then rolled to a stop against the tree trunk as more bullets cratered in the ground beside her. The bullet strikes suggested the direction of the shooter. Ever so slowly, she edged her gaze around the side of the trunk. She only had a second of viewing before more bullets gouged bark off the tree, pieces landing on her head. But it was enough. She saw the muzzle flash. The gunman was about a hundred yards away, downslope, partially concealed by a cluster of manzanitas.

She peeked around the wide trunk again, intentionally drawing fire. Eruptions of dirt marked the impacts in a line only inches away. She twisted to a kneeling position on the opposite side of the tree. She fired as the barrel leveled on the manzanitas where she'd seen the muzzle flashes.

The gunman fired back, but his aim was off, having expected she would be on the other side of the tree. He got off three shots before she connected on him. The small-caliber, high-velocity bullet ripped through the gunman's shoulder, at the base of his neck.

She kept firing, aiming at different locations behind the waist-high shrubs, where she imagined the shooter might be. Ten shots fired, then twelve. Finally, with no more return fire, she stopped.

She scanned the likely hiding spots within two hundred yards of her location, pointing the M4 Carbine everywhere she looked. The gunman who'd been wounded by the improvised mine hadn't moved. With her ears ringing from the gunfire, she couldn't hear if he was moaning.

He might have bled out.

She continued to search for targets for a full minute, before concluding that it was probably safe. With her weapon still shouldered and pointing forward, she descended—first, to the manzanitas where the shooter had been. She approached from the side, giving the bushes a wide berth. As she cleared the dense foliage, the prone body of the gunman came into view. The top left of his chest was soaked with blood. Still keeping the barrel of her weapon aimed at him, she reached down and pressed against his neck—no pulse.

Next, she advanced toward the log where she last saw the injured man lying. She kept her vigil, the barrel pointing everywhere her gaze turned. But it was quiet, and nothing was moving.

As the man came into view, she saw he'd squirmed to a sitting position with his shoulders resting against the smooth wood of the log. He attempted to raise his rifle, one hand still pressed against his leg wound.

"Don't do it," she said. "Your partner is dead. Toss the gun to the side, or I'll put a bullet through you, too."

After a moment's hesitation, he did as instructed, and she closed the gap. She stood over him, barrel inches away from his head.

"Are you armed?"

He shook his head.

"Open your jacket—slowly—and show me."

With one hand, he spread the lightweight jacket aside. No holstered handgun or knife.

"Keep that hand up. The other can stay on your wound. Are there anymore?"

He tried to sit straighter, pain electrifying his body as the injured leg shifted ever so slightly.

"Just the three who are meeting the gunsmith Turner."

"They're no longer in business. Anyone else?"

He shook his head as he glared at her.

"You sure? Only the five of you?"

"That should have been enough. There was only supposed to be two of them."

"What can I say? Bic has more brains than you cowboys gave him credit for."

"You carrying a first aid kit?"

He shook his head. "No."

"Let's see what it looks like. Move your hand."

"I'm bleeding."

"And you'll keep on bleeding if we don't dress that wound. Now move your hand."

A nasty ragged gash, four-inches long, extended across the top of his thigh. Dark red blood flowed from the laceration.

Danya narrowed her eyes in concern. "Okay. Put pressure back on the wound."

With a sigh, she placed her left hand into a cargo pocket in her trousers and removed a sterile compress, a packet of QuikClot® powder, and an elastic wrap of the type used for sprained joints. She always carried just enough first aid supplies to handle an emergency.

"This is all I have with me. There are more medical supplies with the mules." She handed over the items. "Don't apply it too tight and cut off the blood flow to your leg."

She sized him up, keeping some separation, while he completed dressing his leg. He was pale, and perspiration dappled his face—signs that shock was setting in.

"What's your name?" she said.

"Who's asking?"

"Look, pal, you don't have many options. This will be a lot easier if I know what to call you."

"Gordon. My name is Gordon."

She had already noticed that neither of these LAD soldiers were wearing packs, just a small cargo pouch hung from his belt. "Okay, Gordon. Who has the money?"

He stared back at Danya.

"I asked you a question." She kicked his leg, eliciting a yelp.

"Okay. Take it easy. Karl has it. In his pack."

"All of it?"

"Yeah, all of it."

"Good boy."

She backpedaled several steps and grabbed a straight and stout branch. It wouldn't work as a crutch, but could be useful as a walking staff.

She tossed it to him. "Can you make it down the hill and to the middle of the meadow?"

"I'm not going anywhere with you," he said.

"Have it your way. You can stay here and try to make it out on your own, if you feel lucky. My bet is that you'll bleed out before you cover two miles. Or you can cooperate. In which case, you might make it out alive. The choice is yours."

His malicious glare softened just a bit, and he struggled to his feet, leaning against the log and supporting his weight on the one good leg. Danya picked up his weapon and slung it across her shoulder.

"Turn around. Hands on your head."

He had to lean over the log to comply, while supporting his weight on the one leg. Danya pressed the steel barrel hard against his back, and with her free hand, patted him down. Clean.

"Okay. Let's go."

Danya didn't bother to retrieve her gear. She could do that after she completed the job.

Slowed by her hobbling prisoner, it took twenty minutes to descend and cross the meadow to meet Bic and Eddie. They'd had enough sense to gather up the weapons from the fallen LAD gunmen, which were now placed atop one of the rifle crates.

"We heard an explosion and shooting," Bic called, as he jogged toward Danya and the stranger, leaving his nephew behind with the cache of weapons.

When he got within ten yards, panting from the exertion, he said, "You all right?"

She nodded. "Two came up the backside of the ridge. I killed one. This guy here is Gordon. He tripped one of my mines. Looks like a nail ripped a wicked gash in his leg."

Bic had already noticed the bandage and that he was limping severely.

"Are you and Eddie good?" she said. "No one is hurt?"

"We're fine, thanks to your sharp shooting. They would have killed us, for sure."

She resisted the urge to say I told you so, and instead looked beyond Bic, to the merchandise. Eddie was standing guard, gripping his rifle with both hands.

"We got the money!" Bic said. "It was in the backpack. That

one over there was carrying it." He motioned to the prone figure. "Hundred-dollar bills. All of it."

"Where's the pack now?"

"It's with Eddie." He paused. "What are we going to do with the guns and stuff?"

"I'll deal with that. You just keep an eye on Gordon. He's not going to run away, and I already searched him. Just have him sit, and don't get too close. And keep your eye on him. Understand?"

Bic nodded. "Yeah, sure."

She glanced at her watch. It was early afternoon already. The cloud cover remained, but at least it wasn't dropping lower. Still, she would need to move quickly before darkness set in.

She crossed over to Bic's nephew.

"Hey, Eddie. Everything good?"

He nodded emphatically. "Boy am I glad you're on our side. That was some shootin'."

"We have a change of plans, and I need your help."

"Sure. What do you want me to do?"

"First, remove the tops of all six rifle crates and lay them on the ground. Let's make sure everything is still there."

"Okay, but they only removed and tested one rifle."

She smiled. "Let's just be sure, all right?"

Eddie shrugged and then placed his rifle on the ground so he had both hands free to complete the task. Danya picked up his weapon and placed the sling over her shoulder, along with the other rifle she'd taken from Gordon.

With the lids already pried open, Eddie was soon done with the task.

"Now what?" he said.

"Place one of these cases of dynamite in each crate with the rifles. Place the boxes of ammunition in the crates, too."

"Why?"

"Because we can't take these guns with us."

"Hey," Bic called, and jogged closer. "What are you doing?"

She spun on him, her carbine pointed at his chest. "These guns and explosives are not coming back."

"Why?" Bic said. "I could find another buyer. There would be another job for you to provide security."

"It's not happening." Her voice was firm, backed up with the muzzle of her rifle. "You better put your gun down."

Bic's eyes widened. "Okay. Whatever you say." He dropped the carbine.

She nodded for him to step aside, and then gathered his gun, adding to her growing collection.

"Help your nephew. And be gentle. That stuff is shock sensitive."

Each case held fifty pounds of high explosives, and with the rifle crates side by side, that meant the dynamite cases were also side by side. All she would need is one detonator, and the entire cache, all three hundred pounds, would explode.

When the two men had completed the task, they stepped away, allowing room for her to check their work. She shed the three carbines from her shoulder into the nearest rifle crate, and then retrieved a stick of dynamite.

She looked at Bic and then Eddie. "You would be safer to gather up Gordon and the mules, and move away to where the trail we came in on enters the meadow. That's the way home."

"What about you?" Bic said.

"I've got to gather up my gear on the hill. Then I'm departing in a different direction."

"What about your pay?" Bic said.

She reached inside her jacket pocket. When her hand emerged, it held a radio-controlled detonator.

"I'll wait until you and the animals are all at the edge of the meadow. Now get going."

Bic turned for the pack that held the money.

"Leave it," she said.

Bic pointed at the pack in exasperation. "But that's the money."

"Toss it here." She kept her carbine trained on the gunsmith.

"But—"

"Do it. You're in no position to argue the point."

Thud. The pack landed at her feet.

Without lowering the gun, she opened the pack with one hand

and reached inside to grab a bundle of bills. It still had the bank wrapper indicating the stack amount. She tossed it to Eddie, who caught it with both hands. Then she threw a second bundle to Bic.

"You get to walk away free men. And you each have $10,000 cash, unreported income."

"But you can't do that," Bic said. "It's not fair. That money is mine."

"You'd both be dead if it wasn't for me. Now get out of here before I change my mind and decide not to be so generous."

Slowly, Bic turned and took two steps, then stopped.

"What about him?" He pointed at Gordon.

She shrugged. "I really don't care much. You have the first aid kit, and if he's bleeding a lot, apply a new bandage. But if you and Eddie are half-decent men—which I believe you are—then you'll make sure he gets proper medical attention. If it were me, I'd drop him off at the nearest medical clinic and drive away. No questions asked. Get my meaning?"

With head hanging low, Eddie led the mules away, following his uncle.

She made quick work of inserting a detonator into the stick of dynamite, then returned it to the case with the other yellow sticks. She inched away toward the hill, keeping a close eye on the trio to make sure Bic didn't dash back to disarm the explosives. It was slow going with the limping man, but they eventually made it to the edge of the meadow. She was at the base of the hill as she watched them disappear from view. The last she saw was the swishing tail of a mule.

She tucked in low behind a boulder, then activated the detonator and pressed the switch. Her actions were rewarded with a deafening blast and a powerful shockwave that hit her hard, even at a thousand-yard distance. She gazed around the boulder and saw black stick-like objects, which she surmised were assault rifles, hurling through the air in all directions. The cattails and shrub willows within fifty yards were flattened, and a large crater now occupied the location once held by the guns, ammunition, and explosives.

She rose to her feet. With the pack of cash on her back, she ascended to the sniper hide and gathered up her rifle, spotting scope, and the few remaining items from her daypack. After placing the articles of importance on top of the bundles of bank notes, she left the daypack behind. With the Nosler rifle on her shoulder and the carbine in her hand, she moved on to the mines. They had to be disarmed and retrieved. Although the pack was stuffed full, she managed to get the unexploded munitions inside, and the top flap secured. She stashed the detonators in a cargo pocket of her pants, safely removed from the explosives.

Her GPS showed the path to her exit location. It would be a five-mile hike, and she had two hours until sunset. Plenty of time. But the mission wasn't truly over until she was out and far away.

The clouds started to lower, and within minutes, she was hiking in mist that would provide cover, as well as attenuate sound. A few hours ago, she dreaded the fog. Now, she welcomed it.

A good omen.

CHAPTER 5

NUNAVUT, NORTHERN CANADA
MAY 13

THE ARTIC SUN CAST LONG SHADOWS across the flat, glistening white plain on the shore of Bathurst Inlet. Natan Kudloo and Duane Kotierk, both Inuit, had been driving their snowmobiles hard through the night, thanks to a full moon. Each was pulling a sled, and on each sled was a half-ton machine encased within a rusted steel cage. The cylindrical machine was three-feet tall and painted mint green, with dozens of vertical metal fins spaced evenly around the outside.

Natan clasped his mitten-covered hands against his shoulders, trying to stimulate blood flow into his arms. Although dressed in traditional furs, chill had set in from the long drive through the frigid air. He opened the top of his thermos bottle and swigged tepid coffee.

"I could use something hot to drink," he said.

Duane surveyed their destination, the outpost of Umingmaktok. The settlement was divided by a runway. On one side were the old Hudson's Bay Company buildings, and the co-op store. On the other side was the main residential area.

"This place has been deserted for years," Duane said. "We don't have time to make a fire and boil water. I doubt they left any generators and fuel behind."

"Maybe I can heat what's left of my coffee on this machine." Natan pointed at the cargo on the sled attached to the back of his snowmobile, recalling how snow kicked up from the track on his snowmobile quickly melted when it settled onto the pale-green machine.

"You don't want to get too close to those things, or you might begin to glow at night." Duane chuckled.

He removed a satellite phone from a saddle pack, and trudged toward the nearest building.

"Come on. We can call from inside. There won't be any wind. At least it will feel warmer."

Inside, the wood-framed building was empty—no furnishings of any kind, not even a simple chair or stool. No pictures or decorations on the walls. Even the light fixtures that had once hung from the ceiling were gone. Remarkably, all the glass windows were still intact.

"It's nice they left the door unlocked," Natan said.

"Why not? Nothing to steal." Duane removed his mittens and pressed a series of numbers on the Iridium phone keypad.

After a few seconds, the call connected.

"Ranger here. What's your status?"

The characteristic clipping of the voice communication provided the only differentiation between the satellite communication and a typical cell call.

Duane replied, "Roger. We arrived at the air strip."

"Confirmed. Flight is inbound. Advise local weather conditions."

"Clear sky and mild westerly wind. Shouldn't be any problem for the pilot."

"Roger that. Will relay your report. Thank you for your service."

"Okay, Ranger. Say, any reason we need to stick around? We'd like to get back to our village. I mean, if you don't need our help."

"No, you should go. When the plane arrives, they're going to open the casings. But they have proper safety gear, and you don't want to be anywhere nearby when they do to that."

Natan and Duane mounted their snowmobiles and sped off.

Without the trailing sleds, they soon left the abandoned outpost behind.

The de Havilland DHC-2 Beaver buzzed the dirt airstrip at two hundred feet. The iconic aircraft was a favorite of bush pilots flying the backcountry. With a single wing that stretched over the cabin, a square-shaped fuselage that tapered rearward to the tail, and a short, fat nose, the plane had a distinctive appearance.

Although the pilot was concerned about any objects on the runway, she was especially anxious about caribou. Running the single-engine aircraft into a herd of the ungulates, also known as reindeer, would be disastrous for the mission. She executed a low altitude buzz that would surely frighten away any wandering beasts.

Seeing nothing untoward on the short strip, she banked and lined up for the approach. Her three passengers tugged one last time on their seatbelts. The oversized tires kissed the frozen surface and the Beaver bounced once, then twice, before settling down and coasting to a stop near the main buildings.

"Nice landing," said one of the passengers, who'd introduced himself as Jerry. "Looks like you've done this before."

"More times than I can count. I used to fly bush in Alaska and the Northwest Territories."

She didn't look to be older than thirty-five, but she carried herself with confidence and handled the aircraft like a seasoned professional. With a chiseled jaw, pronounced cheekbones, and eyes that matched the blackest obsidian, Sacheen Crow Dog was from the Raven Clan of the Tlingit tribe. She had learned to fly a fixed-wing aircraft before she'd learned to drive.

The tribal elders taught the traditional ways in what seemed a doomed effort to preserve the clan's heritage and culture, including the Tlingit language. Sacheen had benefited from the passing of knowledge, and like all First Nations people, she sought to live in harmony with Nature.

Her father was a fishing and hunting guide, and he eventually earned enough to buy a small Cessna bush plane. He taught her to fly—initially, fixed-wing aircraft. And later, helicopters. Sacheen worked for her father for thirteen years, before he died from bone cancer. It was during those guided outings that she was first exposed to life outside the limited world of her extended family and clan.

Her father's customers were mostly well-heeled white men who came to the far north in search of adventure—or so they said. Without exception, they were arrogant men who did not appreciate Nature, and expected to be waited upon like royalty.

She and her father rose early every morning, and were the last to retire at the end of each long day. She cooked the meals, and cleaned up camp, while her father prepared the horses, guided the parties, field dressed the game they shot, and skinned out their trophies. All the while, the pompous rich white men would boast about their skills and accomplishments. At night, they'd drink whiskey until they were intoxicated, which amplified their rudeness and disrespect.

Although her father urged her to have patience with the ignorance of his clients, she soon tired of their behavior. Wasn't their lack of knowledge that grated on her, but their unwillingness to admit their ignorance and to seek understanding and enlightenment. It was all too clear to her that the effort she and her father put forward for their clients was not appreciated. Regardless of how hard they worked to satisfy their patrons, it was never sufficient.

Unlike her father, who was one with the creatures that inhabited the untamed forest and wild rivers, the men who booked hunting and fishing trips knew next to nothing about the natural world. They did not understand or appreciate the moose and caribou they hunted, or the salmon they fished from the rivers. They saw the animals as merely objects to be taken and counted. And later, once the stories had lost their luster, the objects were to be forgotten.

Sacheen appreciated the gifts of Nature and all that Mother Earth offered to her people. Millenia ago, her people had learned to survive and thrive through the sacrifices of the sacred herbivores and omnivores that roamed the forests, and from the fish that swam the rivers and coastal bays. Each life that was taken had to serve a purpose—that is how the spirit was honored. To waste any part of the sacrifice was to dishonor the spirit, to devalue the life that had been taken.

Sadly, the white men neither shared, nor honored, her cultural heritage and values. They came to her ancestral lands with the singular goal of taking—not because of need to survive, but simply because they could.

Once the propeller on the nose of the Beaver came to a stop, Sacheen opened the cabin door. She pointed to the two sleds left by Natan and Duane.

"There's your project," she said. "We don't have much time. Only a couple hours before the sun sets. I want to take off while we still have at least a sliver of daylight to see the length of the runway."

"No problem," said one of the men.

He was of average height and build, like the other two passengers. They all appeared unkept, as if they hadn't shaved or washed their hair in days.

Sacheen had hired them from Dutch Harbor. They were commercial fishermen, but were lured by the promise of a big payoff for what she'd described as a few days' work. All three men were flown on a commercial airline to Yellowknife, which is where she'd picked them up in the de Havilland Beaver.

They unloaded their tools and a portable generator, and set to work.

"I don't think I've ever seen a contraption like this before," Jerry said. "What is it?"

"A special type of generator," Sacheen said. "They don't make them anymore, and I've been hired by the government to decommission these two so they don't rust and contaminate the land and water."

She was satisfied with telling the men part of the truth, but they didn't need to know everything.

"Whoa, whoa, whoa. You didn't say anything about toxic shit."

"Just relax, Jerry. Your job is only to cut open the outer shell. Inside is a cannister about this big." She used her hands to indicate the size. "It's gray, about the color of pencil lead, and it contains the chemicals the government doesn't want to corrode and leak out. According to the Ministry of Environment, there's nothing to worry about. They just want me to turn in the cannisters."

"You're sure?"

"Look, if there was a health risk, do you think I'd be standing here next to those machines?"

Jerry held her gaze for a long moment.

"No, I guess not." He faced his two colleagues. "Come on. Let's get the generator fired up. Looks like the shell is steel, so that means we gotta use an abrasive blade on the angle grinder to cut through. Let's make four cuts from top to bottom, then see if we can peel the sides away like an orange."

One of the men said, "You mean, like a banana."

Jerry rolled his eyes. "Whatever. Orange, banana—what difference does it make?"

The racket from three grinders' spinning abrasive discs cutting through the steel drowned out the rumble from the portable generator. As the orange sparks flew, the men focused through clear plastic face shields, careful not to cut too deep. Fortunately, the outer casing was mild steel and only about two-millimeters thick, so the spinning discs made quick work of the cuts.

With the scores completed on both generators, the men silenced the power tools and picked up steel pry bars with gloved hands. An occasional grunt punctuated the exertion required to force the quartered sections of the steel casing to separate. But leverage and brute strength won out, and the men folded the sections back to reveal an aluminum lining bolted to the base. After removing the fasteners, they lifted the lining off and discarded it to the side.

"Looks like lead sheet," Jerry said, referring to the final layer of packaging. "These things must weigh a ton."

"There must be several hundred dollars' worth of scrap aluminum and lead," one of his coworkers said.

"It'll cost more than that to fly it out of here," Jerry replied. "Come on. Let's peel this lead back. The cannister should be inside."

"Doesn't look like any generator I've ever seen," said the other worker. "There should be coils of copper wire and big magnets."

Jerry shrugged. "What do I know? But she did say it was different, and that's why the government wants to salvage the inner portion."

"Hey, where is she, anyway?"

Jerry looked around, and not seeing her, shrugged again.

"I don't know. Maybe she went into one of the buildings, looking for a bathroom. Who cares. Let's get this done."

Removing the soft lead sheet was easy work, exposing a gray graphite cylinder about sixteen-centimeters tall and twelve centimeters in diameter. In contrast to the arctic air, the warmth emanating from the cylinder was obvious.

Jerry removed a glove and moved his hand close.

"That's a nice hand-warmer," he said. "Wonder what it is?"

"Hey, guys," Sacheen called, from the doorway of the largest structure.

It was the old co-op building, and designed with just one large room for meetings and other social gatherings. The windows had been boarded over.

"Why don't you take a break and come on inside. I found a bottle of whiskey."

The three men strode toward the building, eager for a break and a strong drink. They pushed through the open doorway and stopped just inside the large room. The only light entered through the opening they'd just passed through.

"Where'd she go?" one of the men said.

They all searched the empty space for her.

The door slammed shut, leaving them in total darkness.

"What the hell?"

"Sacheen, where are you?" Jerry called, fear creeping into his voice.

"I can't see shit."

"Use the light on your phone," the other man said.

Three cell phone lights clicked on, providing meager illumination. The room was empty.

Jerry approached the rear door and tested it. The doorknob turned, but the door was stuck and wouldn't budge.

"Sacheen," Jerry called again, his voice trembling.

From outside the old co-op, having just wedged a thick board between the door latch and the plank stoop, she could hear their muted calls. She hurried to the front of the building. Using a heavy timber brace, she barricaded the front door, then closed a hasp to the doorframe and secured it with a padlock. Given enough time and effort, she figured they would break out through one of the doors, or maybe by kicking out the boards covering the windows. But it didn't matter. She only needed thirty minutes, and she'd be taxiing down the runway and taking to the sky.

Sacheen still had one task to complete. Donning a lead-lined radiation suit she'd removed from a compartment at the rear of the Beaver, complete with head covering fitted with leaded-glass goggles, she used a set of long-handled tongs to remove the graphite cylinder from each generator. One at a time, she carried them to the same storage hold at the back of the aircraft. Inside the compartment was a lead box with two slots just big enough to cradle the cores. She replaced the heavy lead cover and completed one last check to make certain the deadly cargo was secured. After closing the hatch, she slipped out of the bulky suit.

Once strapped into the cockpit, she started the engine. While it was warming, she keyed the radio.

"Ranger here. Cargo is secured."

"Roger that. What about the hired help?"

She gazed toward the old co-op building.

"I think the radiation sickness will get them before they die of exposure."

Then she increased power to the engine and began her takeoff roll. A minute later, she was airborne and flying south.

CHAPTER 6

HATFIELD, OREGON
MAY 17

DANYA ROLLED HER SHOULDERS and tilted her head from side to side. She'd been behind the wheel of her pickup for hours, and her back and neck were stiff. The two-lane blacktop traced a path across flat valleys separated by low mountain passes.

The drive was far from challenging, and boredom was slowly taking over, eroding her habitual state of attention. More and more frequently, she was glancing at the dashboard, checking that her speed was within two miles per hour of the posted limit. Her grip on the wheel was firm to ensure she tracked an even course between the lines. With hardly any other vehicles on the road, even minor infractions of the traffic code could attract the attention of a lone state trooper—and a chance run-in with the police would be unfortunate. For both parties.

In the distance, she saw two grain elevators and a couple low buildings. *Maybe a truck stop. If there's a gas station, maybe they have a restroom and a coffee shop.*

She slowed and saw the signage, and then the fuel pumps. Ever mindful of the vintage Airstream RV she was towing, she applied the brakes with steady pressure and coasted beside the pumps. She stepped out and stretched her body, arching her back. Her brunette hair extended just below her shoulders in graceful curls.

A young woman approached from the open door to the mini-market.

"Do you have a restroom?" Danya said.

"Inside. Fill it?"

"Oh, yeah. Regular, please."

Just outside the market door, an old hound with a graying muzzle and oversized floppy ears was reclined on a pillow, enjoying the sun's warmth—a contrast with the brisk air. Later in the day, the creature would, no doubt, saunter off in search of shade. Danya leaned down and scratched the fella on the head. He groaned and stretched his legs before relaxing again.

She heard a horn toot and brakes squeal as another pickup with faded paint and dented fenders pulled to an abrupt stop at the fuel pumps on the opposite side of the island. She watched as the driver jumped out and removed the gas cap. He seemed to be in a hurry, saying something unintelligible to the attendant, who was doing her best to ignore him.

As Danya entered the market, the aroma of freshly brewed coffee was a pleasant change from the harsh scent of petroleum. She navigated through the narrow aisles packed with snack foods, magazines, and sundries—a compromise between the necessity to carry varied inventory, and limited space.

The store was empty. Still, she looked back over her shoulder before entering the restroom—a practice drilled into her over years of training.

It felt invigorating to walk, even a short distance, after sitting for…she glanced at her watch. She'd been driving for a little over four hours, and her athletic frame protested such a long spell of inactivity.

After washing up, she wove back to the cash register and coffee machine. She was pouring a steaming cup when the female attendant, having finished the immediate task at the pumps, re-entered the store. The young woman appeared harried as she crossed behind the checkout counter. Her straight, coal-black hair was tucked behind her ears and tied in twin braids that extended to the middle of her back. Her mocha eyes were set above high cheekbones, and her skin was tanned as if regularly exposed to sunshine, but still smooth and youthful.

"Anything else?" the attendant said, her mind clearly on other matters.

"Just the coffee." Danya pointed to the cup.

As she reached into her pocket for some bills, a man with short blond hair entered and strode up to the counter. He leaned forward, resting on his hands, with a devilish grin plastered across his face.

"Come on, Toby. I know you want to."

Toby turned to face the man. "Cole, I told you *no*. Now leave me alone." Her voice crackled with fear and embarrassment.

The man reached across the counter and grabbed Toby's arm.

"Listen—"

Danya jabbed a finger into his shoulder. "I don't think you're listening, mister."

He looked at Danya, acknowledging her presence for the first time.

"This ain't no concern of yours, lady."

"She said no."

Cole released his grip and squared off with Danya. At six-one, he was six inches taller, and she estimated he weighed about 190 pounds. His physique was trim and fit, suggesting he might be a manual laborer. Still, his behavior was sloppy and overconfident. She had encountered men like him before—bullies who relied on bluster and intimidation to exert control over others. But when pushed into a fight, they lacked the skills of a warrior, and were almost always decisively beaten.

"I'm just asking my lady friend out on a date. Now go along and mind your own business."

Toby had backed as far away from the counter as she could, her back pressing against a rack filled with packs of cigarettes.

"Please, Cole," she said. "Just leave."

He snorted a laugh. "Or what? What are you gonna do?"

"I'll call the sheriff."

"Now you and I both know that ain't gonna do no good. Hell, it'll be at least an hour before a deputy shows up. That's if they even bother to send a car. Which they won't."

"Listen, Cole," Danya said. "Is that your name?"

He faced her again, annoyance replacing the jovialness.

"What is your problem, lady? Just leave your money on the counter and move along. Or—"

"Or what?" She took a half-step closer.

Cole pinched his eyebrows. "Don't start something you can't finish. I can break you in half with one hand."

With a blur of motion, she punched him in the face. He stumbled backwards, tripped, and fell into an ice bucket loaded with soft drinks. He swiped a hand across his nose, leaving a bloody smear on his upper lip and cheek.

"That was your first mistake, Cole," she said. "Learn from it. You'd best get on your way."

His gaze flitted from Danya to Toby, and back again. Then he pushed himself to his feet. Wiped the blood from his nose again, and glared at Toby.

"You're gonna regret that." He stumbled out the door and paused next to the resting hound to regain his composure.

The dog objected to his presence with a growl.

Cole lashed out with a vicious kick into the dog's ribs.

"You need to get your dog under control, Toby, or I'll file a complaint with animal control. Or maybe I'll just shoot him myself."

In four strides, Danya was on Cole, ramming the heal of her hand into the base of his skull at the juncture with his spine. He stumbled forward, his arms tingling from the blow. But he didn't go down. Instead, he turned like a wounded beast. His face was a mask of rage as he pulled his arm back, signaling his intent to strike.

She kicked him between the legs, and he bent forward, hands cupped over his groin. Then he dropped to one knee, his head drooped. Strings of saliva hung from his open mouth before breaking off and falling to the pavement, where it mixed with splattered blood.

"I warned you, Cole. That was mistake number two. Now get out of here while you can still walk." She turned to finish paying for her gas and coffee.

“Watch out!” Toby shouted.

Danya spun on her heals and raised her arm as a shield to the unseen attack…*mistake number three.*

She deflected the roundhouse punch aimed at her head, and returned a blow to Cole’s solar plexus. He gasped, eyes bulging and mouth open as he struggled to suck in air. She grabbed his ears and rammed his face downward as she thrust her knee upwards. The cartilage in his noise succumbed with a sickening crunch, leaving a bloody imprint on her jeans. She released her grip, allowing the limp body to crumple onto the pavement.

The final encounter had taken less than two seconds. Toby watched from the doorway, her hand over her mouth and her body trembling.

“Are you okay?” she squeaked out.

Danya retrieved her cell phone and punched the buttons.

“I’m fine,” she replied. “But your friend needs some medical attention.”

“9-1-1. What is the nature of your emergency?”

“I’m at a gas station on Highway 39, near the California border. There’s an adult male who appears to have fallen and smashed his face. His nose is bleeding pretty badly, and he’s unconscious. I think he needs an ambulance.”

There was a pause, and then the voice said, “You said Highway 39. Are you at Hatfield?”

“Just outside, on the Oregon side of the border.” She gave the name of the gas station.

“What is your name and phone number?” the voice said.

“Just get an ambulance here, quickly.” Then she disconnected the call.

“Thank you,” Toby said. “That creep and his brother started bothering me a month ago.”

“Did you file a complaint with the sheriff?”

Toby rolled her eyes. “Yeah, but it didn’t do any good. We’re in Klamath County. And only about five hundred feet away,” she pointed to the south, “is the California border. That’s Siskiyou County. That’s where Cole and his brother have their ranch.”

"I see. So the Klamath County sheriff doesn't want to get involved in a cross-jurisdictional complaint."

Toby nodded. "They took my statement. But the deputy said that since Cole and his brother were only verbally harassing me, and they reside in the neighboring county and state, it was unlikely they could do much."

"Has Cole ever threatened you before?"

"Not directly, no."

"But the meaning was clear?"

Toby nodded again and wrapped her arms around her chest.

"He said that I needed a man around for protection. That all kinds of bad things could happen to people out here."

"Do you live alone?"

"I live with my mother. She inherited a hundred acres from my father, just a few miles east of here. She's old and needs someone to cook and clean up the house. We lease the grazing rights and get a little bit of income from that, plus what I can make from pumping gas and working the store."

"The owner treats you well?" Danya gazed over the store's exterior.

The construction was dated, but appeared to be maintained.

"Pays you a fair wage?"

Toby shrugged. "Missus White—that's my boss—she's all right. Pay is minimum wage, but she's pretty nice about giving me time off if I need to take care of Mom. We make do. Watch our expenses, and all. Somehow we manage to cover the medical bills…most of the time. Mom has Alzheimer's and high blood pressure."

She stared at Toby, whose eyes glistened with gathering teardrops, and she was chewing on her lower lip.

"Do you have a gun?" Danya said.

Toby raised her eyebrows. "No," she said. "I wouldn't know how to use one if I did."

"Any brothers or cousins nearby who can stay with you for a while?"

Toby shook her head. "I don't have any family in the area except for an aunt, my mother's younger sister. She lives in Klamath Falls.

She visits us sometimes and stays for a while. She's going to be here in a few days to take care of Mom. I'm supposed to go with a group of people to San Francisco for a couple days. It's a protest against social injustice, but I don't know if that's a good idea now."

Danya placed some crisp bills into Toby's hand.

"That should cover the gas."

Toby looked at the wad of hundred-dollar notes.

"That's way more than the cost of the gas. I can't accept this."

"Yes, you can. Take your mother with you. Who knows? She might enjoy it. Anyway, give this some time to blow over. Right now, Cole is going to be looking for trouble. In a week or two, he'll have calmed down."

"You sound like you know the type of person Cole is."

"I've dealt with a number of men like him. They prey on those they perceive to be weak and defenseless. But when someone stands up to them, they quickly back down."

Toby shook her head and offered the money back to Danya.

"Mom doesn't do well in a new environment. If her routine changes, she's easily confused. If we go stay in a motel or campground, she's likely to just walk away when I'm asleep or in the shower."

"Then you go away for a while, and have your mother stay with your aunt."

"We've tried that before, and it didn't work. Mom became very upset. She walked out of the apartment one day while my aunt was working. Fortunately, the police found her the next morning. She was cold and dehydrated, but it could have been a lot worse."

Danya glared at Toby. "He'll be back. You know that. I may have broken his nose, but he'll be treated and released. And he'll be looking for payback."

Toby dropped her head, and tears traced two lines down her face.

Danya sighed. "Is there a campground nearby? Someplace I can park my trailer and stay for a few days?"

"Nearest campground is about fifteen miles south of here, beyond Tulelake Wildlife Refuge. The campgrounds fill up quickly, though, and unless you have a reservation, you probably can't get a spot. But you can park at my house." Toby's face brightened. "There's plenty of room inside the barn, and I can give you an extension cord to plug into."

Danya considered the offer, knowing where this was headed. Her number-one objective in life was to shun attention, avoid contact with law enforcement, and live anonymously. The later had forced her to adapt to an existence off the grid by using forged identification, no permanent address, and paying for everything with cash. Since holding down a job was contrary to those requirements, she used her considerable skills to liberate ill-gotten funds from gangs engaged in criminal commerce. Typically, she preyed on Mexican drug cartels running operations on both sides of the border.

It was bad enough that she'd assaulted Cole. She should have walked away—after all, it wasn't any of her business. She could have simply paid for the gas and coffee and moved on. By now, she'd be miles away, and with no entanglements.

But that wasn't her style—not anymore.

She didn't know how many of the men and women she'd killed truly deserved it. A lot, she hoped. But she would often lay awake at night, wondering how many of her victims were innocent. Or at worst, guilty of far lesser crimes that didn't justify the penalty she'd administered with ruthless efficiency.

The logical part of her mind argued that she could still leave before the ambulance arrived. She could probably trust Toby not to share her license plate number or the description of her vehicle—a red Ford pickup towing an Airstream trailer. But to be safe, she could sell or abandon the truck later—today, even—and buy a used SUV or pickup from a private seller.

As logical as the plan was, she dismissed it.

"Okay," she said. "Why don't you give me directions, and I'll get away from here before the ambulance arrives."

Toby shared her address, and then said, "You aren't running from the law, are you?"

Danya considered how to answer. If she was truthful, Toby

might feel compelled to share information with the sheriff. Besides, what would be gained by explaining that she was wanted by multiple domestic and foreign agencies?

"I just don't think it'll be helpful if I'm here. You know, in case Cole comes around. Just tell them exactly what I said on the phone. You found Cole unconscious, lying on the pavement, and you assume he fell on his face."

"You think they'll believe me? I mean, it sounds pretty lame."

Danya smiled. "Cole doesn't have the appearance of an overachiever. Besides, who's going to dispute your story?"

"Cole might. He could call the sheriff."

"Which is why I won't be here. Besides, Cole isn't the kind of guy who wants to have anything to do with law enforcement, or admit that a woman kicked his ass. Just stick to the story, okay? You'll be fine."

Toby forced a smile and nodded. "Thank you."

Danya turned and strode toward her truck, then called, over her shoulder, "You can thank me when this is over."

CHAPTER 7

FEARING THAT TOBY'S MOTHER MAY NOT REACT WELL to a stranger parked on her property, Danya decided to wait alongside the county road at the entrance to the long driveway. Two log posts on either side of the gravel drive supported a wood plank engraved with the words RIDDLE RANCH. She coasted to a stop on a long and wide shoulder that also sprouted a bank of mailboxes, which she took care not to block. An oak tree provided shade from the afternoon sun. If anyone bothered to ask why she was parked alongside the road, she would feign being lost and ask for directions to Lava Beds National Monument, which she knew to be many miles to the south.

Shortly after 5:00 p.m., Toby stopped at the row of mailboxes.

"You didn't have to wait here," she said through the open window. "The driveway is just ahead."

"I didn't want to disturb your mother. I'll follow you."

Toby led her to the barn. It was about fifty yards behind the house. The weathered structure was dark gray, with no trace of ever being painted. Two large doors provided access, one on each gabled wall at opposite ends of the barn.

"Your family name is Riddle?" Danya said.

"Yep." Toby extended her hand. "Since we haven't formally met, my name is Toby Riddle."

"Danya." She shook Toby' hand.

"Just Danya? No last name? Mysterious."

"Biton. Danya Biton."

"Hmm." Toby gazed at Danya, taking in her features.

Before her stood a woman in her late thirties, with tanned skin, a high forehead, and a long and thin face. Her hair was a few shades lighter than her dark brown eyes.

After thoughtful consideration, Toby said, "Let me guess. French?"

Danya shook her head. "Israeli. My family is Jewish."

"Oh. I've never met anyone from Israel. Your name is beautiful. Does it have special meaning?"

"According to my mother, my father insisted on naming me Danya. In Hebrew, it means *judgment of God*. And you? I'm guessing American Indian, Modoc or Klamath."

Toby raised her eyebrows. "Yes, and yes. My father's side of the family traces its lineage to the Modoc, but my mother is from the Klamath tribe. We have deep roots here, going back countless generations."

"It shows in your eyes. This land is important to you."

"I've never had much interest in traveling. This is my ancestral home. I belong here. Even if there are jerks like Cole to contend with."

"Don't worry about him."

Toby found comfort in her words. The woman was strong and confident.

"Park anywhere you like," Toby said. "There's an electrical panel just inside the door, and outlets at both ends of the barn. I'll get an extension cord from the house."

Danya pushed the heavy door to the side. It slid open with a screech. Inside, the barn was one large open space. The roof was easily thirty-feet high at the ridge, sloping down to ten feet at the side walls. At one time, it was probably filled with bales of hay. But now it was empty.

She flipped a switch on the wall, and three overhead lamps turned on, providing scant illumination. The empty space seemed to absorb the light, leaving the walls dark and barely visible. The floor was hard-packed gravel, with dark oil stains here and there.

She turned at the soft crunch of gravel to see Toby holding out an old, heavy-duty electrical cord.

"Looks like the barn isn't used much anymore," Danya said.

"There was a time when Dad grew alfalfa on the ranch. He'd harvest it and store it here to keep it dry, then sell to other ranchers during the winter months. That was a long time ago. I was just a little girl."

"What happened?"

"Dad passed away, and Mom got ill. It cost more to hire laborers than we could make by selling the feed. So I got a job at the gas station. A couple of the neighbors pay to have their cattle graze on our land."

"What about you?" She studied Toby.

There was much more to this young woman than she was letting on.

"Not much to say. I go from day to day, making sure Mom's okay." Toby sounded uncomfortable with the subject.

"That's it? What about your future? What are you aspiring toward?"

"Yeah, right. I'm an American Indian. My people have no future," she said, in a bitter tone. "Why do you think those guys bother me?"

"You mean Cole?"

Toby nodded. "And Craig. That's his brother. They're just reflective of the white man in general. They carry the attitude that my people—me—have no rights. In their eyes, we aren't even human."

Danya's eyes filled with sorrow. She was a newcomer to the oldest racial conflict of the New World. But such irrational prejudice based on race, tribal affiliation, and religion marked the history of mankind. It seemed to be a uniquely human behavior, one that was at the root of the vast majority of global conflicts, suffering, and death. She was intimately aware of the pain such thinking had caused in Israel and the Middle East.

"I'm sorry. But surely attitudes are changing. I mean, the issue of racial inequality and injustice is at the forefront of the national dialog. It's in the news every day."

Toby rolled her eyes. "Listen closely and let me know when that dialog extends to the Indigenous Peoples. If you're black, brown, yellow—sure, then white people are *sensitive,*" she made air quotes with her fingers, "to treating you fairly. But if you're red, like me, forget it. We're still invisible. Forgotten by everyone. More than five thousand Native American women go missing every year, and we are ten times more likely to be murdered than the national average. We suffer the highest poverty rate and the lowest employment rate of any racial group in the US. One in four American Indians suffer from food insecurity. Forty percent of housing on reservations is considered substandard, compared to six percent throughout the rest of the country. Statues of Confederate generals are removed from public parks and university campuses, and yet the twenty-dollar bill features the portrait of Andrew Jackson, who waged brutal campaigns against the tribes to push them off their ancestral lands, relocating tens of thousands farther west."

Danya lowered her eyes. "I'm sorry."

"Our struggle spans centuries, and was far more brutal than even slavery."

"Okay, I see your point."

"No, I don't think you do. That's just the tip of the iceberg. For as long as this country has existed, my people have been systematically lied to by the United States government and every agency working on its behalf. Treaties my forefathers signed with the government were broken. My ancestors were murdered by soldiers in a protracted war of genocide. They even used smallpox as a weapon against my people. Following admission into the Union, California offered a bounty for Indian scalps, and legalized enslavement of Native Americans. These crimes are not discussed outside of history books. We have no advocates arguing for our rights. No one speaks on our behalf to demand proper compensation for the land and wealth stolen from all Indigenous People, by white settlers."

Danya was shocked. Timid Toby had a beast inside, and she'd just glimpsed it.

"Why don't you?" Danya said.

"What?"

"Why don't you advocate on behalf of your people?"

Toby squared her shoulders and raised her chin.

"I will make my voice heard. One of many. After decades of inactivity, the Movement is being revitalized."

"Movement?"

"The American Indian Movement, or AIM."

"Catchy."

"I wasn't even born yet when the founders of AIM joined the occupation of Alcatraz."

"The prison?"

"Former prison. It's on an island in San Francisco Bay."

"Yeah, I know where it is. Al Capone was jailed there."

"And a lot of other really bad men, like Machine Gun Kelly and Whitey Bulger. They say no one ever escaped. But I'm not sure I believe that."

"What happened to AIM? I've never heard of it."

"If you lived in America in the 60s and 70s, you'd be familiar with the Movement. It even influenced Hollywood. Marlon Brando asked Sacheen Littlefeather, an actress and activist for Native American rights, to represent him at the 45th Academy Awards, and decline his Best Actor Award for his performance in *The Godfather*. She was both White Mountain Apache and Yaqui."

"I didn't know," Danya said.

Toby shrugged. "Following many protests—some violent—the public seemed to lose interest in AIM by the late 70s. The organization suffered from poor leadership, including scandals, and eventually split into two factions. But it remains active. My generation hopes to revive the Movement. Maybe in my lifetime, we can finally make a difference and achieve equality and justice for all races."

"I hope so. If your energy and enthusiasm are indicative, then I know you will be successful."

Toby's eyes brightened. "Hey, why don't you come with us?"

Danya pinched her eyebrows. "To where?"

"To Alcatraz. That's where we're going to have our first of many peaceful protests. It's a fitting location—the place where the Indian Rights Movement first gained national attention. It would be good to include your voice, your presence. We want to show that we have a diverse base."

"I see. And a Caucasian face would help with that."

"Not just Caucasian. All colors, all people."

Danya thought about the invitation. Since she'd just completed a job a week ago, she didn't have any place she needed to be. Maybe it would help ease the guilt for past sins if she did participate. But first, she'd have to do some research on the American Indian Movement. Her prime rule was to avoid contact with the authorities. And participating in a protest, no matter how peaceful the intentions, could easily escalate into trouble.

"Maybe. But first, we have a more pressing issue to deal with."

"Right. Cole. You have a plan?"

"I always do."

CHAPTER 8

LEAVING THE AIRSTREAM TRAILER PARKED inside the large farm building, away from public view, Danya drove her pickup to the backside of the barn, close to the range land, where it wouldn't be easily seen from the road, but still afforded a view of the house. She didn't expect the confrontation with Cole would escalate too far, so she didn't feel the need for a firearm. Instead, she placed the combat tomahawk on the passenger seat, within easy reach. A certain intimidation factor came with brandishing the time-proven weapon. There, she waited, inside the truck cab, for Cole to show. Of course, there was no guarantee that he would. But if she was reading his character correctly, he'd be steaming with humiliation, and looking to get even with Toby.

The hours slowly ticked by, until it was well-after midnight. The night sky was clear, and the moon was just beginning to rise on the eastern horizon. Danya shook her head, fighting the urge to close her eyes. It would have been nice to have the radio playing something obnoxious—maybe a right-wing or left-wing radio talk show. She found the talking heads to be reliably ignorant and offensive—just the right mix to cause enough irritation to help fight off the fatigue of an all-night stakeout.

She was beginning to think Cole wasn't going to show. Maybe he'd gone home, wallowed in self-pity and alcohol until he was drunk, and fell asleep. Plausible, but it didn't fit the type a man she knew him to be. No, he'd be back to take out his rage on Toby. If not tonight, then tomorrow night, or the next. For sure, he would return.

She unscrewed the cap on the Thermos bottle and poured out the last few tablespoons of coffee. She downed it in one gulp, and wished she had another full bottle of the steaming-hot brew. She placed the cup on the floor and then looked out the windshield again. Her pulse quickened as she recognized a flicker of motion. It was only there for an instant, but she was certain there was movement in the bushes near the back door. Anyone else might have written it off as a trick of tired eyes and dim light. But she knew to trust her senses. Doing so had saved her life on more than one occasion.

She looked from side to side, taking advantage of the greater night-vision sensitivity of the human eye just off direct center of one's field of vision. After nearly a half-minute, she saw it again. As the shrubbery shook, a dark figure rose and glided toward the door. Soon followed by a second figure.

The scene was suddenly bathed in bright light when she turned on the truck's headlamps. In the light, she recognized Cole. His nose was covered in a white bandage, and the skin surrounding his eyes was blackened from bruising. The second man bore a striking family resemblance. *Probably his brother Craig.*

"Stop right there, Cole." She slid from the driver's seat, tomahawk in her grasp.

Cole and his brother faced her, shielding their eyes.

"Who are you?" Cole said.

"What? Forgot about me so soon? That hurts." She closed the distance to the two men, and stopped several yards away.

Each man still had a hand raised in a vain effort to block the glare from the headlights, which were on high beam.

Cole said, "Step away from the light so I can see you."

They were both gripping truncheons, their knuckles appearing white in the light.

"Put the clubs down and go home," she said.

"Why don't you come over her and make us," Craig said.

"Take a look at your brother. You might want to rethink that."

Craig charged her, his club raised, prepared to strike. She held her ground until the last moment, then ducked and stepped inside his outstretched arm. When he swung the club down, all he got was air.

With both hands locked on the tomahawk, she rammed the heel of the handle into Craig's solar plexus. His eyes bulged, and he grunted as the air was forced from his lungs. Stunned and gasping for breath, he was hunched over, frozen in time. She whipped the flat side of the steel head across his temple. Craig staggered to the side before collapsing.

At the sight of his brother falling, Cole became enraged.

"What did you do to him? I'll kill you." He charged and took a sideways swipe with the billy club, aiming for her head.

She ducked and swung the tomahawk low, the spiked end piercing deep into his thigh.

"Ahhh!" he screamed.

Danya ripped it out, tearing the flesh with the sharp point. She pivoted to the side, taking Cole's club hand with her. Choking up on the handle of the tomahawk, she used the sharp blade like a knife. With a downward slash, she cleaved a laceration into his forearm just below the elbow. He dropped the truncheon and cried out again.

She released her grip on Cole and stepped backwards to open up a few feet of separation. Then, still clasping the bladed weapon near the head, she swung the lower part of the handle across the back of Cole's head. He tilted forward and dropped to a knee before arresting his fall.

Craig began to stir, one eye already swollen shut, and a massive bruise discoloring the flesh on the side of his face and head.

Danya wasn't even breathing hard as she stood over both men.

"It's over," she said. "You're both finished. Now get the hell off this property. You're trespassing. That means I can continue to beat the shit out of both of you if I so choose."

Cole stretched out his good hand for the bludgeon. He managed to wrap his fingers around the handle before she smashed her foot on the club, squashing his fingertips in the process, and eliciting a yelp as he worked his hand free.

"Nope. The blackjacks stay here. Both of 'em."

"Jesus, lady." Cole's voice was anemic—not at all the defiant and threatening personality she'd met before.

"Consider this a warning. Don't ever bother Toby or her family again. Do you understand me?"

No reply, so she planted her heel in the middle of Cole's back.

"All right, all right," he said.

"Now leave. And if I ever even *suspect* you've hassled Toby, I'll be back. And I'll kill you. You'll never see it coming. Just boom, and you're both dead. Have I made myself clear?"

The two nodded. "Don't worry. We won't bother Toby no more."

"Oh, I'm not worried. But you should be," she growled.

Cole and Craig scampered down the driveway and out of sight. Danya picked up the two clubs and tossed them into the garbage. She heard the door hinges squeak, and then a soft voice.

"Danya? Is that you?"

It was Toby. She was wrapped in a blanket, standing on the top step.

"It's me," Danya replied. "You won't be hearing from those two again—ever."

"Cole and his brother? They were here?"

"Yeah. Just left."

"I don't get it. What did you say to them?"

Danya smiled. "Let's just say I was able to convince them of the error of their ways."

Toby noticed the steel tomahawk, the business end hanging below Danya's knee.

"I'd imagine that," Toby pointed at the weapon, "had something to do with your powers of persuasion?"

"Oh, this?" Danya slipped the handle beneath her belt. "Yeah. Maybe a little."

CHAPTER 9

Duck Valley Reservation, Nevada
May 17

IN THE HILLS, ABOUT TWO MILES EAST of Owyhee Road, a small team of technicians was busy at work. The double-wide trailer that served as their laboratory was adequate, but primitive. Still, they made do with lead shielding and down-draft chemical hoods—eight of them—that vented through the floor of the trailer. The hoods themselves were nothing more than five-sided rectangular boxes, with the sixth side, the front, a clear glass sash that could be raised or lowered.

The technicians stood before the chemical hoods. Their arms, clad in black elbow-length rubber gauntlets, were inserted into the boxes where they worked with corrosive acid. The heavy gloves, lined with a thin layer of lead foil, made even routine finger movements awkward and strenuous.

In half of the hoods, small piles of ceramic pellets were digested. As the acid did its chemical magic, noxious orange-brown fumes were given off, and these had to be ducted to the outside. Once the pellets were dissolved, the resulting solutions were then concentrated, and finally, evaporated to dryness in the other four hoods.

All but the front sash of each hood was wrapped in layers of lead sheet to contain the radiation. To protect the workers—who had to spend time in front of each hood—they were covered in lead-lined suits. Plus, their daily time in front of the hoods was limited to avoid the onset of radiation sickness. This requirement did not significantly limit productivity since the lab was outfitted with cameras for remote monitoring, and the dissolution process, as well as the drying process, proceeded with little in-person oversight from the technicians. The cameras were monitored from a second trailer nearby, which served as the living quarters.

Unbeknownst to the technicians, the radiation monitor each wore had been calibrated to give a false low reading. The job only required two days, insufficient time for the symptoms of radiation exposure to develop. And long-term effects would be of no concern.

After a full day of round-the-clock effort, the ceramic pellets were digested and dried to yield a colorless powder. In this form, the powder was soluble in water—an undesired property. The technicians further heated the powder in air until it decomposed. This process was also completed inside the down-draft chemical hoods. The result—a water insoluble material that was packaged in lead straws, each holding about a gram of radioactive strontium-90. The straws, each about twenty-centimeters long, were crimped at both ends and placed in grooves in graphite trays. A cover, also made of graphite, fit over the trays to secure everything in place.

Sacheen monitored the technician's progress from the monitors in the second trailer. She'd been paying close attention to their work from the moment she'd delivered the fuel cannisters from the two thermoelectric generators that had been partially dismantled on the shore of Bathurst Inlet. Russia had deployed more than a thousand of the generators decades ago. Unsecured, now they littered the Arctic, leaving their deadly contents free for the taking.

After flying the de Havilland DHC-2 Beaver at tree-top level across the border, she'd made one clandestine fueling stop at a remote ranch, landing on a long and straight dirt road that led to a rustic barn. The owner of the ranch had made a nice profit for less than an hour of work pumping fuel into the Beaver, and for keeping his mouth shut.

Gassed up, she'd completed her flight, landing on a primitive dirt landing strip on the reservation. A simple metal structure served as a hangar for the aircraft as the precious, yet deadly, cargo had been offloaded for further processing.

The graphite containers were stacked next to other boxes, similar in appearance, but filled with lead straws containing cobalt-60 oxide. Another radioactive material, the source had been metallic rods of cobalt-60 used in medical imaging. Like the ceramic pellets, the cobalt rods were also dissolved in acid, and then converted to a water-insoluble powder suitable for aerial dispersion.

"The irony of this location hasn't been lost on me." She was sitting at the de facto kitchen table—a simple six-foot plastic folding table.

Across from her sat Leonard Cloud. Like Lewis Blackhawk, he was from the Shoshone tribe and had lived on the Duck Valley Reservation most of his life, having left only long enough to complete a college education at the University of Tulsa.

Leonard's eyes were dark and clouded with anger.

"It was here," he said, "on this reservation, that the family of my uncle was murdered by government agents. The date is forever burned in my mind. February twelfth, 1979."

"Your uncle was a great leader and spokesman for the Movement, for our people," Sacheen said.

"It came to him naturally. His passion as an outspoken activist in support of Indigenous-People's rights is well-documented and serves to teach new generations. It is fitting that we are continuing the fight for respect and dignity for all tribes."

She reached out and wrapped her hands around Leonard's.

"The atrocities committed by the government against our people will never stop," she said. "Not until we strike a devastating blow. One which the Washington politicians could only imagine in their darkest nightmares. The time for murdering our people, for treating our people like feral dogs, will come to an end. We will force them to recognize our sovereign nations and personal freedoms. Sacred lands which were illegally taken from our ancestors will be ours once again. Wealth, which was stolen from our forefathers, will be returned."

"It is unfortunate that the Council elders do not approve of our methods."

"They are fools," she hissed.

"You shouldn't let it upset you so. They are old men who can't see the truth. Together, we will transform the Movement. Our vision is true. Tens of thousands of our brothers and sisters will follow our leadership. The time for patience is over, while the time for action is upon us."

She rose from her chair and walked around the table, then sat on Leonard's lap and cradled his face in her palms.

"It is our destiny to carry forward the fight that many of the great chiefs from generations ago had undertaken," she said. "And we will be victorious."

Leonard wrapped his arms around her to pull her closer, and kissed her passionately.

She pushed away. "Later, my wild buck." She wore a coy smile. "The technicians will soon be finished."

None of the workers lived on the reservation. They were all Caucasian and Hispanic, and had been recruited from a couple drug labs that operated in remote swaths of northern Nevada. They were all outlaws with criminal records for drug dealing and possession. They'd been working in meth labs—a dangerous job that required attention to detail, commitment to following directions to the letter, and the ability to synthesize dangerous chemicals while wearing personal protection gear. This typically comprised gauntlet-style neoprene gloves and a full-face respirator.

They'd eagerly accepted the temporary job Leonard offered at three times their normal compensation. Half was paid upon arrival at Leonard's lab, and half was promised upon completion of the job.

Leonard sighed. "I suppose you're right." He patted her on the butt as she rose. "Besides, I have a trench to dig."

As Leonard was walking to the backhoe, the door to the lab opened.

One of the technicians called out, "Hey, man. The job's done."

They no longer wore the bulky hazmat suits and gloves.

Leonard turned to face the worker, and pointed toward the other trailer.

"You can go inside and clean up, have some whiskey. Sacheen has the remainder of your pay."

Sacheen heard the sound of the backhoe diesel engine firing up as the five technicians entered and sat around the table.

"We passed Leonard outside. He said you have our money."

"Yeah. And whiskey," another said.

"I'd settled for a night in the sac with you," said a third, with lust-filled eyes.

"Settle down, boys." She reached into a kitchen cabinet and tossed a cloth bank bag on the table.

Bundles of hundred-dollar bills spilled out. The five men all grabbed for it at the same time.

"Ten grand for each of you," she said. "Just as Leonard promised. There are five bundles there. Each still has the currency strap applied at the bank. That's ten thousand dollars per bundle. Count it if you like."

"I believe I will. Not that I don't trust you. But just to avoid any mistakes."

"Knock yourself out." She retrieved a bottle and five shot glasses from the cabinet, and placed them on the table. "Help yourself to a drink. You deserve it. You all did a good job."

The technicians powered down two shots each, sharing trivial banter and occasional laughs, before taking a breather and returning to counting the cash. The smallest man at the table was the first to feel the effects. His arms, overcome by the force of gravity, fell to his side, the half-filled shot glass crashing to the floor.

"What the hell?" said another.

Then he, too, slumped in his chair. Soon, they all were immobilized. They were still breathing, and their eyes still moved about, communicating terror.

The diesel engine had quieted, and Leonard entered through the door. He paused, surveying the limp bodies surrounding the table.

"Shit. What did you give them?"

She smiled. "Conium. It's an alkaloid extracted from hemlock. Works by paralysis."

"You mean, these guys aren't dead? They're just paralyzed? I thought you were going to poison them."

She nodded. "That's what I did. Given enough time, the paralysis will stop their heart and respiration, but the skeletal muscles are affected first."

"No kidding. And fast, too."

"Yeah. I guess I did put a lot of the alkaloid in the whiskey. I wasn't sure how much they would drink. As it turns out, they drank plenty."

Leonard poked one of the men in the shoulder. Motionless, he stared back with listless eyes.

"Well, then, let's get on with it," Leonard said. "You take their feet, and I'll grab their arms."

One by one, he and Sacheen carried the paralyzed men out of the trailer, to the trench he'd just dug with the backhoe. Standing at the edge, they dropped the bodies in. Side by side, Sacheen and Leonard looked into the deep trench. The victims were still alive and breathing shallowly. Those who had come to rest on their back looked up in abject horror, knowing what was about to come.

"Say goodbye," Leonard said to Sacheen, but also to the paralyzed men.

She waved. "Bye-bye."

Leonard climbed into the seat of the backhoe and started the engine. A puff of sooty smoke belched from the exhaust before the engine settled into a throaty rumble. He moved the hydraulics control levers to scoop a bucket full of dirt, and dumped it over the bodies. He repeated the process over and over.

In five minutes, the trench was filled.

CHAPTER 10

THE SOUND OF THE TOILET FLUSHING awoke Leonard. Sacheen was at the sink, splashing water on her face. The nausea had subsided almost as fast as it had come on.

Leonard turned onto his side. The glow of the nightlight glistened off her sweat-soaked body, and he admired her curves through sleepy eyes.

"Is everything okay?" he said.

She patted her face dry with a hand towel.

"Yes. Just a dream."

"The white wolf again?"

She nodded and returned to the bed. Sitting next to her lover, she drew the sheet up, covering her breasts.

"I was in the mountains, at the edge of a meadow. The white wolf came to see me. She had two pups this time. They played like puppies do while I stroked her head. I was staring into her blue eyes, and when I looked up, the entire pack was there."

"This is a good omen. The wolf is cunning, aggressive, dangerous. The white she-wolf is your totem, a true representation of your spirit."

"How can you be so sure?"

With his fingertips, Leonard moved some raven locks from her cheek.

"This is not like you to second-guess our resolve," he said. "Talk to me. Together, we can solve any problem, any challenge."

For the third time in less than a week, she'd suffered nausea in the early morning hours. And along with the brief periods of sickness, her emotions were amplified. At times, she felt deep-seated resentment toward the American Indian Movement for not doing more to win basic civil rights for American natives. It was why she and Leonard had founded the Indigenous Peoples Movement.

If AIM had done more, taken decisive action instead of just talked, I wouldn't be forced to do these things. Why does it have to be me? Why Leonard? The old men, the tribal elders—it's their responsibility to look after their people.

She wanted to tell Leonard what she was feeling, the changes she was going through. But there was never a good time. In a while, he would know. He would see her belly expand as the seed of a new generation grew.

What world will our child be born into?

She looked into Leonard's eyes. "It's nothing."

"You have had many dreams of the white wolf. But those never bothered you like this. Tell me about it. It will help you clear your mind."

"The wolf, her blue eyes are like glacier ice. Beautiful and hard. But this time, I sensed fear in her eyes. It felt like she wanted me to meet her pups, to take care of them."

"Why would she want you to care for her pups?"

"I don't know. In my dream, I was looking into her blue eyes, and then the pack was just there. The pack was fearful. In my dreams, it's like I can sense the thoughts of the wolves."

"In the wild, a wolf pack isn't afraid of any predator. Not even a bear."

"But the white wolf *is* afraid. And I think she feared for her pups, too. And then, across the meadow was a flock of sheep. The pack started to stalk the sheep, but then a shepherd appeared from the middle of the flock. There was only one shepherd—a woman with brown hair. But I don't recall what she looked like. She was wearing a white robe, so she blended in with the sheep. And she held a wooden crook. At first, she didn't see the wolf pack approaching.

But before they could single out an old ewe, the shepherd saw them."

Leonard was fully awake now, listening intently to Sacheen's dream.

He said, "One shepherd against an entire pack of wolves wouldn't stand a chance. The pack would easily single out an old or sick sheep and take it down."

"Except that's not what happened. While the white she-wolf watched, the shepherd threw off her robe. She was firing a submachine gun at the other wolves. She killed all of them, until only the white wolf was left. Then it's like I was seeing through the eyes of the white wolf. I was the wolf. I charged at the shepherd. She had her gun pointed right at me. I heard the gunshots, expecting the bullets to find their mark, but they didn't."

"Did the she-wolf get the shepherd?" Leonard said.

Her voice barely above a whisper, Sacheen said, "No. I woke up."

"It's only a dream. It can't hurt you. Besides, I can tell you with certainty that one hunter against an entire pack of wolves wouldn't stand a chance. The wolves would encircle the shooter and kill him quickly."

As comforting as Leonard's assurances were, Sacheen couldn't shake the feeling that her dream was a harbinger of things to come.

CHAPTER 11

ALCATRAZ ISLAND, SAN FRANCISCO BAY
MAY 22

PREDICTABLY, THE TRAFFIC SOUTHBOUND on I-5 moved along at five to ten miles per hour faster than the posted speed limit, and Danya made good time. She and Toby passed the hours conversing mostly about Toby's family and life as a Native American living off the reservation, in a community dominated by ranching. As she learned, Cole hadn't been the first white man to threaten Toby.

Shortly following a rest stop near Willows in the northern Sacramento Valley, Toby turned an inquisitive eye to her new friend.

"You haven't said much about your life."

"Not much to say."

"Really? I mean, the way you took Cole down, and his brother, I'd have thought you're ex-military. In Israel, women serve in the military, right? Combat, too, I've heard."

"Nah. Nothing that exciting."

"Is that so? You didn't learn to fight like that in school, or by being someone's secretary."

Toby's probing was met with silence. Danya stared ahead at the road, watching the white line zip by. Her thoughts drifted back in time. She placed an elbow on the arm rest, and two fingers against her temple—a habit when she was deep in thought.

Had it already been several years since she'd entered the Oregon wilderness with her team of four operators? Her callsign had been Artemis—the hunter. She recalled with clarity killing the Oregon State trooper near the crest of the Cascade Mountain range. The trooper had gotten the drop on her team members, and disarmed them all at gunpoint. But not her. She'd slipped away. Out of sight of the officer, she crept up on him from behind, placed a gun to his head, and pulled the trigger. No guilt, no remorse. Just doing the job.

At the time, the job had sounded simple enough—terminate an American civilian who'd stumbled upon secret information dating back to June of 1967. Knowledge of a long-forgotten event that had transpired during the Six Day War, when Israel was fighting the Arab Coalition for its very survival. The secret was supposed to have been buried deep—so deep it would never surface.

But somehow it did.

Although the information was of no strategic importance so many decades after the war, it was still considered to be a significant liability for the Israeli prime minister, potentially endangering Israel's relationship with the United States.

The problem had to be rectified, and Mossad dispatched Danya to lead a team of four operators already living under cover in the US, to clean up the mess. Tracking down the American was easy, and terminating him *should* have been a simple affair. After all, he was just an ordinary civilian.

Toby's voice brought Danya back to the present.

"You okay?"

"Yeah. Just thinking."

"About what?"

Danya remained silent.

"Come on," Toby said. "I've shared almost my entire life story."

"Yeah, don't expect me to reciprocate."

With coffee in hand, Danya and Toby boarded the ferry at the Alameda Ferry Terminal, on the Oakland Inner Harbor. Before leaving the Riddle Ranch, Danya had left her trailer parked inside the old barn. She didn't want the hassle of towing it through traffic, or to run the risk that it might be vandalized in the ferry terminal parking lot. It would be safe in the empty barn until she returned in a few days.

Expecting that her daypack would be subject to inspection prior to boarding the ferry to San Francisco, she made sure it didn't contain any knives or firearms. However, she left the binoculars in the pack rather than risk having the expensive optics stolen from her parked car. Besides, she expected the views from the small island near the mouth of the bay to be spectacular.

After disembarking in San Francisco, the pair walked a short distance to Pier 33, where they boarded a second ferry. It was a beautiful spring morning in San Francisco, with a cool, gentle breeze blowing in from the bay. She was glad she was wearing a bulky hooded sweatshirt to ward off the chill that persisted despite the sunshine. They sat with many other Indigenous People for the short boat ride to the landing dock on Alcatraz.

"You have an unusual name for a woman," Danya said.

"I'm named after Toby Riddle. She was an important Modoc woman who served as an interpreter during the Modoc War."

"I haven't heard of the Modoc War."

"It was in the 1870s. The government wanted to force the Modocs onto the same reservation as the Klamath tribe. Have you heard of Captain Jack?"

Danya shook her head.

"He's a famous Modoc Chief. He led a band of warriors into the lava fields to resist the army. The lava fields are rugged and extremely difficult to pass through. Captain Jack was a brilliant tactician. He held off the soldiers for many months. Anyway, in 1873, Toby Riddle overheard a plan to attack the US Peace Commission when she delivered a message to the Modoc leaders, which included Captain Jack. She told the Commission of the plan, but they didn't heed her warning. Some of the commissioners were killed, but Toby saved the life of Alfred Meacham. He was the Oregon Indian Superintendent."

"What happened after the war was over?" Danya said.

"The Modoc tribe was forced off their ancestral lands in northeastern California and southern Oregon, the rich lands around Tule Lake and Lost River. Some were relocated more than a thousand miles to the Indian Territory in Oklahoma, while the remainder were resettled to the Klamath Reservation."

"I think I'm beginning to understand why this protest is important to you," Danya said.

"It's important to all my people. The Modoc War was late in the history of the white expansionist policies. Those policies resulted in all American Indians eventually being forced onto reservations. Think about it. Can you imagine that being done today?"

"Those were different times," Danya said. "A lot has changed since the nineteenth century."

"Times always change, I suppose. Eventually."

"What do you mean?"

"I'm just saying the obvious. Ever since Europeans set foot on this continent, the red man has been treated as a second-class citizen, at best." Toby paused, then whispered, "At worst, we've been treated as vermin—to be exterminated."

"I'm sorry. I didn't know. When I was in school, only the highlights of American history were taught." Danya paused in reflection. "Perhaps I should learn more. It seems this dark passage of your history has similarities to events in my country."

Toby looked into her eyes, searching for any sign of deceit—a ploy to pretend to be sympathetic. But no such evidence was there.

"What was wrong then, is still wrong now," Toby said. "The United States must acknowledge its crimes against humanity, committed in the name of westward expansion."

Danya reflected on the history of her homeland. Founded in May 1948, the State of Israel was literally carved out of the Middle East by the victorious allies, following the end of World War II. The land was taken from Palestine, against the wishes of the Palestinian people. The result was conflict that, to this day, has not been resolved. A festering wound that showed no sign of healing.

She reflected on the Palestinian people, who were evicted from their ancestral homeland. *Was their plight really any different from that of Native Americans?*

Finally, Danya said, "Do you think your protests will bring about the change you seek?"

Toby sighed. "Truthfully? No, not in my lifetime. Eventually, I think attitudes will change. I mean, just look at the progress the civil rights movement of the 60s brought about. But almost six decades later, there's still work to be done. And that civil rights movement has never extended to my people."

"I hope this is the beginning of that change," Danya said. "I truly do."

"Thank you." Toby reached out for her hand. "I'm very lucky to count you as a friend."

"How many protestors do you expect?"

"I'm not sure. Maybe as many as a hundred."

Danya surveyed the faces on the ferry.

"I don't think there are that many on this boat."

"Don't expect every protestor to look like an Indian. I mean, you're participating, right?"

We'll see. Danya was still apprehensive about placing herself in a situation that might involve police interaction.

"Besides," Toby said, "more may arrive on later ferries."

The ship slowed as it approached the dock, and with a small bump of the fenders, came to a stop. Once the mooring lines were secured to bollards fore and aft, the gangway was put in place, and the passengers offloaded in single file.

Many peopled milled about the dock area, seeing the structures of the former penal institution up close for the first time. The large apartment block dominated the view. It was originally constructed as barracks for soldiers when the island was a military prison, and then remodeled to provide housing for correctional officers and their families when the prison was transferred to civilian control. High up on the wall of the five-story building was a sign identifying Alcatraz as a federal penitentiary. Just above the sign, in red, was the greeting *Indians Welcome*. Hand-painted in 1969, it was a reminder that the former federal prison was occupied by indigenous Americans.

Danya and Toby followed a sea of people moving past a block of restrooms, toward the old guard tower.

"We're supposed to meet at the base of the tower," Toby said. "I think we're going to be given pamphlets to hand out to visitors. And maybe some signs, too."

"Why Alcatraz?" Danya said.

"This is where the modern movement really began. According to the 1868 Treaty of Fort Laramie, any unoccupied land could be rightfully reclaimed and taken back by the tribes. Since President Kennedy closed and abandoned the prison here in 1963, it was our treaty right to claim this island. Plus, it's only a mile or so from San Francisco. Initially, it was mostly a student group that had organized in the Bay Area. They called themselves Indians of All Tribes. On November twentieth, 1969, a boat carrying members from twenty tribes landed on Alcatraz. That initial group numbered seventy-nine, and included family members, women, and children. More activists came later."

Danya said, "Being in the middle of the California Bay Area would make this a convenient, and strategic, location for a protest."

"Yes, but it was also symbolic. Alcatraz was federal property. And Indians of All Tribes was taking it, just as the federal government had taken our lands."

"What happened? Why didn't the movement continue to gain momentum?"

Toby shrugged. "Hard to say. I think the public lost interest in yet another civil rights movement. Maybe they thought AIM was too militant. You know, not long after the occupation of Alcatraz, there were conflicts between Indians and the FBI, at Wounded Knee and Pine Ridge. Those events turned public opinion against us. And many of my people still don't trust the FBI."

Off to the side of the path, a group of people were gathering flyers. Toby grabbed a few dozen sheets, which consisted of a list of broken treaties dating back two hundred years. At the bottom was a chronological list of several massacres carried out by the US Army, against native populations, mostly women and children. On the reverse side, a historical black-and-white photo documented Native American corpses littering the village at Wounded Knee. Another showed a mass grave with bodies of Indian women and children stacked three-deep. The flyer was professionally produced with high-resolution images. The organization's web address was provided at the bottom of the page, beneath the photos, along with a call for support.

"Offer these to everyone you see," said the organizer, a barrel-chested man in his late twenties.

He wore a ball cap embroidered with the words *American Indian Movement* overlaid on an eagle feather.

"Ask people to write their representatives and demand recognition of tribal rights guaranteed by treaties," he said.

"What are these for?" Toby picked up an arm band from the table next to the flyers.

The barrel-chested man said, "It identifies you as a member of the protest. Put one on your arm, over your clothing so it's easily visible. Take one for your friend, too. We want everyone to know who's here peacefully supporting our cause."

Toby picked up two and handed one to Danya. They were printed on some type of durable paper, like the wrist bands they put on hospital patients, but many times wider. The design was a copy of a classic Plains Indian beadwork band, a style worn by warriors.

"These are beautiful. My name's Toby." She extended her hand to the organizer. "I'm from the Modoc and Klamath tribes."

"Nice to meet you, Toby. I'm Clyde Means." His grip was firm.

Several protestors were hoisting signs and chanting, attracting the attention of some of the visitors.

"Stay nearby," Clyde said. "We're expecting more supporters on the next ferry. It will arrive in about thirty minutes. We'll get everyone organized on the dock, and then shoot video for the news stations."

"Are you expecting any reporters?" Toby said.

"I hope so. Nothing confirmed yet, but we put the word out."

Danya looked across the dock and saw a gathering group of park rangers taking note of the protestors. If they decided to question the demonstrators, she didn't want any part of it.

"Why don't you stay here," she said to Toby. "I know this is important for you. I'm going to take a short walk, and then I'll be back when the next ferry arrives."

"But I thought you were also going to participate?"

"Don't worry. While everything is getting set up and organized, I'd like to at least see the outside of the cell house." Danya pointed toward the highest location on the tiny island, where the imposing three-floor concrete blockhouse stood next to the tall and slender lighthouse. "Besides, I'll bet the view from up there, across the bay to San Francisco, is amazing, and I don't know if I'll ever be back here again."

Toby smiled. "Of course. I'm sorry. I was being selfish. Take lots of pictures. I'll see you in a bit."

Alcatraz Island was nicknamed *The Rock* for good reason. It was a robust mountain peak that protruded through the bay, leaving the tip exposed. This solid foundation gave work crews a good footing for the structures they would build there—apartments and barracks, a chapel, administrative buildings, and the iconic cell house, which was located on the very top of the island. Due to the steep slopes dropping into the surrounding water, the boat landing had to be cut from rock, leaving a steep escarpment where the excavation had ended. The old barracks building was located at the north end of the landing, with the back of the large structure almost touching the stone ledge.

Leaving Toby with the protestors, who were swelling in number, Danya followed the main pathway from the dock, up toward the cell house. The grade was surprisingly steep, and passed beside the guardhouse and through the sally port about a hundred yards beyond the guard tower. The sally port was constructed with an outer wall and an inner wall to create a strong defensive position. A massive door was hinged from each wall. Illustrating the serious intentions of the fortification, an iron muzzle-loading cannon was mounted on a carriage within the sally port. The gapping maw of the cannon pointed down the slope, toward the dock. Had it been loaded with grapeshot and fired, it could have taken out a hundred invading troops charging up the path Danya had just walked.

Just inside the sally port, she turned and gazed back toward where she had come from. Several park employees, clothed in dark green jackets, were talking to Clyde Means while the demonstrators continued waving their signs and chanting. But after a brief conversation, the rangers dispersed again.

Hopefully, the park staff would allow the protest to continue without anyone being detained. Danya knew it was supposed to work that way, as long as there wasn't violence.

A young couple entered the sally port, and she quickly turned again to admire the view across the bay, to Treasure Island, and beyond to Berkeley, just like she imagined thousands of tourists did every day. The pair paused at the breach end of the large-bore gun while the woman read from a guidebook.

"The island is perfectly placed to protect San Francisco Bay. It was originally built as a fort. But the Civil War didn't reach this far west, and the fort didn't see any action."

Her male companion slapped a hand on the steel gun barrel.

"So they eventually converted it to a prison," he said.

"That's right. First, a military prison. And then, for civilian criminals."

The young man gazed across the cold waters of San Francisco Bay.

"I have to admit," he said, "I'd be intimidated about trying to escape if I was locked up here. Assuming you eluded the guards and didn't get shot, that swim is a long one."

"And the water is really cold. Plus, they say the currents are very strong. If you were swimming for shore when the tide was going out, you'd probably get pulled out into the Pacific Ocean."

"Did anyone escape? Make it out alive?"

"Maybe." She ran her finger along lines of text in the guidebook. "It's controversial. It says here that three inmates executed a daring plan. It was really cool, when you think about it. They made a movie about the escape. Anyway, they were never seen again. And their bodies were never found, either."

The couple exited the sally port and strolled up towards the cell house, which appeared to be the main attraction.

After snapping several photos across the bay, Danya ambled on. Ahead was the empty shell of what used to be the post exchange and officers club. There, the path made a sharp 180-degree turn and continued to climb. At the next switchback, she opted to go straight ahead and enter the large, flat parade ground. A few other visitors were milling about, mostly enjoying the spectacular view.

Eventually, she wandered to the edge of the grounds facing south. She was unable to see the courtyard adjoining the dock area, as the view was blocked by the tall barracks building. But the view of San Francisco was stunning. She meandered across the parade ground and toward the southern edge of the island, where she found herself standing alone on the edge of a bluff overlooking a rocky shoreline.

Given her military training, it was obvious to Danya that the extreme topography and commanding views made Alcatraz a strong defensive fortification. The steep rocky slopes reminded her of the mountainous terrain where she had hunted the American many years before. The memories were still vivid, as if it had all happened only weeks ago.

Her intelligence sources had said the American was just an ordinary man, lacking any military service or martial training. That assessment couldn't have been further from the truth. After he lured her team into the Cascade Mountains, he proceeded to use the boulder-strewn slopes and tree cover to his advantage, picking off the Mossad team members one by one, using only a hunting rifle.

Danya shook her head. Life was so much simpler when following orders was all that mattered. *How many of those orders were morally wrong?*

Her introspection was interrupted by a pair of seagulls diving off to her side to snatch a few morsels from a dropped cereal bar. A short distance beyond the squawking birds, a sign pointed to the Agave Trail, but a gate was closed at the trail head.

She drifted closer. A map posted next to the gate showed the trail extending down from the parade grounds, to the edge of the bay, then wrapping around and finally connecting to the ferry dock. Another sign read that the trail was closed due to nesting seabirds.

She looked toward the water lapping at the rocky shore, and spotted a man and a woman at the water's edge. They were facing the bay, squatting.

Some people just won't follow the rules.

After watching the pair for a minute, she started to turn, but something odd caught her attention. It appeared that the man had retrieved something from the water's edge and placed it inside his waistband. His shirt covered whatever it was.

Whatever the two were doing wasn't her business, so Danya turned and strode across the parade grounds.

CHAPTER 12

LEONARD CLOUD RETRIEVED A PISTOL from a black water-tight bag that was wedged between two stones in the shallow water. Only hours before, under cover of darkness, an accomplice clad in a black dry-suit, and being pulled by a battery-powered underwater scooter, had transported a cache of water-tight bags to this particular spot on the shore, near the Agave trail. The accomplice had made the journey from a thirty-six-foot sailboat bobbing a half-mile off the shore just south of Sausalito. Tethered to the stern of the sailboat was a futuristic-looking watercraft. With a bubble-shaped enclosure tall enough for twelve adult passengers and one pilot to stand upright, the Jet Capsule appeared top heavy, but in fact, was designed for speed and agility.

After a quick check that the magazine was loaded, and a round was chambered, Leonard stuffed the pistol, a Beretta 92, inside his belt and then pulled his shirt in place to cover the handgrip.

"We'll come back later for the rest of the gear," he said. "First, we need to secure the island."

He climbed the trail to the parade ground, with Sacheen two steps behind him. She had a sweater tied around her waist to hide the Beretta handgun she had at the small of her back.

After climbing over the gate and earning disapproving glares from three nearby tourists, the two strode down to the dock. The ferry had just finished unloading, and was about to begin accepting passengers for the ride back to Pier 33. Several park rangers were maintaining an orderly line. All carried holstered sidearms, in addition to handcuffs, pepper spray, and a radio hanging from their utility belts.

Leonard approached one of the rangers, who was standing alone, a couple dozen yards from his colleagues. Like the other park service staff, he was wearing green trousers and a dark green jacket with a park service patch on the shoulder. The rangers were all watching the flow of people away from the ferry, and the short line ready to board.

Leonard nodded as Sacheen strode up to the visitor's center. A middle-aged man and woman were receiving directions to the cell house. Some of the tourists who had just arrived were finding their way to the museum and movie theater inside the barracks building. She ignored the people traffic and kept her eye on Leonard, who was standing to the side of the armed ranger when he pulled out his pistol and pressed it against the man's side. The ranger started to reach for his weapon, but stopped when the gun barrel was pressed harder into his flesh.

"Good. Now call your buddy over. And don't do anything stupid. Got it?" Leonard reached around behind the ranger to confiscate his pistol, and glanced at it before placing it underneath his shirt. "Nice weapon. Smith and Wesson, M and P. Forty cal., I'm betting. Would be a shame if I had to shoot you with your own service piece."

The ranger nodded almost imperceptibly.

"Hey, Stuart. This gentleman here has a question about the park that I can't answer. Thought you might be able to help him."

"Yeah, sure."

As Stuart approached, he sensed something wasn't right. But it was too late. He was within a few feet of his colleague when he saw the gun.

"Nice and easy," Leonard said, his gaze locked with the park ranger's. "I'll take that weapon." He tucked it between his waist and belt, with the other Smith & Wesson.

Sacheen had acted as soon as Leonard had drawn his gun. She

drew up close behind the female park ranger and pressed her gun into the woman's back, Sacheen's sweater draped over her weapon and arm. Unlike the staff manning the dock, this ranger was not carrying any law enforcement tools.

"Clasp your hands together in front of your body, nice and friendly like."

The woman complied, adopting a normal appearance, and doing her best to hide the terror she felt. Oblivious to the drama, people were moving about, absorbed by the historic sights on display.

Sacheen whispered in the ranger's ear, "Anyone else working here?"

"No. Just me."

"Good. Do you have a family?"

The ranger scrunched her brow. "Huh?"

"Do you have a family?" Sacheen repeated, with more intensity.

The woman nodded. "Yes. My daughter is three. Please let me go."

"If you follow my directions, you'll see your daughter again. But if you don't…"

"Don't kill me. Please. I'll do whatever you say." Her voice trembled.

"Good. We're just going to take a short walk. And be cool so you can go home and be with your little girl."

They strode to Leonard, Sacheen a half-step behind the woman. The gun, obscured by the sweater, never wavered from the ranger's side.

There were two other rangers within sight on the dock, but they were occupied with the ferry boarding. Without lowering his gun, Leonard instructed Sacheen to handcuff the three park staffers together, in a tight circle. Unless someone looked closely, it would appear they were all huddled in conversation.

"You." Leonard poked Stuart with the gun barrel. "Radio your friends to come over."

Because Stuart's hand was cuffed to the man next to him, it took some coordination, but he made the radio call.

"Be there in a minute," a voice squawked over the radio. "Need to finish boarding these people first."

"Tell him you have a situation and need both men to help you now."

Stuart did as instructed. The urgency of the message brought the two park rangers right away.

"What's the situation?" one of them said, when only feet away.

Sacheen and Leonard discretely rotated their guns into view, using the handcuffed federal employees as shields. If the rangers attempted to draw their weapons, they and their colleagues would certainly be shot dead.

Leonard said, "Both of you, put your hands on your head. Don't try to be a hero, and you'll be released unharmed."

Sacheen kept her aim on them while Leonard removed their weapons and bound their hands behind their backs. The crowds milling about the dock area, combined with the passengers boarding the ferry, served to conceal the detainment of the park rangers. But some had glimpsed the pistols, and word was spreading.

"Stuart, can you radio the ferry?" Leonard knew they were running out of time.

So far, the plan had unfolded exactly as expected. But they still had one more objective to achieve before moving to the next phase of their mission.

Stuart nodded.

"Good. Tell them to wait. There's an emergency, and you are bringing an injured person to board the ferry."

"But no one's hurt," Stuart said. "The message would have come across the radio if there was an injury."

He smacked Stuart across the back of his head.

"I can change that. You want me to?"

"No. I'll radio the ferry. Just relax, okay?"

A mother pushing a stroller scurried away after approaching close enough to see the brandished guns. She was pointing and speaking frantically to other tourists.

"I am relaxed," Leonard said.

The park ranger made the call.

"Good boy," Leonard said. "Are there any more armed rangers wandering about?"

"No. Just us. We're to make sure nothing crazy happens as people disembark from the ferry."

"You mean, like us?" He motioned to Sacheen. "Guess you didn't see that coming."

In a shaky voice, Stuart said, "There are volunteer guides up at the cell house."

"Volunteers?" Sacheen said. "You mean, they are not armed?"

She exchanged a nervous glance with Leonard.

"No weapons," Stuart said. "They're history buffs. They guide the tours."

Leonard ground the barrel of his pistol into Stuart's side, and leaned close to his ear.

"You'd better be right."

Two young men with military-style haircuts, wearing Bermuda shorts and pastel sweaters, approached Leonard. They'd heard people talking about the disturbance, and seen many pointing their cell phone cameras at the close group of rangers.

While two paces away, to Leonard's side, one of them said, "Hey, man. Is there a problem?"

Leonard spun and pointed the Beretta at the man's face.

"No problem. Now just back up with your friend while you both are still able to stand."

With hands raised, the two men inched backward and dissolved into the crowd, which had moved away, creating an empty buffer space around Leonard, Sacheen, and the park employees.

"What are you going to do?" the female ranger said, her voice cracking.

"It's your lucky day," Sacheen said. "All of you are going home."

"You won't get away with this," said one of the park rangers. "Someone is certain to have called the police."

"I really couldn't care less," Sacheen said. "I just want all of you off my island."

Then she and Leonard herded the handcuffed rangers onto the ferry. Dozens of visitors were gawking from a distance. Nearly all were talking on their phones or taking video.

At the sign of the handcuffed park employees being herded onboard at gunpoint, a ferry crewmember raised his radio and began speaking loud and fast.

"Put the radio down, mister, and step aside." Leonard motioned with the Beretta.

With raised hands, the crewmember complied. No sooner was the last person onboard when the mooring lines were cast free and the ferry engines churned, pushing the boat away from the dock.

Sacheen was on the radio right away.

"The ferry dock is cleared of armed park rangers. Send in the Jet Capsule now. With all these tourists on their phones, it won't be long before a police boat arrives onsite."

Over the radio speaker, a tinny voice replied, "The boat is loaded and ready. We've just been waiting for your signal."

Leonard said, "Let's get the rest of the supplies."

He and Sacheen hopped over the gate at the point where Agave Trail split off from the dock. It was about a half-mile to their stash of weapons, and they covered that distance in a few minutes.

Tucked in amongst the tide pools were three black zippered bags with floatation cells. From a distance, one could hardly discern the bags from the barnacle-covered rocks. Leonard grabbed two and handed them to Sacheen. Then he retrieved the final bag, which was longer and heavier than the others. Both labored to carry the bags up the trail, and emerged on the parade grounds above the ferry dock.

Deciding it was time to check in on Toby, Danya was retracing her route, following the pathway downhill. From within the sally port, looking through the downhill gate, she saw the dock directly ahead, and noticed a group of park rangers seemingly having a discussion with the two figures—a man and a woman—she'd observed recently in the off-limits area at the water's edge.

"Wonder what that's about?" she mumbled.

While she watched, the park staff members were ushered

toward the ferry. They boarded, and then the ferry departed. Toby was still with the group of demonstrators conversing amongst themselves and seemingly oblivious to whatever was going on with the group of uniformed employees about a hundred yards away.

Danya removed the binoculars from her daypack and leaned against the wall of the sally port to stabilize the image. She scanned across the throng of people, those closest using their phones to photograph and video whatever was going on. The man and woman jogged off the dock and onto a trail that wrapped around the southern end of the island.

They're going back to the same spot. Must be something more that they need.

Although Danya never completely relaxed, she certainly had not been in a vigilant state on this visit to Alcatraz. She had agreed to accompany Toby in the capacity of a tourist to what she expected to be a peaceful protest, combined with some sightseeing. She was still working through the reason why she felt this was important to do.

After hours of quiet reflection, she was still searching for an answer. She couldn't help but see similarities between the displaced American Indians and the displaced Palestinian people. But there was more—a feeling of collective guilt. She was, after all, Israeli by birth. Even more, she had served her government within the Institute for Intelligence and Special Operations. In Hebrew, the agency name was *HaMossad leModi'in uleTafkidim Meyuḥadim*—universally known as Mossad.

The events she'd witnessed over the last ten minutes had set her senses on full alarm. In her capacity as an assassin for Mossad, she'd been trained to observe the actions of people, to be suspicious, to anticipate the worst that others might do, so as to pre-empt an attack.

Her training and years of experience taking down terrorists and other enemies of the State told her that everything was wrong with the present situation. But she was no longer a Mossad agent. She'd been on the run and off the grid ever since she'd failed to follow orders and terminate the American civilian in the rugged mountains of Central Oregon.

That mission had started off well enough. And by all indications, the target had no idea he was being hunted by a pack of trained assassins. Perhaps the unfortunate run-in with the state trooper was an omen.

Danya and her team tracked the target into the wilderness, and it was soon apparent that he knew the terrain well. As her team began taking losses, she realized the American wasn't just a simple civilian, as she'd been led to believe. Turning the tables, *he* had become the hunter. He was cunning and fought fiercely. After killing three of her teammates, she managed to corner the man and his dog, a red pit bull. Both had been wounded. Ever loyal, the canine had suffered grievous injuries defending his master.

From only a few yards away, she could have killed the man easily. She looked into his eyes and read his pain, fear, and confusion. Although she didn't know the details of the secret information he supposedly possessed, it was clear he was no threat to her country. He was a nobody who had unfortunately been in the wrong place at the wrong time.

She hesitated, questioning whether she was truly acting justly to protect her homeland. That brief moment of introspective returned a most unexpected answer.

That encounter was an epiphany for her. The American was not a terrorist, and he presented no clear or credible threat to the State of Israel. For certain, he was dangerous when provoked. But he'd acted in self-defense. Assuming the intelligence was correct, he had simply stumbled upon some documents—secrets close to fifty years old—that might prove a political embarrassment for the Israeli prime minister.

Danya had killed many times for her country. It was a skill she was proficient at. But those cases were always unambiguous—terrorists, or financiers for terrorists. *They deserved to die, didn't they?*

But this American was neither.

She made a snap decision, one that would change the course of her life.

She spared his.

The price was steep. Disavowed by her country, hunted by her former employer, and wanted for murder in the US, she was constantly on the run—no official identity, no permanent address, no close relationships. To survive, she applied her considerable talents to liberate ill-gotten gains from criminal enterprises. And when judgment day came, she hoped and prayed that her late attempts at redemption would tilt the scale in her favor. Even if only a little.

She replaced the binoculars in her daypack, wishing she had a weapon. *That must be it. The security prior to boarding the ferry was good enough that it would be impossible to smuggle a gun on one's person. They must have had a couple weapons stashed along the shore. But why go back?*

As soon as the thought entered her mind, she knew the answer.

And it sent a shiver down her spine.

CHAPTER 13

VERNON THUNDERHAWK CLIPPED THE RADIO to his belt and then climbed aboard the Jet Capsule bobbing behind the sailboat just south of Sausalito, where they'd spent the night. He worked his way past the twelve well-armed warriors sitting in two rows on either side of the yacht tender. Heavy-duty water-tight cases were aligned on the deck along the center line of the 7.5-meter boat. Large teardrop windows on the port and starboard side of the enclosed yacht tender provided excellent visibility for those inside.

After taking the solitary seat at the bow of the craft, Vernon turned the ignition key. The 370-horsepower engine came to life with a throaty rumble. A crew member on the sailboat cast off the stern line and pushed the Jet Capsule away. Vernon engaged the jet drive and eased the hull clear of the sailboat. Then he applied full throttle, and the small boat jumped to speed. The bow rose on the bay, and the Jet Capsule reached its maximum speed of thirty-five knots. They would arrive at the ferry dock in less than five minutes.

He estimated it would take the police considerably longer to arrive in their Zodiac, assuming they were patrolling in the South Bay. If not…well, Leonard would deal with them.

Vernon followed a course south, directly for Alcatraz Island. He glanced at the radar display. A couple small blips showed from sailboats far to the east. So far, there was no indication that the Coast Guard had dispatched one of its coastal patrol boats. He reasoned that the San Francisco police would be the first to respond with their marine unit. And if they couldn't resolve the situation, then the Coast Guard and the FBI would be summoned.

The radio on the console of the Jet Capsule was tuned to channel sixteen, allowing him to monitor all emergency traffic. It had been quiet.

But that was about to change.

"Mayday! Mayday. Mayday. This is the *Alcatraz Flyer*. Gunmen have seized the ferry dock on the island. Over."

The police Zodiac had been cruising past several marinas south of the Bay Bridge when the call came in.

"*Alcatraz Flyer*, this is SFPD Marine Unit Two. Come again?"

"Police Marine Unit Two, this is *Alcatraz Flyer*. I say again. Two armed persons have taken control of the boat dock on Alcatraz. Request immediate assistance. *Alcatraz Flyer* is returning to Pier 33 with five park rangers and my crew. All rangers were disarmed by the gunmen. Dozens of civilians, maybe more, are on the island, and presumed to be hostages."

Officer Tozer cranked up the twin ninety-horsepower outboards, and in moments the twenty-one-foot Zodiac, with a crew of two officers under Tozer's command, was rocketing at fifty knots. Officers Lopez and Brandt were sitting low in the boat, holding on with both hands to avoid being bounced into the bay.

Keeping one hand on the throttle and the other on the wheel, Tozer guided the rigid inflatable toward the former maximum-security prison, bouncing across the wave tops. The cool salt air tugged at his navy-blue cap. Sunglasses protected his eyes from the gale-force wind.

"Call it in," he told Lopez.

Officer Lopez reported to dispatch and received confirmation of multiple 911 calls from Alcatraz. Fortunately, there were no reports of injuries.

About five hundred yards from the dock, Tozer was the first to notice the bubble-shaped yacht tender round the north end of the island. It was moving fast, and on a course that would intercept with the police Zodiac.

"Lopez," Tozer shouted, to be heard above the buffeting waves and wind. "Hail that motorboat and order them to steer due east, away from Alcatraz."

Onboard the Jet Capsule, Vernon clearly heard the call from the SFPD Marine Unit. The expansive sloped windscreen provided an unimpeded view forward and to the sides. He'd been focused on the island shore, aiming to skirt close to the rocky shoreline, and hadn't seen the rigid inflatable boat approaching from the southeast at a high speed. Upon hearing the radio call on channel 16, he scanned to the left. The white spray of seawater caught his attention first. Then he realized the spray was generated by the Zodiac.

He judged his distance to the boat dock. *I can make it first. Leonard had damned well better be ready, because that police boat is going to be right on my tail.*

Vernon held the throttle advanced to its stop, and angled even closer to shore, trying to cut yards off the distance he had to travel. He refused to reply to the radio call, in part because he was focused on navigating the boat at maximum speed in proximity to a rocky coastline.

With the dock only a hundred feet away, Leonard cut the engine. The small Jet Capsule bled speed rapidly, but it still hit the wood and steel edge of the floating pier hard enough to crack the fiberglass gunnel. Onboard, the men were jarred by the impact.

Sacheen was ready on the dock, and she threw a line to the yacht tender. One of the men emerged from the cabin and grabbed it to pull the small boat snug. There had been no time to hang bumpers, and the once-beautiful hull was taking a beating.

A deep, sharp report split the air. It sounded nearby, but there was no one on the ferry dock firing a gun. A second gunshot soon followed, echoing off the hard surfaces of the concrete buildings.

"Everyone off, now," Sacheen said.

She was the only woman among the combatants, and she weighed half as much as the largest of the twelve men, but there was no mistaking that she was in charge.

Men poured out the rear cabin hatch as fast as a football team running onto the field. Everyone had a weapon in hand. Many also carried a sturdy plastic case in the other. In seconds, the boat was emptied, Vernon being the last to disembark.

On the dock, the roar of engine horsepower cut through the air. It was the Zodiac, and it was close.

A third gunshot, and the engine noise was cut back.

Vernon spun around to face the bay. He couldn't see the Zodiac, but he knew it had to be close. He jogged over to see around the hard-top canopy on his craft. There it was, not more than seventy yards away. The police boat was turning in a tight circle. Thick smoke billowed out of one of the twin outboard engines, but the audible signature of one engine running meant the Zodiac wasn't dead in the water.

He pulled his handheld radio from his belt, and checked that it was on channel 16.

"Police boat, listen carefully. You will get only one warning. Leave the vicinity of Alcatraz Island immediately."

Lopez snatched the mic from its cradle, not waiting for Tozer's order.

"Screw you, asshole."

"Not what I had in mind," Tozer said. "But right to the point."

Brandt was at the stern with a fire extinguisher. He'd just emptied the contents on the damaged engine.

"The starboard engine is ruined. Looks like it took a round through the block. I shut off the fuel to it. Port engine appears to be operational."

"Who's firing on us?" Tozer said.

Lopez was looking through a set of marine-grade binoculars.

"I didn't see any hostiles on the dock when we were hit," he said. "But a dozen armed men were on that tender. And now they have their guns trained on us."

"Shit!" Tozer said. "We can't take them on directly with only pistols."

He steered farther into the bay, where he maintained a position about eight hundred yards away, out of range of typical military assault rifles. While Lopez and Brandt kept a close eye on events through binoculars, Tozer keyed the microphone.

"Dispatch, this is SFPD Marine Two. We've taken fire from assailants on Alcatraz. No injuries, but one of my engines was shot up and is not functional. We count…"

He looked to Lopez, who replied without taking his eyes away from the optics. "I count thirteen—no, make that fourteen hostiles. All armed with shoulder-fired small arms. They're lined up on the dock as if they're daring us to come in."

Tozer keyed the mic again. "Fourteen armed assailants. Small arms. Unknown number of hostages."

"Roger," came the reply from dispatch. "Hold at a safe distance. Over."

Taking advantage of the temporary lull, Tozer decided to take stock of his boat.

"Any damage other than to the starboard motor?"

A half-minute later, Brandt said, "Fuel tank is secure. No leaks. No damage that I can see to the buoyancy tubes."

The radio chirped to life. "Dispatch to Marine Two. You are ordered to hold at a safe distance. Beware of increased maritime traffic."

"Roger that, Dispatch. Marine Two will hold at eight hundred yards."

"What do you think command is up to?" Brandt said.

"I'll wager they called the Coast Guard," Lopez replied. "I think the Coasties always have at least one patrol boat on station at Yerba Buena Island. Even one of those boats will rip a new one in those assholes."

"They could use the hostages as shields."

"Maybe," Lopez said. "But my guess is they'll shit their pants and drop their weapons when the Coast Guard pulls up. I have activity."

Brandt and Tozer each grabbed binoculars and spied the dock area. It was difficult to get a clear view, given the distance and rocking of the Zodiac.

"Looks like they're splitting up," Brandt said.

"Yeah," Lopez said. "A group of four assailants took off up the path."

"I see 'em," Tozer replied.

The group had already passed through the sally port, and was nearing the top of the island.

"They're heading for the cell block," Tozer said. "There'll be a lot of tourists inside the old prison."

"That's only the half of it, boss." Lopez kept looking through the optics. "Look back at the dock area. They're rounding up the hostages."

With the threat from the police watercraft eliminated—at least for the moment—Sacheen had ordered most of her team to gather up the civilians who'd been gawking at the spectacle unfolding before their eyes. She ordered four of her soldiers to herd the tourists into the movie theater room of the old barracks building, while another team was dispatched to take control of the massive reinforced-concrete cell house. The remaining men on the dock set to work making preparations for the next phase of the operation.

With her pistol tucked in her waistband, Sacheen approached the Indigenous American protestors. The group numbered about twenty, and like most of the other civilians, they had their cell phones out and were taking pictures.

She addressed the group. "My brothers and sisters, you are witnessing a historic event. Today marks the beginning of a new era. An era in which we will finally have our rightful lands returned. An era in which we will regain our sovereignty."

A murmur swept through the protestors. They all held her gaze while the dock landing was being cleared of tourists, all shepherded at gunpoint into the old barracks.

"We share a common heritage," she continued. "My name is Sacheen Crow Dog. My mother gave me the name of the great activist and Hollywood actress, Sacheen Littlefeather, and I carry forward her work with pride. I invite you to join our cause—the Indigenous Peoples Movement. Claim your place in history, alongside my warriors."

Toby stepped forward. "I came here to protest peacefully. To educate people about the inequalities our people face. Violence is not the path I have chosen."

Sacheen approached Toby until they were face to face.

"And what nation are you from?"

Toby raised her chin. "I am Klamath and Modoc."

Sacheen drew her lips tight in a mocking grin. "You say violence is not your path. But the Modoc have often chosen violence against the white man to resist oppression and resettlement."

Toby stared into her eyes. She, too, knew her people's history. In the eighteenth and nineteenth centuries, nearly all nations fought bloody battles against the US Army and white settlers intent on taking Indian lands. In most cases, the land was protected by treaties which were conveniently broken for monetary gain.

"You have a strong spirit," Sacheen said. "What is your name?"

"Toby. Toby Riddle."

Sacheen's eyes widened. "You don't say. Now that *is* interesting. Are you related to the famous Modoc of the same name?"

Toby straightened her posture and pulled her shoulders back.

"I am. She was named Winema by her people, before she took her English name. And she was my great-great-great-grandmother."

"I see." Sacheen paused. "One of my passions is the history of our ancestors. I've studied the chronicles of the North American Indigenous People, focusing on the past one hundred fifty years." She placed a finger to her lips, then wagged it at Toby. "If I recall correctly, Toby Riddle—"

"Winema. Her name was Winema. It means *woman chief*, in the Modoc language."

Sacheen smiled, but it did not reach her eyes.

"As I recall, *Winema* was employed as an interpreter during the Modoc War of the early 1870s. It was in that capacity that she earned her notoriety, if I'm not mistaken."

Toby's face flushed at the insult. "You mean, her fame."

"You are reimagining historical fact. Winema was a traitor. She married a white settler and then betrayed her own people during the Modoc War."

"It is you who is twisting history to suit your purpose. Yes, it is true that Winema shared information she'd overheard from a council of Modoc warriors. They were planning to murder the peace commissioners rather than allow negotiations to continue that would have ended the war. She cautioned General Canby of the planned ambush, but Canby ignored her warning and went on with the meeting. Winema was there serving as translator. None of the commissioners carried weapons. They were meeting with Captain Jack, the Modoc Chief, and other tribal leaders. Captain Jack shot Canby in the face. Other Modoc warriors killed Reverend Eleazor Thomas. The other commissioners were wounded, including Alfred Meacham. Winema saved his life, preventing Captain Jack from taking his scalp."

"Even by your account, Winema betrayed her tribe. She sided with the white man."

"She was on the side of the Modocs, trying to prevent their slaughter. She knew, as Captain Jack did, that the Modocs could never win the war. There were too many US soldiers. A negotiated peace was the only solution. After the murder of General Canby, the Army sent one thousand soldiers to drive my people to the Klamath Reservation, and to the Indian Territories, more than a thousand miles away."

"Peace." Sacheen scoffed. "Captain Jack was a warrior. He did not support peace with the settlers. He knew that only by force could his people have their homeland."

Toby shook her head. "Captain Jack's Modoc name was Kintpuash. And he and Winema were cousins. Perhaps that is why Winema was able to freely access the Modocs during the peace negotiations. Regardless, initially Captain Jack did believe in the negotiations. It was only later that he reluctantly agreed to go along with the other Modoc leaders in the plot to murder the commissioners."

"Captain Jack was hanged," Sacheen said. "Winema chose to save a white man over her own flesh and blood."

"Murder is immoral and unlawful. Winema did what was right. Many whites were sympathetic to the plight of the Modocs. But that changed with the murder of Canby. The cowardly attack on the peace commissioners played into the stereotype crafted by those in favor of exterminating the Indigenous Americans."

"And how would you say the nations have fared over the past one hundred fifty years of negotiated peace with Washington?"

Toby remained silent. She had come to join the protest to draw attention to the inequities Native Americans had faced since Europeans first colonized the Americas. But there was nothing to gain from further debate.

"It's different now," Sacheen said.

"And how is that?"

Toby didn't buy it. Change would come slowly, as social transformation would require generations to alter their biases, as well as societal norms.

"The nations never united to fight their common enemy—the US government," Sacheen replied. "We are united now. But more importantly, *now* we can fight for our rights, using superior weapons and tactics. The politicians cannot resist."

"And if they do?"

"Then they will taste the bitterness of our resolve. We cannot lose this time."

Toby shook her head. "Why do you think you can beat the government? They command the police, as well as the most powerful military. What do you have? A dozen warriors with rifles?"

"We have a weapon that will turn their cities into uninhabitable wastelands. Come, join us." She stepped back from Toby and cast her gaze across the protestors. "All of you. Join us. Be united with your brothers and sisters. Together, we will gain our rights which have been denied for so long. Our ancestral lands will be ours once again."

"No," Toby said. "This is not the path our forefathers would have taken. They understood that bloodshed would only lead to more bloodshed. Never to peace."

"Anyone who wishes to join our Movement," Sacheen said, "step forward and stand by my side."

None of the protestors moved.

"Very well. Then you are traitors to your people." She turned to one of her men. "Take them into the building. Treat them the same as the other hostages."

CHAPTER 14

AT THE SIGHT OF THE FERRY TENDER coming into the dock at high speed, and expeditiously disgorging its armed passengers, Danya turned and ran back through the sally port. Whatever was happening, it wasn't good, and she needed to separate herself from the throng of tourists.

On the uphill side of the gate was the military chapel and the derelict electric repair shop. Neither building was open to the public, and the wide walkway angled past the front of the buildings before turning sharply back and sweeping around the rear of the structures as it climbed to the cellblock. She hopped the metal fence skirting the edge of the paved pathway, and scurried down the narrow alley between the two buildings. She used the structures to conceal her presence from the four armed men she saw running up the path.

She worked her way to a position near a corner of the chapel where she was above the footpath, yet could still observe the events unfolding on the ferry dock and the adjacent courtyard.

The three gunshots she'd heard had the characteristic deep boom of a large-caliber rifle. Her suspicion was confirmed when she saw smoke billowing from the engine on the Zodiac about half a mile from the edge of the dock.

There's a sniper out there somewhere. Through her binoculars, she saw the SFPD emblem on the inflated buoyancy cell.

The presence of a large number of armed men—presumably terrorists—was unsettling. Her immediate priority was to evade detection and capture.

What are they after? If she could figure out their plan, she would be better able to resist.

Escape was an unlikely possibility. The very reasons that these facilities were constructed on this rocky island in the middle of San Francisco Bay made escape virtually impossible. Unless, that is, she could steal the futuristic-looking yacht tender.

Danya had no idea how she could steal the boat from right under the noses of the terrorists, or if she could get any of the captives safely on board and ferry them across the channel to San Francisco.

One step at a time. First, identify the objective. And then develop the plan.

With so many hostages under the control of the terrorists, there would be no rescue. The sniper shot that had disabled one of the outboard engines on the police boat was a clear message to stay away. Any attempt to storm the island from marine craft, or from the air, could precipitate a slaughter of dozens, maybe hundreds, of innocent men, women, and children. She had no idea how far this radical group might go if threatened, but she'd certainly had dealings with Middle Eastern terrorist cells that would not hesitate to execute hostages to keep the military at bay.

From her concealed position next to the chapel, she glassed the dock landing. Her interest settled on the group of protestors. She could clearly see Toby engaged with the armed woman. Danya was too far away to hear what was being said, but at least there weren't any guns pointed at Toby.

Following a lengthy exchange, Danya watched as the protestors were led away at gunpoint, to the same building where the other civilians had been taken. She surmised that they were all being held in a large room in the barracks building. Unfortunately, during her brief tour of the island, she had not entered the former barracks, and had no idea of the layout.

But that was only part of the problem. She was confident another group of tourists, those who'd already begun touring the cell house, were also being held as hostages in the former maximum-security prison. Two groups of civilians at two locations was a nightmare scenario. Any attempt to forcibly execute a rescue would quickly degrade to a bloodbath.

In the courtyard between the ferry dock and the barracks, Vernon was overseeing preparations for launching the drones. He had just a small group of gunmen under his direction, most having been assigned to keeping an eye on the two groups of hostages. Several of the largest cases were open, revealing many quadcopters and radio controllers. Another case, uniquely yellow, was nearby. It would remain closed until the drones were ready to fly.

Meanwhile, armed with a Barrett M82 .50-caliber rifle, Leonard had set up his sniper hide about halfway up the slope that extended from the dock and courtyard, to the parade grounds. He was positioned next to the largest tree, a trunk two feet in diameter, with his body concealed behind deciduous shrubbery. The heavy rifle rested on a bipod and was fitted with a high-power telescopic sight. From his position, he had an unobstructed view of the ferry landing and the bay beyond.

His eye was close to the scope, his lips drawn tight. His body was rigid, and he remained motionless, even as Sacheen joined him.

"What is it?" she whispered, when she was close to his side.

"A Coast Guard cutter is sailing in our direction." His face remained glued to the eyepiece.

Sacheen looked out across the bay and spotted the white bow wake created by the white and orange vessel approaching fast.

"Sooner than I'd thought," she said.

Leonard removed his eye from the scope and faced her.

"It's a small patrol boat," he said. "Probably from the base on Yerba Buena Island. It lacks any large weapons. Still, it will have two bow-mounted .50-caliber machine guns. And a crew of ten or more men with light arms—rifles, shotguns."

"They won't dare fire upon us and risk harming the civilians," she said.

"They would not do so knowingly, I agree. However, they don't know where the hostages are being held. And they could wreak havoc on the fleet of drones. Should you have the men move the drones to cover? Maybe up to the cellblock? It has thick concrete walls."

She shook her head. "At the rate that cutter is approaching, we don't have time to move the drones." She placed a hand on his shoulder. "I need time to get the Folgore recoilless rifle positioned and loaded. You have to slow them down, maybe with a distraction."

A wicked grin formed on Leonard's face.

"I can do that."

She ran down the slope and across the courtyard. Stopped before one of the sentries. He was a mountain of a man, standing six-and-a-half-feet tall, and weighing 275 pounds—all muscle.

"Charlie, help me with the Folgore. We need to position it up there." She pointed to the parade ground above and behind the barracks. "We'll set it up behind that pile of rubble. We have to hurry."

Charlie slipped the sling of his MP5 over his shoulder, and grabbed the handle of a long black packing case. Most men would have struggled with the weight, but not Charlie. He lifted the case with ease before balancing it on his shoulder. Sacheen grabbed a smaller container that held four high-explosive rounds, and jogged up the slope to the elevated parade ground, passing Leonard on the way.

She reached her destination first, and selected a V-shaped recess where two large piles of rubble merged. The low heap of rocks and broken concrete was formed when the government bulldozed the former correctional officer's residential apartments, which had been located on the parade grounds. The entire prison facility might have been demolished had it not been for the creation of the Golden Gate National Recreation Area in 1972—the congressional Act that brought Alcatraz under the administration of the National Park Service.

Carrying the heavier load, Charlie was only seconds behind her. He placed the container on the hard surface with a grunt, and flipped open the latches, then threw back the lid. Before him was a long dark-green tube with a bulbous flare that marked the rear end. An optical ranging and sighting system was mounted near the middle of the tube. A tripod was clamped to the tube just in front of the sight, and the legs were folded forward in line with the eighty-millimeter barrel. With both hands he pulled the recoilless rifle from the foam padding. Once the legs were splayed, the tripod supported the weapon and allowed full movement side to side, as well as elevation.

Sacheen dropped to one knee and sighted along the length of the barrel.

"Good," she said. "We can fire on anyone approaching the dock."

The mounds of debris were twenty-feet wide and extended ten feet beyond the rear of the recoilless rifle. Nothing was going to shoot through that.

"Do you know how to operate this weapon system?" she said.

Charlie nodded. "Yes," he said, in a raspy baritone. "We've been trained to handle every weapon we have. And we all can fly the drones, too."

It was a goal both Leonard and Sacheen had insisted upon—redundancy at every level. Losses were not only possible, but likely, and success meant that each team member had to be able to do the job of any teammate that might fall.

"Good," she replied. "See that Coast Guard cutter?" She pointed across the bay.

It was close enough now to distinguish details, even without the aid of optics.

Charlie nodded.

"It's coming for us," she said. "When it nears the island, they'll throttle back the engine and slow. When it's within range, you are to fire upon it. Aim for the pilothouse first, then for the gun mounts on the bow. If you have any rounds left, try to blast a hole in the hull at the water line."

"I can do that," he said.

"I can't stay here and load for you."

He shrugged. "They say this is a two-man weapon system. But we trained to load, aim, and fire with only one person."

She slapped him on the shoulder and ran back down the slope to Leonard's hide.

CHAPTER 15

AS THE COAST GUARD CUTTER BORE DOWN on the island, the .50-caliber pedestal-mounted machine guns fore of the super structure came into view. Behind each gun was a Coastie wearing a bright orange floatation vest.

"I need you to slow down that cutter," Sacheen whispered, only inches away from Leonard's ear. "Create a diversion so they can't use their speed and mobility against us."

His eye was glued to the telescopic sight on the rifle, his finger slowly applying pressure to the trigger. The police Zodiac was still circling seven hundred to eight hundred yards away. It was a long shot, but easily within range of the Barrett. The three police crewmen busied themselves between talk on the radio and glassing activities on Alcatraz.

Boom!

The sharp report startled Sacheen, but not Leonard. His shoulder absorbed the recoil, just as it had the hundreds of times he'd fired the weapon on his remote ranch on the Duck Valley Reservation, honing his marksmanship to the point that he could hit a man-sized stationary target at one thousand yards, eight out of ten tries.

The semiautomatic action of the Barrett chambered another round. A second later, he fired again.

Sacheen trained her binoculars on the police boat. Dense

black smoke emanated from the second outboard engine, and the craft was drifting. One of the air-filled buoyancy cells was rapidly deflating. The crew was absorbed in emergency activity. While one was talking on the radio, the other two seemed to be franticly assessing the seaworthiness of their boat.

Leonard fired again. The round punctured another buoyancy cell, imparting a severe list to the small boat. As one, all three police officers pitched over the side into the cold bay water.

"There's your diversion," Leonard said. "The cutter has no choice but to stop and fish those officers out of the water."

She smiled. "Perfect."

From her concealed location next to the old military chapel, the rifle reports sounded muffled to Danya. She surmised the shooter was on the far side of the barracks building. She raised the binoculars again, in time to see a bullet take out the second outboard engine on the police Zodiac. Time to leave her cover and enter the conflict.

The most direct route to the far side of the barracks was back through the sally port to the main path. But with five or six armed guards busying themselves on the dock, that route was a nonstarter. Another option was to skirt the rear of the barracks. The ground behind the building rose steeply, held in place by a retaining wall forming a slot, or narrow path just wide enough for building maintenance. Tracing the top of the wall, the walkway to the parade grounds was elevated almost to the roof of the barracks. She reasoned that if she followed that slot, it was unlikely anyone would see her unless they were on the trail directly above. If that were to happen, she'd be trapped. Although far from ideal, it was the best option she could come up with.

More rifle shots provided encouragement to move. Fortunately, the back wall of the barracks was devoid of windows. She advanced in a low crouch. Far above her head, and much farther to the right, was the massive concrete cell house atop the island. The slot she was moving in limited her field of view, and she still had no definitive idea where the sniper was positioned.

Before she reached the end of the building, the rifle shots ceased. She paused and dropped to a knee, scanning above and behind while listening for sounds of danger.

Nothing appeared out of place, and she resumed her advance. As she neared the end of the building, a wing of the barracks extended across her path, forcing her to detour. At the corner of the structure, she paused again, searching for the presence of danger. All seemed normal, and then she heard a *swoosh!*

Like the gunshots, the sound originated from some undetermined location in front of her position.

The Coast Guard cutter was already slowing. It circled around the disabled Zodiac as the captain maneuvered between the island and the police officers treading water. He reversed engines and brought his boat to a full stop, using the hull and large super structure as a shield from further gunfire while three Coasties threw life rings overboard. The crewmen then walked the lifelines to the stern of the boat, where a ladder was mounted to the hull.

On the bow, the machine guns were aimed toward the ferry dock.

"Seaman," the captain said. "Fire a short warning burst into the water, near the edge of the ferry landing."

The Browning M2 machine gun burped for a second, sending a half-dozen shells into the bay water, and a fountain of spray high into the air.

The cutter was drifting, its bow coming around fully to face the island only seven-hundred yards away.

"Recovery complete," a junior petty officer reported to the captain. "We have all three men safely onboard. No injuries."

A streak of fire and white smoke lanced out from the plateau halfway to the top of the island. Two seconds later, a thunderous explosion engulfed the pilothouse. Dagger-like shards of glass from the windows were blasted inwards. The razor-edged fragments sliced through clothing and flesh, killing two, and injuring the captain.

The blast took out most of the bridge controls and electronics. Unable to change engine speed, the boat limped forward. Fortunately, steering was still operational.

In unison, both machine guns cut loose, aiming at the origin of the rocket. The Coasties fired short, controlled bursts. The rapid, staccato reports were deafening, and masked all other sounds on the cutter. And then, just as suddenly as it began, the gunfire stopped.

The boat bobbed on the water while the crew took stock. On the stern deck, crewmen led the three police officers, each wrapped in a blanket, below deck, where they would be relatively safe and out of the way. A chief petty officer scrambled to climb the ladder to the pilot house, fearing the worst.

Gunfire erupted again. But this time, single shots, and the report was distant and not so loud. Leonard took advantage of the nearly stationary gunners on the bow of the boat. He fired, and the shot narrowly missed a Coastie standing behind one of the Browning machine guns. The close miss spurred her to return fire, but she didn't know where the rifle shots were coming from, and so aimed at the approximate spot the rocket had been fired from.

Bullets impacted the rubble pile at the edge of the parade ground, ten yards above Leonard. He adjusted his aim and slowly applied pressure to the Barrett's trigger.

Boom!

As Leonard recovered from the recoil, he saw the bullet strike the Coast Guard gunner. Her body fell backwards onto the steel deck plates. He observed her through the scope for a moment longer, and failing to see any movement, concluded she was dead.

The other gunner unleashed a torrent of lead into the rubble pile. Leonard moved his aim and fired. The gunner fell to the side as if his legs were pulled out from under him. He writhed, clutching his thigh where the bullet had passed through thick muscle.

With the machine guns silenced, Charlie again took careful aim with the Folgore ranging and sighting system. Satisfied, he pressed the firing button, and a rocket streaked forward and slammed into the super structure directly behind the port machine gun. He used the five-power sight magnification to assess the damage from his two hits. Two large holes were evident in the super structure, and the pilothouse looked to be in ruins.

The cutter turned hard to port to escape the rocket fire. With half her crew dead or wounded, and a severely damaged bridge, she was out of the fight.

Charlie loaded and aimed. The boat was just coming around, offering a broadside shot. The perfect setup, and he fired.

The rocket raced forward in a shallow arc. It impacted the hull three seconds later, amidships and just above the water line. A near-perfect shot. The five-kilogram high-explosive warhead blasted a gaping hole in the thin steel hull. A geyser of water shot up and away from the explosion. Cold bay water was pouring in, even before the spray settled.

CHAPTER 16

WHITE SMOKE FROM THE ROCKETS was drifting above Charlie's firing position on the edge of the parade grounds. Danya scrambled up the slope, shielded from Leonard's view by the thicket of trees and bushes surrounding him.

As she cleared the lip of earth and landed on the parade grounds, she realized the rocket launcher was at the southern-most edge, fortified by a large pile of broken concrete and scattered rocks. As she approached, another rocket was fired. She gazed across the water in time to see the warhead explode upon the side of the cutter, at the waterline. The Coast Guard cutter had taken a beating, but at least for now it was still afloat.

Danya cautiously rounded the nearest rubble pile. As she cleared the mound of debris, she spotted Charlie kneeling with the Folgore above his right shoulder. He was so focused on aiming, that he didn't notice her approaching.

She recognized his concentration for what it was, and knew he was about to fire the weapon again. The cutter was a sitting duck. She had to interrupt the shot.

Danya wrapped her hand around an apple-sized chunk of concrete, and heaved it.

The concrete struck Charlie on the back of his shoulder just as he pressed the trigger. His body jerked to the side, sending the eighty-millimeter high-explosive warhead off on an errant trajectory. It exploded on the water, fifty yards off the stern of the retreating cutter.

Stunned, Charlie turned on his attacker. He managed to rise to his feet just as she slammed into him, her arms out and shoulder down for the tackle. Although she was half of Charlie's weight, her mass and speed were sufficient to drive him backwards, knocking the Folgore off its stand. He was pushed back two paces before his heel stopped against a large stone at the base of the rubble pile. With his feet stuck, momentum carried him onto his back, and he slammed against the concrete and rock scree. Her shoulder drove the air from his lungs with an *umpf!* She pushed back, trying to separate from the giant, but was locked in placed, pinned to his chest with his arm. Then, with his free hand, he punched the side of her face. She shook it off and punched him, but the strike was weak. She swung again, but couldn't get enough freedom of movement to land her fist with force.

As long as Charlie held her tight, she had no leverage to trade blows. He pummeled his fist into her head and face again. Her vision blurred for a second, before clearing. She had to break his grip before he pounded her unconscious.

She latched her fingers onto a piece of concrete, but it was too heavy to move.

Wham! The blow connected with her temple, causing her vision to go black and her strength to ebb. She shook her head and blinked.

His fist landed again, high on her cheekbone, and starbursts of multicolored lights danced across her blackened vision. A few more blows like that, and it would be all over. She kept feeling with her right hand for something hard and heavy, passing over chunks that were too large, or simply immobile.

Anticipating another strike, she turned her head to the right just before Charlie's meaty fist connected with the back of her skull. She thought she heard the crack of knuckles on bone. Her head hurt like hell, but it wasn't debilitating like the strikes to her temple and face.

Then she wrapped her hand around a chunk of rubble that filled her grip. It weighed about a pound, and she accelerated it toward Charlie's head with all the force she could muster. The mass of concrete delivered a satisfying thud when it connected with his head. She felt his grip slacken, and pushed herself free. She brought the bludgeon down again, slamming it into his forehead in a lethal blow.

Charlie's arms fell limp. She tossed the chunk of concrete aside, revealing a blood-filled depression in his forehead.

"I don't think they'll be back," Leonard said.

He'd left his sniper hide and joined Sacheen on the dock where others were busy preparing the drones.

"They'll try again," Sacheen said, "but not right away. First, the local police and FBI will need to coordinate. Probably Homeland Security, too, since the Coast Guard is under their command."

"How long do we have?" he said.

"Plenty of time to get the drones prepared, and send an even stronger message."

Eight quadcopter drones were in a line, spaced several feet apart, in the middle of the courtyard. Each was equipped with an ultra-miniature camera. Originally developed for the US Army, the camera and integral transmitter weighed less than an ounce, and were capable of sending real-time video over the cellular network. With a range of over eight miles, the drones could transmit live video from San Francisco, and cities along the East Bay—Richmond, Berkeley, and Oakland.

Each drone was flown using a radio controller modified with a high-power transmitter. By clipping a cell phone to the controller, the pilot would have direct observations of the transmitted video, making immediate in-flight course adjustments if necessary to avoid interception.

Vernon Thunderhawk was supervising the preparations.

"As soon as we run a system check to verify comms and video," he said to Sacheen, "the first drone will be flight ready."

She was observing the men carryout the preparations.

"Good," she replied. "Once the drone is ready, get suited up and insert the payload. Load up the other drones, too, and stage them along the edge of the dock, far enough away so as not to irradiate our warriors. Understand?"

He nodded. "No problem."

"Good."

"What's the destination?"

"San Francisco. Think you can pilot the drone to Pioneer Park?"

"With Coit Tower standing as a guiding beacon, it will be easy." He smiled.

"Complete the preparations, but do not launch until I return. I want to speak with someone."

Sacheen strode to the barracks entrance. She wanted to try once more to convince Toby to join her cause.

Upon entering, she found herself in a gift shop. Beyond the gift shop was a movie theater which normally played a short documentary film about the former prison. A couple minutes of the film told the story of the brief first American Indian occupation in 1964, followed by the more widely known occupation spanning from November 1969 until June 1971.

She surveyed the crowd of hostages. It wasn't long before she spotted Toby sitting with her back against the wall and her knees drawn up against her chest. She approached and sat next to Toby.

After a moment, she said, "I'll make sure someone distributes water. I don't think there's much food to be had. Mostly just some candy in the gift shop. I'm sorry. I'll ask one of the warriors to distribute what we can find for the children."

Toby fixed her gaze on the far side of the room.

Sacheen said, "Everyone will be released before long. Maybe a day. Two, at most."

Toby remained silent.

"It's not my wish to harm these people. But this action is necessary. Your spirit is strong. You should stand with your people."

Toby turned to Sacheen, her eyes filled with anger.

"You have no right. These people you have kidnapped, and now threaten, what have they done to you? What have they done to any of the tribes?"

"The wars between American Natives and the federal government never ended," Sacheen said. "In the 1960s and 70s, many brave people risked everything to raise awareness for the rights of Indigenous People. The American Indian Movement, and Indians of All Tribes, carried our message to the public. Even as we protested peacefully, the government assaulted and murdered our young men and women."

"Past transgressions do not justify your actions," Toby said. "One can always find some historical wrong that was done to one group or another. The cycle of violence has to be broken."

"Spoken like a true idealist." Sacheen paused, but Toby offered no reply. "Have you suffered any mistreatment, any violence at the hands of the police or white mobs?"

Toby thought of the harassment and threats from Cole and his brother, but decided to keep that to herself.

"I'd imagine you have," Sacheen said, "but would rather lie to yourself than admit the truth. Your home in Southern Oregon, near the Klamath Reservation, is fertile land, ranch land. Lots of rednecks there, right?"

"Bigots are found everywhere, even in the tribes."

"I'm not your enemy," Sacheen said. "Haven't you ever yearned for a family?"

Toby gazed back in silence, but her eyes said what her heart felt.

Sacheen nodded. "I don't want to be a revolutionary. But if not me, then who? How long must we wait patiently before our children have a future? Before the chain of poverty is broken?"

Toby slowly shook her head. "This is not the way. We will never win by force. Hasn't history taught you anything?"

Sacheen gazed at the ceiling. "Would you have me bring a child into this world to life on the reservation?" She wiped her eyes, the back of her hand coming away moist. "I can't do that. What kind of person does that make me?"

"I don't know."

Sacheen cleared her throat. "Our people have tried negotiating with the government. We've tried protesting for our civil rights. We've demanded to be treated equally. It doesn't work."

"Our people have lost many battles, but not the war."

She appraised Toby again. She saw strong character, loyalty, determination, honesty, intelligence. Traits that would make her a good spokesperson to carry their message to the public. Plus, she was a young and attractive woman, with obvious Native American features. She would be the perfect image of the Indigenous Peoples Movement, IPM.

"Come with me." Sacheen held out her hand. "There's someone I'd like you to meet."

Toby eyed her before relenting, concluding that there was little to lose by going along. Side by side, they walked out of the former barracks.

Leonard stood arrow-straight in the middle of the paved courtyard between the ferry dock and the barracks. The Barrett rifle was slung diagonally across his back. His eyes were narrowed, and his lips pursed in a studious mien. He was gazing across the bay, at the receding Coast Guard cutter, with a countenance devoid of any expression that might convey regret or remorse.

"Leonard." Sacheen approached from behind. "I'd like you to meet Toby."

The two women stood side by side, and Leonard turned to face them.

"Toby is from the Modoc and Klamath tribes. She came here today with about two dozen other protestors."

"I see." Leonard looked beyond her, to the building where the tourists were being held. "Why are you with them?"

Toby turned toward Sacheen. "Well?"

"I invited Toby and all of the other activists to join our cause. In the meantime, I thought it best if everyone was together inside. That way, we can make sure no one is accidentally injured."

His gaze moved from Sacheen back to Toby.

"I assume Sacheen has explained our objectives?"

"She said your goal is the return of historical tribal lands and sovereignty for First Nations People. Personally, I can't begin to imagine how you plan to achieve that."

"You don't agree with our aims?" Leonard said.

Toby shook her head. “Not at all. Of course, I agree with your goals. But this isn’t the nineteenth century anymore. Time has moved on. What once was sacred hunting grounds two hundred years ago, is now covered by cities, highways, factories, and farms. Are you proposing all that is taken down, bulldozed? And what of the people who inhabit those towns and cities?”

“It would be a fitting turn of the tables for the white man to be forced onto reservations,” he said. “But no, that is not our idea. However, an appropriate sum should be paid to the tribes for the use of our land.”

“You really think you can achieve that?”

Leonard shrugged. “Why not? There is precedent. Eminent domain allows the government to seize private land, provided compensation is paid to the landowner. The government has already taken our lands—sacred lands. They just haven’t paid for them yet.”

Toby had to admit that there was a certain amount of logic to what he was saying. But she also knew that logic and reality didn’t have to be one and the same when it came to governance and politics.

“It’s going to take more than a sit-in on this island to convince even the state government, not to mention the federal government, to accept your proposal. The expense could be astronomical.”

“All to be negotiated,” Leonard said. “But likely in the hundreds of billions of dollars.”

“Do you really think you can win?”

“We do.”

“Yeah, right.” Toby chortled. “And what have you been smoking?”

Leonard narrowed his eyes. “We have the means to make this happen.”

“Oh, really? Let me tell you something. Whoever you are negotiating with is just going to play along, tell you what you want to hear, until they manage to sneak a SEAL team, or whatever, onto this rock. There will be a gunfight. It will probably be ferocious. And you and all your men will be killed.”

“We have the hostages. How many?” he said to Sacheen.

“Over two hundred.”

“You’re not that naïve,” Toby said. “Or that stupid. Let me do the math for you. Let’s say you have two hundred hostages, and you want two hundred billion dollars. That’s one billion per person. Who’s gonna agree to pay that? No one will.”

Leonard turned his head to Sacheen, smirking.

“You’re right. She is smart. And cool under pressure.”

Toby said, “My advice—cut your losses while you are still breathing.”

“Your life hangs in the balance, too,” Sacheen said.

Toby rolled her eyes. “Tell me something I don’t know. Whatever happens to me is beyond my control. The two of you,” she pointed at Leonard and Sacheen, “you’re making the decisions. Not only concerning your lives, but the lives of everyone here. Every man, woman, and child here is innocent. They have no say in your dispute, or ability to influence the outcome.”

Leonard said, “Ever since Europeans landed on the shores of America, our ancestors have suffered. They were innocent, too.”

“No one can change what happened hundreds of years ago.”

“If you think this is only about historical grievances, you’re mistaken. Let me explain my family history.”

“Will I find this interesting?” Toby raised her eyebrows.

“Hear me out before you judge.”

Toby frowned. “Fine.”

Leonard nodded. “Let me begin with introductions. My name is Leonard Cloud. And this,” he waved a hand toward Sacheen, “is Sacheen Crow Dog, a member of the Raven Clan of the Tlingit tribe. My family owns a small parcel of land in northern Nevada, on the Duck Valley Reservation. I grew up there in a modest house. My mother was Shoshone-Paiute, and my father was of the San Carlos Apache Nation. None of this will have any significance to you, but I want you to understand my cultural identity. *Our* cultural identity.”

Toby nodded.

“For you to understand my passion, you need to know my recent family history. The brother of my mother was John Trudell. He died a few years ago. Do you know of him?”

"Yes, I do. Didn't he broadcast the radio program from Alcatraz, during the occupation?"

Leonard nodded. "That's right. My uncle was among those idealistic protestors who came to Alcatraz in 1969. He broadcast on the UC Berkeley radio station at night. They called his show *Radio Free Alcatraz*. Anyway, he remained active in the leadership of the American Indian Movement—what some called the Red Power movement—for many years. In fact, he was the national chairman of AIM throughout most of the 1970s. The Movement was mostly peaceful, but there were a few exceptions."

"You mean the incident at Wounded Knee?" Toby said.

"The standoff lasted seventy-one days. Two of our people were murdered by federal agents."

"My recollection is that gunfire was exchanged by both sides," Toby said. "Law enforcement officers were also injured."

Leonard nodded. "And during the trial that followed, in which the government sought prison sentences for my brothers, the US District Judge saw through the charade and dismissed all charges due to government misconduct. It was not the last time that AIM protestors were railroaded. My uncle, he didn't trust the FBI. He was protesting in Washington, DC, in 1979, and he burned a US flag on the steps of the FBI headquarters. He said it was because you burned the flag if it was desecrated, and the treacherous actions of the government amounted to dishonoring the flag, the nation. Twenty-four hours later, his family was murdered in a house fire."

"Murdered?" Toby raised her eyebrows.

"That's right," Sacheen said. "Of course, the tribal authorities investigated, but they were in league with the FBI."

"Another conspiracy theory?"

"There are many facts not included in the government's account," Sacheen said. "During the 1970s, there was a lot of tension and conflict between the FBI and American Indians, mostly members of the Oglala Sioux Nation. You should research the Pine Ridge and Wounded Knee incidents. There is good reason to believe that the FBI was working to suppress activism they viewed as radical. They funded a group of counter-activists, under the direction of Dickie Wilson, who rose to be tribal president of the Oglala Sioux in a rigged election. He established a special police force that violently opposed peaceful protests for Native American rights."

"My grandmother was murdered in that house fire," Leonard said. "Along with my uncle's wife and unborn child, and their three young children. My cousins."

Toby looked into Leonard's eyes, seeing genuine grief.

"I'm sorry. That was a violent period in American history. The Black Power movement peaked. So did the organization of Latino farm laborers."

"True. And Native Americans were not spared from the wrath of an oppressive government. In June of 1975, two FBI agents entered the Pine Ridge Reservation. You know, that was a dangerous time on the rez. Dickie Wilson's vigilante group wanted to keep the status quo, to keep the red man under the thumb of the Bureau of Indian Affairs."

"I know something about that," Toby said. "Those two lawmen were murdered in cold blood. You can't justify that."

Leonard's mouth turned down. "And by what evidence do you conclude it was murder? Because the FBI said so? As I said, that was a dangerous and violent time on the reservation. Everyone was poor. They knew nothing else their entire lives. So when two strangers come into the community in everyday cars, not wearing any uniforms, and produce weapons—tell me, how would you respond?"

Toby didn't want to dwell on how she would react. She wanted to think she was better than to give in to fear and popular prejudice. But was she deceiving herself?

When Toby didn't reply, Leonard continued.

"You know, there were a lot of people there, all shooting their guns. Who fired the shots that killed the FBI men? Everyone fled afterward. They knew it was bad, and that it would only get worse. Two of my brothers in the Movement were arrested and put on trial. But the judge agreed that they'd acted in self-defense. Only later was Leonard Peltier arrested in Canada and extradited to the US. The

FBI had learned from their previous failures to get convictions in federal courts, so they had written statements from a few members of the tribe that implicated Mister Peltier in the murders. That was enough for a guilty verdict, even though those witnesses told the court their statements were forced by the FBI."

"I sympathize with your frustration over what you see as a miscarriage of justice. I really do. But 1975 was a long time ago."

"And I have a long memory. The relations between Native Americans and the US government have been festering, like a fetid wound that won't heal, for a hundred fifty years. It was no coincidence that the agents were killed on the Pine Ridge Reservation. That is part of the Sioux Nation. The Sioux signed a treaty with the government in 1868, that promised a vast territory, including the Black Hills, in perpetuity. That promise, like so many others from the white politicians, lasted only a few years, until gold was discovered in the Black Hills. The Sioux were forced off their land. Naturally, without compensation. Then the government built a monument on lands they'd stolen by chiseling the faces of four US Presidents into sacred Lakota Sioux granite."

"History cannot be changed," Toby said. "In time, the rights you seek—we all seek—will be realized. But only if your organization works with the politicians to make that change through law."

"No. The politicians cannot be trusted. They are only interested in their own financial reward."

"If you fight the system, you'll only lose."

"My uncle and my brothers in AIM, they all tried to work with the system. We have been trying for more than four decades."

"These are different times. You can't hold on to the anger forever."

"I can." Leonard's eyes smoldered with the fire of repression. "The federal government has never stopped waging a war of deceit and violence against Native Americans. Sacheen and I have dedicated our lives to correct this wrongdoing. We have forsaken our own family so we can be the voice of right and reason that will be amplified ten-thousand-fold. The heinous and cowardly crime against my family that took my kinfolk from this world so many decades ago triggered a cascade of events that is about to reach its climax. When our work is done, Sacheen and I will live the remainder of our days in peace on my family's land, where we will raise our children. The end will be the beginning of a victorious movement, having gone full circle. Our people will break the chains of oppression, shake free from the cycle of poverty and crime. Only then will our spirits rest, together as one."

Sacheen embraced Leonard, and he returned the tender show of affection.

Toby felt mentally exhausted, finding it difficult to process everything she'd been told, and to check it against what she thought to be the truth. The facts were fuzzy, at best, having been reported by mainstream news media, with their obvious biases toward the status quo, and history written by stodgy scholars sympathetic toward European perspectives.

"Look, I understand that a lot of bad things have happened," she said. "And I'm sorry. But what does any of this have to do with me?"

Leonard and Sacheen exchanged a knowing glance.

"We believe you are a person of integrity and strong will," Sacheen said. "We also believe that you love your cultural heritage and wish to better the lives of your tribe, and all tribes."

Leonard said, "It is time for all who identify with their native cultural heritage to stand together."

"You still haven't shown me why you believe you can achieve your objectives. And if it means killing even one of the hostages, count me out."

Sacheen said, "As I told you before, we do not plan to harm any of the hostages. For their own safety, it was necessary to move them to secure locations. My warriors are there not to harm them, but to protect them."

Leonard's gaze met with Sacheen's. She nodded in response to an unspoken statement.

Then he faced Toby. "It is time to reveal our plan."

CHAPTER 17

DANYA REMOVED THE MP5, spare magazines, radio, and folding knife from Charlie's dead body. Fearing that she could be discovered at any moment, she needed to move. But to where? The clear decision was back to the barracks. She knew that many hostages were being held within the large building, including Toby.

Maintaining a low crouch to avoid presenting her profile above the lip of the parade ground, she darted toward the building. She was exposed to observation by anyone in the cell house, but she hoped they were occupied watching their prisoners, rather than gazing outward.

Her training by Mossad had included military and guerilla tactics for house-to-house fighting, and a principle of those lessons was to fight from top to bottom, if possible. In urban combat, whoever occupied the upper floors had significant advantages over an opposing force on lower floors. The question was, how to gain access to the top floor of the barracks without being seen or heard.

She was still dashing toward the building when an idea came to mind.

The barracks was a huge, five-story structure—nearly as large as the cell house—and shaped like the letter L. The longest portion paralleled the ferry dock, with a short wing that stopped where the terrain rose steeply to the flat parade grounds. She slid down the slope to the building, using the natural vegetation to remain hidden from view of the terrorists working below in the courtyard adjoining the dock.

At the third and fourth floors, the barracks building was wrapped with a continuous deck, so narrow that it appeared more like a walkway. Pillars stretching between the third and fourth floors joined the decking. A row of tall windows, each about three-feet wide, and spaced five feet apart, provided for an abundance of light and fresh air at each level.

At the corner, a large drainpipe funneled rainwater from the roof to the ground. She rapped her knuckles against the pipe. It felt sturdy, and the black color with streaks of rust suggested it was made of cast iron. *Should be strong enough. Assuming there aren't any cracks.*

With the MP5 slung over her head and shoulder, she grasped the drainpipe and started climbing. The rough and weathered iron abraded her hands like she was gripping sandpaper. At least it wasn't slippery. She squeezed with her thighs, and her boots also achieved a solid hold, helping to propel her upward in short order. She completed the twenty-foot climb to the third floor in about a minute, and hoisted herself onto the narrow deck.

So far, she hadn't been seen. But now she was more exposed to observation from the cell house, given her elevated position.

She drew the knife, and with her free hand, started checking the windows. The first one was locked. She moved to the next—also locked. But at the third window, her luck changed, and the sash rose smoothly.

Not seeing anyone in the room, she climbed through the opening and closed the window, careful not to make a sound. The ten-foot ceiling made the room feel larger than its actual size. The floor was covered with stained oak boards, and wide molding trimmed the door and window. It appeared to be an office. A plain metal desk sat to one side, and cardboard file boxes were stacked against a wall next to two four-drawer metal file cabinets. Above the dark-wood door was a closed transom window.

Slowly, she turned the antique doorknob and cracked the door open just enough to peek outside. She glimpsed a wide hall covered in worn carpet. Empty. She opened the door wider and saw many closed doors on both sides of the hall. To the left, the passage ended, but it extended to the right and turned a corner.

She edged out of the office and unlimbered the MP5 submachine gun, raising the buttstock to her shoulder. With her back hugging the wall, she listened for a half-minute.

Silence.

Drawing in a deep breath, she advanced toward the end of the hallway.

The trio crossed the courtyard and stopped about thirty paces from Vernon. He had just removed the hood of his protective garment and laid it on the ground. The suit was silver and bulky, resembling a fire-resistant suit. With the hood on, it covered his body from head to toe. He peeled off the rest of the heavy clothing.

"What is he wearing?" Toby said.

"It's a lead-lined suit," Sacheen replied.

Toby was familiar with lead aprons used in the dental clinic when her teeth were X-rayed. But she'd never heard of a lead-lined protective garment, and she had no idea why the man needed to wear one.

Vernon strode across the separation.

"The drone's ready," he said to Sacheen. "The payload is sealed. It's safe to approach."

"What are you doing?" Toby said.

Sacheen held out her hand toward the drone.

"Come. I'll show you."

The aircraft came into view as they approached. It had six large propellers on arms that symmetrically stretched out two feet from the main body. The props were arranged at the end of each arm, around the center of the craft. Beneath the junction of the six arms was a squat metallic cylinder oriented so the axis of the cylinder was vertical.

To the side, Toby saw seven similar drones. Each even had the same short metal cylinder affixed to the body of the aircraft.

"What is that fixed to the drone?" Toby said. "Is it a bomb?"

"Oh, no," Leonard said. "A bomb that size," he pointed to the aircraft, "wouldn't do much damage. Maybe break a few windows. That's about all."

"Then what is it?"

"Inside that chamber is some of the deadliest material mankind has ever made," he said.

Toby's eyes widened.

Leonard continued. "You see, when the atomic genie was released from her bottle, she unleashed more than just the atomic bomb. Thankfully, governments have largely refrained from using such terrible weapons, and they've managed to keep their stockpiles secure."

"At least, as far as we know," Sacheen said.

"But uranium and plutonium used to make bombs are not the only radioactive elements that can cause great harm," Leonard said. "You see, inside that payload chamber is a mixture of strontium-90 and cobalt-60, in the form of a fine powder. Have you heard of these elements?"

Toby stared back in silence.

"No? I'm not surprised. Not the sort of thing one would discuss in normal conversations. Cobalt-60 is used in medical imaging machines and industrial devices, for scanning welds in things like steel pipelines. And strontium-90 was used by the Soviets to make thermoelectric generators. They placed hundreds of these machines at remote beacons in the Arctic to serve as navigational aids. Both materials are highly radioactive, hence the protective suit worn by Vernon as he loaded the capsule."

"If these materials are so dangerous," Toby said, "how did you get them?"

"It's really not so hard if you know where to look. Sacheen took care of the acquisition."

"The cobalt was purchased from a metal recycler in Mexico," Sacheen said. "The strontium was a bit more difficult, mostly because I had to travel to northern Canada to acquire the material. When the Soviet Union collapsed, the government abandoned nearly all of their thermoelectric generators. Not that they were ever secured in the first place. Anyway, it was a simple matter to contract with some enterprising men to scavenge the materials from two of the rusting machines."

"But how did you get that stuff into the country? Don't they have radiation detectors at the borders?"

"Of course. At the major international crossings. But we didn't use those. It was easy to smuggle the material where the borders are unguarded."

Toby folded her arms across her chest.

"So you're going to fly the drone over San Francisco," she said, "and crash it into city hall. So what? City hall will be contaminated, but who's going to care?"

"You misunderstand," Sacheen said. "That's not our plan at all."

"Then what?"

"This will be a message. A warning." Leonard faced Vernon. "Power up the drone and fly low on a direct course for Pioneer Park."

Vernon nodded. He flipped the master power switch on the controller, and all six electric motors turned on with a buzzing sound. He advanced the power setting until the aircraft rose to a hover. Finally, he made some trim adjustments and ensured he had a clear image on his phone clipped to the controller. Then he sent the drone south toward San Francisco.

"Like I told you before," she said to Toby, "we don't want to hurt anyone. Vernon will land this drone in Pioneer Park, with its cargo of radioactive dust still locked away inside the payload capsule. I'll call the police and tell them where to find it and what it contains."

Leonard said, "Once they confirm that we're telling the truth, they will have no choice but to capitulate to our demands."

"They'll never give in," Toby said.

"That would be a mistake," Leonard replied.

"You can call it what you like," Toby said. "I'm just telling you that the politicians will never give in to your demands. You can't blackmail the government. Other people have tried, and it never works."

"True. But that's because the threat was never sufficiently... painful before. This time it will be."

"You just don't get it." Toby raised her voice. "You can nuke city hall. You can nuke the entire block. They don't care. They'll just fence it off, tear everything down, and rebuild."

"You take us for fools if you think we don't know that," Sacheen said, with fire in her eyes.

Leonard motioned toward the other seven drones.

"This fleet of unmanned aircraft has the capability to spread enough radioactive dust to blanket San Francisco, Berkeley, Richmond, and Oakland. More than one and a half million people will be displaced. Thousands will die from cancer within the first year. All of San Francisco, and half of the East Bay, will be uninhabitable for half a century, maybe longer. And that's just the beginning. If we have to, we'll nuke every major metropolis in America."

"My God," Toby said. "You're all mad."

CHAPTER 18

LEONARD LASHED A VICIOUS BACKHAND across Toby's cheek, drawing blood from the corner of her mouth.

"I thought you to be smarter than that. As spokeswoman for all Indigenous People, your voice would carry influence. You could help unite our people for the first time, while building support among other ethnic groups for our cause. Change is overdue. It is inevitable."

He nodded his chin toward the barracks, Sacheen's signal to return Toby to the other hostages. As the two women departed, Vernon addressed Leonard, starting at the video display on his phone.

"Do you really think you can turn her?"

"In time, yes."

Vernon returned his concentration to the flight path of the drone. He had an unobstructed view across the bay, to San Francisco. There were no boats or ships in the path—no doubt the waters surrounding Alcatraz had been closed off to maritime traffic.

He flew the craft at a height of twenty to thirty feet above the water. He didn't think the authorities had any radar system in place that could detect and track the drone, but flying it low was prudent, nonetheless.

Five minutes after launch, the real-time video showed the piers along the north shore. He slowed the drone and increased altitude, flying between the upper floors of the many skyscrapers populating the financial district.

A couple minutes later, he was following the rising terrain, with Coit Tower looming directly ahead. That was his landmark, and he slowed the drone even more. Flying at about the speed of a brisk walk, he brought the hexcopter over Pioneer Park. A large lawn stretched in all directions beneath the aircraft. People were enjoying the park—some playing catch and flying discs. Others stretched out on the turf, reading a book or conversing with friends.

He held it in a hover while Leonard watched the video over his shoulder.

Leonard said, "Hold there while I call the police."

"Battery power is good for another twenty-five minutes of flight," Vernon said.

Leonard dialed 911 while he walked to the water's edge. He was gazing across the bay, imagining the events about to take place.

"I'm calling from Alcatraz," he said. "And I have a very important message for the mayor and the chief of police."

"What is your name, sir?"

"Never mind that. Listen carefully.

"Sir—"

"Shut up. As we speak, a helicopter drone is hovering over Pioneer Park. The drone is carrying a nasty payload of radioactive dust. So unless you want a lot of people to begin glowing, you'd best get the police to clear the park and secure the drone."

"Sir—"

Leonard ended the call, then strode back to Vernon.

"Keep it in a hover for five minutes, then land it on the lawn. And try not to hit anyone when you bring it down."

"Where's the fun in that?" Vernon wore a sly grin.

"Just follow my order. We need to appear reasonable and rational for this to work. If the police and the feds think we're crazy red Jihadists, they'll storm the island, and that will be game over."

"You really think they'd do that, and risk killing the hostages?"

"I have no doubt. The math is easy—sacrifice a hundred to save a thousand."

⌖

Danya approached the bend in the hall. As far as she could tell, the third floor was deserted. But as she reached the corner, she heard murmurs, distant and muffled. *Maybe the hostages*?

She stole a glance around the corner. The path was clear. Midway down the long corridor was a stairway. *Is that where the voices are coming from?*

With silent footsteps, and hugging the wall, she crept toward the stairway. The voices grew in volume as she closed the distance. She paused at the landing. A worn oak railing twisted up to the fourth and fourth fifth floors. It also extended down to the first floor. She cocked her head—the voices were louder, and definitely coming from below.

With a firm grip on the MP5, and the stock against her shoulder, she descended one step at a time. Fearing creaky treads from the aged construction, she gently applied her weight with each footstep and planted her feet along the edge of the oak treads where they were more likely to be secured to the framing.

Following the voices, she descended to the midpoint landing without any issues. As she turned to traverse the final flight of steps, she saw the staircase terminated in what appeared to be a small room on the ground floor. She tiptoed downward. Opposite the base of the stairs was a door with the universal male-female symbol indicating it was a restroom. To the right was a second door. *Maybe that opens onto the room where they're keeping the tourists hostage?*

She eased up to the door and placed her ear close, confirming voices on the other side. Gently, she tested the door latch. It turned freely.

Opening the door, even just a crack, was risky if one or more terrorists was near the door, or in a location where they would see the door open. But there was no avoiding that she'd have to pass through the passage if she was to have a chance of freeing the hostages. While she considered the best tactic, she took in the small space. Leading with her weapon, she checked the restroom. Empty.

There was a third unmarked door tucked away under the staircase landing. A quick inspection revealed it to be a janitorial closet, complete with a variety of cleaning fluids, mops, brooms, rags, paper products, and a laundry sink.

Feeling slightly more secure in her space, she returned to the door she was now certain adjoined the holding area for the prisoners. She put her ear to the door again. The voices were muffled, rendering only occasional words understandable.

Suddenly, a male voice sounded distinct and close.

"Clear the way."

The general chatter ceased. The door latch turned, and then the door opened just a crack. As it did, voices became more distinct.

"If there aren't any tissues in the storeroom, bring out a case of paper towels," someone called, from the distance.

Danya was already moving up the staircase, two steps at a time. If she didn't round the turn at the landing, she'd be spotted for sure.

"Roger that." The guard pushed the door open and strode for the janitor closet.

Peering around the newel post on the landing, Danya was able to snatch a glimpse into the large room through the open door before it swung closed, confirming her suspicions. Although she had less than two seconds to survey the room, she saw several dozen people sitting in groups and talking. She didn't see any of the terrorists, other than the man who'd been tasked with retrieving supplies from the storeroom. He was focused on his errand and didn't even cast a glance up the stairs. His weapon, also an MP5, hung from his shoulder.

A minute later, with a cardboard case of Kleenex® tissues in hand, the guard returned to the large room, giving her a second chance to spy through the open passage until the door automatically closed.

She grasped the opportunity and dashed down the stairs.

It had been agreed that Sacheen would be the spokesperson when conveying the group's demands to the authorities. They were familiar with studies that suggested a woman would be subconsciously perceived as less threatening than a man. Men naturally tended toward conflict, and this trait was most pronounced in male-male interactions. The goal was to work past the initial aggressive response from law enforcement, and get them to reason through the problem.

Once the politicians were engaged and in control, both Sacheen and Leonard agreed, the risk of mission failure was greatly reduced. Local and state political leaders would never accept large portions of the Bay Area being transformed into a radioactive wasteland. The federal government would have no choice but to fall in line. California was simply too populous and too important to allow it to suffer such a preventable disaster.

After one transfer, Sacheen was connected with the mayor of San Francisco.

"This is Mayor Webster. Who am I speaking to?"

"Did your police department pick up the drone in Pioneer Park?"

"They did. And that's quite the stunt you pulled. Do you have any idea how much trouble you and your *associates* are in?"

"Mayor Webster, please. Bluster and threats are not going to be helpful. My pilot flew that drone and landed it safely without harming any civilians. We did so as an act of good faith. It is important that you understand what we are capable of doing. But it's equally important that you understand our intention is a good-faith negotiation, during which harm to innocent civilians can be avoided."

"If that's the case, you'll release the hostages you're holding."

"And give up my leverage? No. Not just yet."

"Okay. You called me. What do you want?"

Sacheen's voice was soothing. "I want to help by showing you what we are ready to deliver. Within a few hours, I'm certain you'll have confirmation that the drone was transporting cobalt-60 and strontium-90. Both are especially nasty radioactive isotopes."

"The cannister is being transported to Lawrence Livermore Labs for analysis," Webster said. "But I've been told that a portable radiation detector showed a high-level reading. For the sake of argument, let's say I believe you. What's this about? Isn't this the point where you make your demands known? Something like millions of dollars in unmarked bills, and a plane to take you out of the country?"

Sacheen chuckled. "You've read too many thrillers. But yes, we do have demands that we will communicate at the proper time. First, I assume the FBI is actively involved?"

"Naturally. Kidnapping is a federal offense. So are acts of terrorism."

"Terrorism? Oh, my. We haven't carried out any such acts—yet."

"Is that a threat?" Webster said.

"Not at all. I'm just being honest. Our discussions will be much more effective if we cut to the chase and speak candidly with each other. Anyway, I'm glad the FBI is engaged. In fact, I'd like for you to have the special agent in charge fly to Alcatraz in their helicopter."

"Why?"

"Because I want to show him the fleet of drones we have, each with their payloads ready and prepped for flight. It's part of my effort to be transparent with you."

"Do you really think the special agent in charge is going to surrender himself to you to become another hostage?"

"As I said, my offer is to show him how serious we are and what we are capable of doing. If you understand that, and accept that, the rest will go quickly, and the scores of civilians I'm holding here can be released."

"How many hostages are there?"

"I'm glad you asked. We completed a head count. Fifty-three children, plus eighty-three women and seventy-two men."

"If you—"

"Relax, Mayor Webster. No one has been harmed, and that is not our intention. However, we will need a food and water drop by evening if we haven't concluded our business by then."

"That's a lot of people. Where are you keeping them?"

Sacheen laughed. "Nice try. Now, getting serious again, you can tell the FBI that we will release ten children to fly back in the helicopter as a show of good faith. The special agent in charge is free to return, too. My offer is good for the next sixty minutes. That's all."

"And if they refuse?"

"Shortly, ten children will be standing on the ferry landing. I'm certain you have us under surveillance, so you'll know I am not bluffing. They'll remain standing there until the deadline. But if the deadline passes, and the helicopter does not arrive per my instructions…well, there won't be ten children standing any longer."

"So much for your pledge not to harm anyone."

"Mayor Webster, I never made any such pledge. I did say it was not our intention to harm any of the hostages, especially the children. Which is the truth. However, if you give us no choice…if you test our resolve…well, then you will need ten body bags for the children I offered. Please. Accept our proposal. It is in everyone's best interests."

Webster scoffed. "You expect me to believe your crap? Whatever your game is, I'm absolutely confident you're only playing for what's best for you."

"I have many drones here, each loaded with the same material you'll find in the aircraft I already delivered to you. Shall we launch the fleet across your city and the East Bay?"

"The Coast Guard will put helicopters in the air and shoot down every one of your toy planes before they cross over land. Face it, you're outgunned and outmanned."

Sacheen smiled. "That would be quite the feat. Our drones are piloted. And from the vantage afforded by the excellent strategic location of this rocky island, we have a clear view across the Bay in every direction. I could order my pilots to fly drones to the north, over San Rafael. South to San Francisco. East to Richmond, Berkeley, and Oakland. Or I could order the drones to fly en mass to the target of my choice. Do you know how hard it is to defeat a swarm of drones?"

Although she didn't expect an answer from the politician, she waited through a moment of silence for theatrical effect.

"The point is, you will have no idea if my drones are in the air or not, because you can't detect them. They fly too close to the water, and are too small to be picked up by radar. You'll never know where they are flying, or when. So save your bluster. It only serves to demonstrate your ignorance."

"The Coast Guardsmen onboard their helicopters will search visually," Webster said. "They're really good at that, you know. Comes with rescuing fishermen bobbing in a stormy sea."

"Plucking a stationary seaman from the ocean is one thing. They are usually wearing an orange life vest and waving their arms. My drones will be moving fast, on an unpredictable course, and are painted blue-gray to match the bay water. But it's your call. I'm simply trying to give you a reasonable alternative. A way to avoid a tragedy of epic proportions. After we've dusted the Greater Bay Area with enough radioactive powder to render it uninhabitable for a century, I'll call the *San Francisco Chronicle* and tell them how you steadfastly refused my request—a simple request, actually—to have the FBI send their special agent in charge here for a face-to-face meeting. Following the meeting, he is free to leave with the ten children. Maybe in fifty years they'll bring daring tourists to the irradiated wastelands, just like they do at Chernobyl. I'll bet they'll even have a tour named for you. Something like, *The Mayor Webster Night Tour. No flashlights needed—the place glows after dark.* Kinda catchy, don't you think?"

The mayor knew he had no leverage, and it galled him to concede, even something so minor as to suggest the FBI agree to the meeting.

"I'll pass along your invitation," he grumbled. "Anything else you'd like for me to share with the feds when I speak with them?"

"Yes, there is. Make sure they only send the SAC and the pilot. No one else. After all, they need to be able to carry the children back. Is that clear?"

"Abundantly."

"Good. Remember, one hour. And trust me, what I have to show them is worth their time."

"And the children?"

"Like I promised, they will be released unharmed. Although the FBI may not report directly to your office, I know you have influence over their actions. I suggest you put your charm and diplomacy to good use."

"You haven't given me much time. What if they don't have a

chopper fueled up nearby, ready to go?"

She exhaled an exaggerated sigh. "I believe that with all the creative minds working this problem, someone can figure out a solution. Now time's wasting, and you have a job to complete. Thank you, Mayor Webster. It was a pleasure talking with you."

She ended the call, confident the authorities would acquiesce to her demand. The offer to set free a group of children was irresistible bait.

CHAPTER 19

AT THE BASE OF THE STAIRCASE, Danya again leaned in close to the door to complete an audio check of the room beyond. She heard nothing alarming, only the muffled voices of many people carrying on normal conversations. She slid the MP5 from her shoulder and stashed it in the storage closet behind the door. Put the extra ammunition magazines inside her pack before placing it next to the submachine gun. Anyone entering the closet would not see the weapon unless they closed the door—possible, but not likely.

The folding knife she'd taken from the big man at the rocket launcher was tucked into a back pocket of her jeans, while the portable radio was clipped to her waistband at the middle of her back after ensuring it was turned off. The oversized sweatshirt easily covered the items, allowing her to blend in with the hostages.

Once again, she leaned in close to the door for one last check. And as before, all she heard was the indistinct chatter of muffled voices. She squatted and delicately turned the doorknob to crack the door open enough for a quick visual survey. All clear except for two armed guards conversing across the large room. Even the nearest clusters of civilians paid no attention to the door opening just a bit.

She pushed it open further. Still squatting, she slid through the opening and closed the door behind her. Thirty feet away, a middle-aged woman sat cross-legged with a group of children. The youngsters were completely occupied, entertaining themselves by playing a card game, seemingly oblivious to the looming threat of harm. The woman, however, raised her head just as Danya was closing the door. She opened her mouth to speak, but Danya preempted her with a finger held to her lips. The woman accepted the message, her glare punctuated by a raised eyebrow.

Danya scooted over to the group and squeezed between a giggly adolescent girl and the woman, who learned toward the newcomer.

"Who are you?"

"The one who got away." Danya said, furtively angling her gaze to take in the room.

"Huh? I don't understand. Why did you come in through that door? Is that a way out?"

"Maybe. Probably not."

The kids paid her no heed as they continued to play the game, which required each to throw cards from their hand, face up, onto a communal pile, which other players would randomly and frantically grab, inevitably resulting in a chorus of laughter.

"Are they going to let us go?"

Although Danya knew the answer, she didn't want to voice it. Since every hostage was a potential witness, no way the terrorists would allow them to walk away. But it was important that the hostages did not give up hope.

"I'm Danya. What's your name?"

"Sue. Sue Kincaid. I teach at an elementary school in Alameda. These are some of my students. We're studying the Civil War. Some field trip." She frowned.

Her brunette hair cascaded in graceful waves before being pulled together with an elastic band just below her shoulders. She wore turquoise-rimmed glasses that rode low on her nose, giving her a scholarly appearance.

A guard meandered toward the group. Danya tilted her head toward the card game while keeping the guard in view through her peripheral vision. Just then, one of the students reached out and snatched the pile of cards, eliciting laughter from the other players. Danya smiled, pretending she was following the play. After a minute, the guard turned and moved away from the group.

Sue had taken notice of her visitor's reaction to the armed man. "Who are they?" she said.

"Does it matter?"

Sue raised an eyebrow again, but didn't voice her thoughts.

Danya said, "Consider them the wolves."

"Then that would make us the lambs?"

"You catch on quickly."

"And what about you?" Sue appraised her new companion. "I don't see you as a lamb."

"Me?" Danya gave a thin smile, but there was no mirth in her eyes. "I suppose I'm the shepherd."

"Did you come to rescue us?"

Danya leaned in close to avoid her voice carrying.

"Not exactly. Look, Sue, it's really important that you remain positive, okay? We're gonna get out of this, and you need to keep a cool head and make sure your kids are safe. They'll look to you for direction. Just play it smart. If there's shooting, get everyone to lay down immediately, okay? No hesitation, right? Just get your kids to lay flat on the floor. You, too."

With her brow crinkled, the school teacher from Alameda stared at Danya.

Finally, Sue nodded. "Okay," she whispered.

Danya turned her gaze back to the card game. The children were so innocent, to the point they could laugh and joke while in the midst of a life-and-death ordeal. Only, they didn't know that. Children never did.

She thought back to another hostage situation that had unfolded halfway around the world. It was less than a dozen years ago, but in other respects, a lifetime had passed since then.

She'd been part of a team sent to rescue a school bus filled with kids. The bus had been hijacked near a farming commune in the Golan Heights. Extremists claiming loyalty to Syria had taken the youths and the driver hostage, demanding that the Golan Heights be returned to Syria. Two days into the negotiation, the bus driver was executed—a single bullet to the head. The entire grotesque event live-streamed to social media.

The Israeli prime minister, with a grim nod, agreed that time had run out. Photographs and real-time video from a high-flying drone confirmed that the school children were being held on the bus. The bus was essentially a solar oven, even with the windows open, and concern over the children's health was high.

Despite warnings that an outright assault was likely to result in collateral damage—optimistic estimates ran as high as half of the children being killed, whereas others feared that all could be lost if the bus was rigged with explosives—the prime minister authorized an elite team, selected from Mossad's best field operators, to engage the terrorists. No ambiguity in the order. The terrorists were to be killed. Surrender was not acceptable. There would be no quarter, no mercy, and no public trial, which other extremists would use as a reason to recruit new Jihadists. No, the terrorists would simply vanish into obscurity.

Under cover of darkness, Danya and three other operators silently landed five hundred meters from the bus. They'd parachuted from high altitude. Their black canopies, shaped like air foils, had allowed the team to literally fly their chutes to the landing zone. The plan was straightforward: Pair up and form two teams. Flank the camp, shoot the terrorists, and extract the children. Although it sounded simple, she knew the truth.

Once the site was secure, a ground team would race in to provide transportation back to safety. Five military helicopters would be in the air and ready to transport the most severely wounded to the nearest hospital. Medical teams onboard each aircraft would include trauma nurses and doctors with the capability to undertake emergency surgery. The mission planners didn't think this was merely a possibility, but rather a guaranteed outcome.

At least one drone was always overhead, unseen and unheard, providing a direct video link. Just before the Mossad team exited their C130 aircraft, the images showed the school bus illuminated by the flickering light from two small fires, one on either side of the school bus. The high-resolution video also revealed the terrorists—

five total—on a roaming patrol around the bus, establishing a perimeter only twenty meters away from the vehicle.

The two Mossad teams, designated Alpha and Omega, landed and released their chutes. After a final update, they split to flank the bus. The black sky was marked by thousands of tiny points of light, but the moon had yet to rise. With the aid of state-of-the-art military night-vision goggles, the darkness did not present an impediment to Danya and her teammates. As if it were a sunlit day, they slipped to their positions two hundred meters from the bus.

She was the spotter. Her shooter was a man named Seth Meier. Before this mission, she'd never met Seth, but their brief introductions onboard the C130 led her to believe he was a disciplined and capable operator.

Once in position, Seth quickly set his weapon—an Israeli Weapons Industries DAN .338 Bolt-Action Sniper Rifle chambered for the powerful Lapua Magnum round, topped with a high-power scope on its bipod—and dropped into a prone position behind the stock. At two hundred meters, he could hit a dime nine times out of ten. And the .338 caliber bullet, traveling more than twice the speed of sound, was lethal.

Danya reached into her pack and removed a high-magnification spotting scope, configured for low-light amplification.

"I've got three tangos," she whispered. "The other two must be on the far side of the bus. Standard AKs fitted with suppressors."

Although not up to the standards of high-quality sniper rifles, the ubiquitous AK assault rifle was, nonetheless, deadly. All the more so at close range.

Seth studied the image in his scope as he traversed the target area.

"Roger that," he said. "Three tangos. They've got no clue they're walking dead men."

"As it should be," she replied.

The sniper team waited in silence for two minutes, until Omega Team radioed.

"In position. We have two tangos in sight. Ready to engage on your order."

Peering through the scope, she studied the situation. Nothing appeared out of the ordinary for a hostage situation. And that nagged at her. *What am I missing*?

No fortification. No visible backup. No heavy weapons. Her deliberation was interrupted by the squelch of the radio.

"Alpha Team, I say again. Omega is in position. We have two tangos. Ready to drop them at your order."

She stole one last, long look through the spotting scope, still unable to put her finger on what was troubling her about the scene only a couple hundred meters away.

She shook it off. Their order was clear. It was time.

Pressing the transmit button on her portable radio, she whispered, "This is Alpha Team. Clear to engage."

Less than a meter away, Seth heard the order and gently squeezed the trigger.

Boom!

Danya was still recovering from the muzzle blast from Seth's rifle when she heard the report, one and a half seconds later, from the first shot fired by Omega. With precision and confidence, Seth had nudged the crosshairs to the next target. He fired. Without waiting to ascertain where the bullet hit, he was on to the third target. All the team members knew that this had to be a coordinated, lightning strike so as to deny the terrorists the opportunity to open fire on the busload of children.

No sooner had the gunfire faded into silence, when a tinny voice came over the radio.

"Two tangos down. All clear."

Danya surveyed the scene through the spotting scope, while Seth did likewise using the rifle scope. Three prone bodies near the front of the bus. Nothing moved.

"Clear," she said into the radio.

Then she removed a portable loudspeaker from her backpack. She held it close to her lips and spoke slowly and clearly.

"Children. Leave the bus immediately. The Israeli Defense Force is here to take you home."

After hearing the verbal message, Omega Team radioed for the helicopters and ground transports to come in. In the distance—muted at first, but growing more intense—she heard the helicopter rotors beating the air as they raced to the scene. She kept her eye to the scope just long enough to ensure her order was being acted upon. The first youth to the door, a young girl, gazed in her direction. For a fleeting moment, she looked into the teenager's eyes, seeing fear mixed with hope.

Satisfied the bus was being evacuated, Danya rose, but only reached one knee before the distinct staccato of AK fire reached her ears.

"Shit." She dropped back to the spotting scope. "We missed one!"

"Not possible," Seth replied.

Through the precision optics, Danya saw the crisp image of children spanning a range of ages, exiting the bus and running into an empty landscape. Then she heard the report of rifle fire again, but she couldn't locate any muzzle flashes, and concluded the suppressors on the AKs were masking the bright flash of burned gunpowder escaping the barrel.

"One of the terrorists is shooting." She watched helplessly as six children fell.

One appeared to be clutching a stuffed animal.

"Kill him. Shoot!" she shouted.

All pretense of stealth forsaken, replaced with a sense of urgency she'd never before felt.

"Where?" Seth replied. "I don't see any movement."

More gunfire, and another four children fell as they continued to pour out of the bus.

"By the front of the bus."

Seth hesitated. "There are three bodies there. No movement. Which one is the shooter?"

"Shoot all of them! I don't care if they're not moving. Just shoot them all again."

While Seth was methodically sighting and shooting, Danya jumped to her feet and raced toward the school bus. The two-hundred-meters distance was nothing for a gunfight, and recklessly close for a sniper team. But now that she was sprinting to reach the children, the distance seemed immense.

She kept pumping her legs and gulping in air as she screamed into the loudspeaker.

"Get down! Get down and lay on the ground."

She'd covered two-thirds of the distance and was close enough to see four or five kids standing together near the door of the bus. It appeared everyone had exited, and thankfully the AK fire had ceased. She took two more strides, when everything before her was engulfed in a brilliant flash of white light. A burst of searing heat hit her, followed by a blast wave a heartbeat later, knocking her on her back, and she was smothered in blackness and silence.

There was no accounting for how long she was out. Maybe only seconds, maybe a minute or two. The next thing she recalled was Seth with a firm hand on her shoulder, calling her name.

"Danya! Danya."

Slowly, she rose, fighting nausea from both the explosive pressure wave and her head slamming onto the earth. Her gravest fears took form before her eyes. The school bus was engulfed in flame, its roof having been blasted away, and the sides peeled back like the yellow skin of a banana. In the flickering firelight, she saw many small bodies lying motionless on the ground, some twisted in unnatural shapes.

All of her training, all of her professionalism, evaporated in that instant.

She wept.

Only seven of the forty-two school children escaped alive. The survivors had all suffered injuries, many life-threatening, and all were evacuated in the military helicopters. The ground vehicles were used to transport the corpses, later to be delivered to grieving families.

The subsequent investigation revealed that one of the terrorists, presumably the leader, possessed a version of a dead man's switch—a failsafe. Every two minutes, he was required to press a button on a remote detonator. If he failed to perform this simple task, fifty kilograms of Semtex packed into the bus would detonate.

Close to the worst possible outcome, but not unpredicted.

The terrorists were left where they fell after having their fingerprints taken and their faces photographed. Then a military demolitions team arrived at the site. By now, a couple days had passed, and the corpses were bloating. Didn't matter to the IDF. What they would do was far more severe than allowing the Muslim cadavers to decay in the midday heat.

The military engineers wrapped each of the five bodies in det cord, which also secured ten bricks of C4 explosive to each body. It was a grisly task, but none of the engineers shied from their duty. The slaughter of the school children fueled a raging hatred that only time could quench.

Once their task was completed, all retreated a safe distance. And then, with cameras rolling, the detonator was pressed. In a microsecond, the remains of the five terrorists vaporized. All that was left was a red mist that slowly settled across the arid land.

In the days following the tragedy, Danya came to realize what had nagged her so much at the outset of the mission. No escape vehicle, no means of egress, other than the bus itself, which was clearly a poor means of escape. The terrorists had never intended to leave alive, nor had they intended to allow the hostages to be rescued. Their aim was to attract global attention to their cause, and to impose a severe penalty upon the Israeli people and government for past transgressions.

Although the Mossad team, under her command, performed like clockwork, they could not prevent a disastrous outcome to the mission. It was a bitter lesson, one that she refused to forget. A lesson that seemed relevant to her current situation.

She surveyed the young faces gathered around her, and vowed to do all she could to prevent any harm to these hostages.

She whispered in Sue's ear, "Did you see any of the terrorists carrying bags or backpacks?"

"No. Just those ugly machine guns, or whatever they are."

Good. Maybe they don't have any explosives.

Danya continued surreptitiously surveying the guards and the features defining the room they were in. There were four gunmen, and they appeared to be more relaxed than they should be. Clearly, they didn't consider the hostages to be a threat. From the far side of the room, she saw Toby enter, escorted by the woman she'd observed previously speaking with her friend when the other people were taken hostage. Toby walked among the assembled people, but didn't seem to have a special destination in mind. The woman who'd escorted her spoke briefly to one of the guards before leaving.

"Remember," Danya said to Sue, "when the shooting starts, hit the floor, all of you. Promise me."

The school teacher nodded. "We will. I promise."

"I need to go see someone. I'll look for you later." Danya rose and walked across the floor to Toby.

At the sight of her friend, Toby smiled and closed the gap.

"Thank God. I'm so happy to see you. I didn't know where you were, or if you were safe. When I couldn't find you, I was hoping you'd gotten away."

"Follow me." Danya led Toby with a hand on her elbow.

They sat on the floor close to the door she'd entered through. She noticed the red mark on Toby's check.

"What happened?"

"One of the terrorist leaders hit me after I called him and his girlfriend crazy."

"The woman that directed you in here—she's the girlfriend?"

Toby nodded. "They asked me to join them. Said they want me to be the spokeswoman for the group."

"Did they say what they want? What their demands are?"

"Nothing specifically. But generally, they want ancestral lands to be returned. I don't know exactly how they think that's supposed to happen. But they have drones loaded with radioactive material, and they said they will release it over the Bay Area if their demands aren't met."

Danya knew the threat, if credible, was a nightmare scenario. In essence, a poor man's dirty bomb, without the difficulty of the explosives. It was a threat Mossad had studied in great detail.

"Did they say what type of radioactive material?"

"Cobalt. And another one, an odd name. It began with an S."

"Strontium?"

"Yeah, that's it. Cobalt and strontium. They flew one of the drones to San Francisco, they said, to a park, and they were going to call the police and tell them where to find it."

"Not a good sign. Do you know how many drones they have?"

"I counted seven lined up near the ferry landing. But maybe they have more. I don't know for sure. Is that stuff—cobalt and strontium—is it bad?"

Danya nodded. "Yeah, it's bad. If they're not bluffing—and we have to assume they're not, since they delivered a sample to the police for authentication—they could render the Bay Area uninhabitable for generations."

"I don't understand. Since this radioactive material is so dangerous, how did they manage to get a hold of it?"

Danya raised an eyebrow. "There are a lot of people who will sell anything to anyone for a relatively modest amount of money. Actually, it doesn't surprise me at all. It was only a question of when, not if."

"We can't let them carryout their plan. We have to do something."

"And we will. Now, tell me everything you can from your conversation. Everything. No detail is too small or insignificant."

For the next twenty minutes, Toby relayed all she could remember. Periodically, Danya interrupted to ask questions.

No sooner had Toby finished, when Sacheen appeared at the doorway.

"That's her," Toby said. "That's Sacheen."

Sacheen was engaged in conversation with two of the guards.

"The police helicopter is on its way in," she said. "It will land here soon. Time to collect the kids."

As if an important question was forming in her mind, she swiveled her head left and right, taking in the large space.

"Where's Charlie?"

One of the guards shrugged. "Haven't seen him. Maybe Dolan knows where he is."

She looked beyond the guard's shoulder. "Dolan. Come here for a minute."

The man shuffled over, his weapon still hanging from his shoulder.

"Yes ma'am." He stood straight.

She demanded respect, but shunned any address with military overtones.

"Why isn't Charlie here helping to keep an eye on the hostages?"

"I don't know, ma'am. Haven't seen him since before we shot up that Coast Guard patrol boat."

She considered his response. "That's the last time I saw him, too. He was set up with the Folgore rocket launcher on the parade ground."

"You want me to go check, see if he's still there?"

"No, I'll radio up to the cell house. They still have four men there. You can go back to watching these people."

She made the radio call, short and to the point. Then she directed the two guards to carry out their task. They moved forward and commenced picking children at random from the seated crowd. A young girl, probably no more than six years old, cried for her mother as she was pulled up onto her feet. The mother reached out, only to be jabbed by the muzzle of an MP5.

"Sit down," the guard said.

"Take your hands off my granddaughter," a voice called from behind the guard.

He turned and faced a gray-haired woman no more than five-feet tall, her face covered in deep creases. As she looked up at the guard, she jabbed a boney finger into his chest.

"If you must take someone, you will take me."

"Suit yourself." The guard shoved her along with the others that had been selected.

It only took a minute to gather up the children, and it caused enough commotion that everyone in the room was staring at the guards.

"Something's not right." Danya whispered in Toby's ear.

Toby stood and strode across the gap to Sacheen and the guards. "Leave the children alone," she said.

Danya had dropped her head and looked away, avoiding eye contact with the terrorists.

Sacheen locked her gaze with Toby's as she closed the distance. "You're in no position to make any demands." Then she faced the nearest guard. "Take her, too."

Toby did her best to comfort the children, many of whom were crying as they were escorted away, not far behind Sacheen.

The thumping sound of rotors beating the crisp air was growing louder.

CHAPTER 20

ONLY TWO OF THE GUNMEN WERE LEFT to guard all the hostages, and Danya decided it was time to make a move. She didn't have to wait long for both guards to be looking away from where she was seated, and when they did, she dashed for the door to the stairway and the storage room.

One of the guards caught her quick motion. "Hey! Stop."

But it was too late. The door was already swinging shut behind her. The guard sprinted across the large room, darting between people sitting in clusters across the floor. He threw the door open, his weapon leveled and ready to fire.

But the anteroom was empty. He looked up the short flight of stairs to the landing and paused, listening for footsteps.

Nothing.

He took two steps and craned his head, searching up the stairwell, expecting to see a shadow or a fleeting glimpse of a hand on the railing as the person dashed to an upper floor. But nothing.

To the right, he opened the door to the restroom and checked the stalls. Also empty. That left only the small janitorial closet. He turned the door latch and threw the door open, expecting to find the woman he'd seen fleeing crouched in a corner, hiding.

The crack of a gunshot was deafening in the confined space. A thin wisp of gun smoke wafted from the barrel of Danya's MP5. The guard stumbled backward two steps, a crimson splotch growing at the center of his chest. The bullet punched a neat hole through his sternum, then exploded in his heart before it shredded a ragged hole where it exited his back, leaving metal fragments in his spine. He lacked the strength to hold his weapon level, and it landed on the linoleum floor with a clank. Then his eyelids closed, and he fell face forward.

Danya's daypack was where she'd left it, behind the door. She removed the spare ammunition magazines and stuffed them in her pocket where she could access them quickly. Then she slipped the pack onto her shoulders. She knew the remaining guard with the hostages would have heard the gunshot. But would he assume it was his teammate who had fired the weapon? Surely there wouldn't be any reason for him to think that *she* was armed and dangerous. After all, for all the terrorists knew, she was just another civilian hostage. Someone's girlfriend, or an adventurous young woman taking in the sights of the San Francisco Bay.

After leaving the storage room, she stopped at the door and listened. The hostages were quiet, no doubt terrified by the sound of gunfire. She pounded her fist on the door, then stepped to the side, pressing her back to the wall.

It wasn't long before the guard approach. "Hey, Dolan. You okay?"

Then he nudged the door open and pressed half his body into the anteroom. From three feet, Danya fired before he had a chance to realize it was an ambush. The 9mm bullet entered his left cheek, traveling upward, and took a generous portion of his brain and skull as it exited his temple.

After dragging his body to the janitorial closet with Dolan's corpse, she scavenged the extra mags from the guards' belts. Well-armed, she entered the room with the hostages. Dozens stared at her, a mixture of fear and shock on their faces.

"It's okay," she said, her voice carrying across the expansive space. "I'm not going to hurt you. I'm going to get help. Please stay where you are. You're safer here."

As she darted across the room for the far doorway, she removed the portable radio from her belt and powered it up. She hoped the terrorists were using only one channel. And she further hoped the radio was still set to that frequency.

She listened for several long seconds before she heard a voice.

"Ma'am, it's Kyle. I came down to the parade ground from the cell house, just like you said. And I found Charlie."

Sacheen turned her back to Toby and the kids. "Kick him in the ass and tell him to get back to work."

"He can't do that, ma'am. He's dead."

"What?"

"Like I said. Someone bashed in his skull with a chunk of concrete."

"Where did you find his body?"

"Lying next to the rocket launcher. Looks like there was a struggle. The Folgore was knocked over."

"Shit," she hissed.

"There's more bad news."

"How can it get any worse?"

"His weapon and extra mags are gone. His radio, too."

She straightened. "Listen up, everyone. Communication security has been compromised. Immediately change to the alternate channel. Spread the word in case someone has the volume turned down and misses my order."

After making the adjustment to her portable radio, she approached Leonard and Vernon, motioning them to a side bar several steps away from Toby, who had adapted quickly to the role of chaperone.

"Charlie's dead. Whoever killed him also took his radio and weapon. Change your radios to the backup frequency. Do it now."

The helicopter was closing fast, and as it neared, the roar of engine and rotors was reaching the point of making conversation impossible. Toby's arms were outstretched, and the children were huddled close, seeking comfort from her presence.

"What is your name?" Toby shouted to the elderly woman, who also had her thin arms wrapped around two children at her side.

"Margaret. I wouldn't let them take my granddaughter." The woman looked across the many small faces, each filled with terror. "Don't you worry about this. You'll all be just fine. And you'll have a story to share with your friends."

The helicopter had taken a hovering position about fifty feet above the flat pavement, drowning any further conversation among the hostages. Once the pilot was convinced it was clear, the aircraft slowly descended.

Shortly after the skids were supporting the weight of the helicopter, the pilot reduced the fuel flow, keeping the engine at idle. The tail was painted midnight blue, with the letters CHP in gold. The passenger compartment was white. A gold seven-point star beneath the words *Highway Patrol* marked this helicopter as belonging to the California Highway Patrol.

The side door slid open, and out hopped a short middle-aged man wearing tan slacks and a dark-blue windbreaker. The letters FBI were printed in bold yellow letters on the breast and sleeves. The man's hair was cropped short, military style, and he wore dark wireframe sunglasses. He held his hands raised as he moved forward.

Sacheen met him halfway. "You must be the federal agent overseeing this affair?"

He nodded. "Name's Flynn. I'm the special agent in charge of the San Francisco office. The mayor relayed your message." He gazed beyond her, to the collection of kids huddled around Toby and Margaret. "I see you kept your word, sort of. You said ten kids. I count nine."

Sacheen shrugged. "The old woman insisted we take her rather than her granddaughter."

Flynn nodded. "Okay. I'm here. Now what?"

"What's with the CHP bird? I was expecting either an SFDP or an FBI helicopter. I don't like the idea of more agencies getting involved. Too much bureaucracy. Too many bosses, all trying to show they have the biggest pair, if you know what I mean."

The FBI man tilted his chin to the side, indicating his ride.

"It's the best we could do with limited time. My office doesn't have the budget for its own aircraft. Neither does the SFPD. But don't worry. Our agreement with CHP is simple. They're only providing transportation—no operational involvement in resolving this affair. They have no jurisdiction. Think of that aircraft as...I don't know...maybe air Uber, if that helps."

Sacheen narrowed her eyes, maintaining a steady aim with her Beretta at Flynn's chest.

"You armed?" she said.

He shook his head. "May I lower my hands?"

"Open your jacket. Slowly. Leonard here," she indicated with a nod, "will make certain you're telling the truth."

The SAC complied, and Leonard completed the pat-down, finding no weapons.

Flynn said, "I understand that you landed a drone in Pioneer Park, with a small load of radioactive material. Too small to be a dirty bomb."

"That's right," she said.

"So what's your angle? Why insist I come out here if you're not going to surrender?"

"It's like I explained to Mayor Webster. We delivered a sample of our capability so you, the mayor, and the governor would understand that we are not bluffing. We are ready to carry out our mission and deliver seven drones over San Francisco and the major metropolitan cities surrounding the Bay. Each is carrying a full payload of strontium-90 and cobalt-60, just like the sample. This negotiation will go much faster if you confirm the threat."

"And I'm supposed to believe your boast because you say so?"

"Not at all. I insisted on this meeting so you can see for yourself. The drones are over there." She pointed toward the edge of the landing, near a block of restrooms. "If you came prepared and have a radiation monitor—as I'm sure you have—you can check each one."

Flynn rolled his eyes. "The detectors we use are very sensitive. A smart person can spoof them easily. Maybe dab the drone with a few flakes of radium paint from an antique clock. Or glue an americium button from a smoke detector, somewhere onto the aircraft. Even the old canary glass that was colored with uranium salts has enough radioactivity to set off our detectors."

"Don't try to con me," she said. "I've done my research. The decay pathway of strontium-90 is pure beta radiation, which doesn't penetrate far, even in air. But cobalt-60 decay involves both beta and high-energy gamma radiation. You'll get a strong gamma signal from it while you're still several dozen feet from the drones. That energetic response doesn't come from canary glass or antique paint."

Flynn frowned. *It was worth a try.* "Yeah, I've got a detector. Mind if I get it from the cabin?"

"Be my guest. But if you turn around with a weapon, you'll be dead before your knees touch the ground. Understood?"

He nodded.

"Oh…tell the pilot to step out. He can leave the engine idling. But I want him out of the aircraft, hands on his head."

"Fine." Flynn strode back to the helicopter.

The side door was still open. On the seat was a black case. He popped open the lid and removed the portable radiation monitor. Then he relayed the order to the pilot. As Flynn returned to Sacheen, the pilot stepped out, standing a few feet from the helicopter. His fingers were laced, and hands pressed against the top of his flight helmet.

Flynn produced the device for her to inspect. "In case you don't trust me. It's a gamma radiation detector. It will not only signal the presence of gamma rays, but also measure their energy. I've been briefed on what to look for. From that spectrum, I'll know if what you say is true."

The device looked like a small tablet, except it was thicker and had yellow rubber armor around the edges. A probe that looked like a microphone was connected to the tablet with a coiled cabled, much like an old telephone cord.

She said, "Too small to hold a gun inside the case. And if it's carrying explosives, you'll be dead, too."

"No tricks. This will record and display the gamma ray spectrum on the monitor. If it's cobalt-60, as you claim, we'll know."

"Good. Then let's get on with it. You capture your spectra, and then take the children and the old woman back. Both are good-faith offerings, proof that we wish to conclude our business fairly and swiftly. In return, you are to pass along what you've seen to the governor. I want to parlay with him immediately."

"And what exactly am I to tell the governor? You've made no demands."

Her aim was threefold: To entrench her position on Alcatraz. Then to show the officials in charge that she had control of the situation. And finally, to give them a negotiation pathway to resolution. She had accomplished the first two of her goals.

"Very well. I'll tell you." She pointed to the second-floor corner of the barracks building, only fifteen yards away.

On the wall, painted in fading red paint, read *Indians Welcome,* and *Indian Land.*

"See that?"

Flynn raised an eyebrow. "I do."

"This is where the movement really came into being. And this is where we will achieve our final victory." She paused, but the FBI agent had no comment. "All lands that were taken from my people through violation of legally binding treaties will be immediately returned to sovereign control of the nations. Where that may not be possible or feasible, fair compensation will be forthcoming within sixty days. No backpedaling, no legal challenges."

Flynn's eyes widened. "Are you nuts? I can't agree to that."

"Of course you can't. You are merely the messenger."

"Let me give you a quick civics lesson. The governor can't agree to your demand, either. This isn't a question that falls under the purview of the state. Congress and the president will have to arrive at a solution."

"Do you think I'm stupid? California is not without political influence. Deliver my message. Convene a press conference. I will deliver a recording of our grievances to be aired nationwide. Once Americans learn how First Nations people have been cheated, persecuted, slaughtered by the federal government, they will stand by our side. With one voice, people nationwide will demand what is right and just—that all land illegally taken from the Indigenous nations be returned to the rightful owners. Congress will have no choice but to heed the people's will."

"The government will never negotiate with terrorists."

She chortled. "We aren't terrorists. We've harmed none of the hostages. In fact, I'm taking extraordinary measures to ensure we have a good-faith negotiation."

"Your men murdered some of the crew on that Coast Guard cutter."

"We were fired upon first. My warriors acted in self-defense."

"You have two hundred eight hostages, all of them innocent civilians being held against their will."

"None have been harmed, and I'm about to release nine children, and a grandmother, into your custody. In return, my demands are modest, only that you deliver my message, along with your data. I believe if you do this, including sharing the evidence of our capabilities that we've given you, everyone—the people and the politicians—will make the right decision."

"You're really going to let me go?" Flynn said.

"Why not? Who better than you to deliver the message—to impress upon the FBI, the SFPD, and the governor, what we are capable of doing?"

"Okay. Let's say I believe you. That helicopter is a Eurocopter AS350. Now, I'm not an aviation expert, but those that are tell me it can transport five adults. And you've released nine children."

"Nine young children. Each weighs less than half a full-grown adult. And the old woman can't weight more than a hundred pounds. Still, that's your problem. Take all, or some. It's up to you."

"If I can't take them all, can I come back for the rest?"

"No. This is a demonstration of good faith. You'd be foolish to read in anything that's not there."

"Very well. Let's see the drones."

"Follow me."

Leonard and Vernon trailed by a couple steps.

"There'll be three guns on you," she said. "So please don't test me. The rules are simple. You can get as close as you want. Not that I'd recommend it. And you are not allowed to touch any of the drones. I suggest you keep a distance of at least twenty feet, unless you want to glow in the dark. As for me and my team, we won't approach closer than thirty feet. Once you've recorded the gamma spectrum from the drones, you are free to leave with the hostages."

CHAPTER 21

AFTER PASSING THROUGH THE CROWD of captives, Danya exited the holding room, into a portico that fronted the barracks building. The leading edge of the roof was supported by concrete pillars spaced about twelve feet apart.

The element of surprise she'd had only minutes ago had eroded, but hopefully had not evaporated. She knew they were aware that Charlie was dead, and they were onto her having a radio. By switching to an alternate channel, her ability to eavesdrop on their communications was nullified, so she turned off the device. She still carried it, though, clipped to her belt. Might have value later.

A gift shop was located at the southeast end of the portico. And directly to the front of the portico was an adobe concrete building with a mission-style gable on each end. It housed the restrooms for the arriving tourists as they disembarked from the ferry. She kept a low profile, shielding herself behind the base of the column closest to the souvenir store.

She was relieved to see Toby standing with a group of children, near the restrooms. But that relief was tempered by the presence of two armed men with their guns trained on the prisoners. A third guard was near the helicopter, gun pointed at the pilot from a judicious distance.

Danya watched as Sacheen conversed with an FBI man not far from the helicopter. Danya was too far to hear what was being said.

Then they turned and walked farther away from the idling aircraft, toward the restrooms. She didn't know what their destination was, or why Toby and the children were present. If they were going to release the children, why were they not already climbing onboard the helicopter? Maybe the helicopter was for a different purpose? But what?

With Sacheen and two of her men escorting the FBI agent away from the scene, that left just three armed guards. If Danya could eliminate them, the children could be flown away to safety. Despite the risk, the opportunity was enticing. She had a good position, with cover and a clear field of fire on the tangos. And they had no idea she was there.

Shouldering the MP5, she leaned around the base of the pillar and sighted on the guard nearest the pilot. Her attack would have to be swift. She had to protect both the children and the pilot so he could fly them to safety.

Taking in the scene one last time, she prioritized the targets.

Danya let out her breath and squeezed the trigger, sending a 115-grain full metal jacket bullet downrange. In a tenth of a second, the bullet struck the guard standing by the helicopter. A crimson cloud engulfed his head just before his legs gave way, and he collapsed in a heap.

Like a robot following a programmed routine, she moved her sight to the next priority.

The pilot's training clicked in, and he was in motion, taking advantage of the ensuing confusion. In three strides, he was at the open door of the Eurocopter, and extracted a handgun tucked away beside his seat. He had his pistol in a two-handed hold, and took aim at the gunmen escorting the top-ranking FBI agent.

Two seconds had passed since Danya's first shot.

Sacheen and the federal agent were in the lead, with Vernon and Leonard trailing. Vernon a little to the side. But they had not confirmed the location of the shooter, and had failed thus far to take defensive positions.

The pilot selected Vernon as his first target. Although he'd have preferred to take down Sacheen, the apparent leader, she was too close to Flynn for a safe shot. And placing a round into Leonard, who was in a direct line with the FBI agent, presented the risk of the bullet passing through and onward into the special agent in charge.

With a firm grip on the pistol, legs slightly apart, the pilot took aim and fired twice.

He was a good shot. He'd practiced often, and had even won a few pistol-shooting matches using the very same Smith & Wesson M&P 40 he was currently brandishing.

The two shots followed in quick succession, and Vernon tumbled forward as if he'd been hit from behind with a sack of concrete. Although the pilot had the drop on Sacheen and Leonard, he still didn't have a clear shot since Agent Flynn was in their midst.

"Drop the weapons," the pilot shouted, hoping the element of surprise would mask his tactical disadvantage.

Toby and the children were frozen in terror at the gunplay going on around them. Toby flinched with each gunshot, and the kids were crying.

Leonard swung around and opened up with the MP5, laying down an arc of bullets that cut through the middle of the pilot. As shock and electric fire from bullets ripping through his abdomen registered in his brain, he squeezed the trigger again, sending his final shot skyward. With blood pouring from his wounds, the CHP officer gazed toward the pale blue sky and took his final breath.

Danya had her sights on the closest guard near Toby and the children. She fired, striking him in the upper chest just a heartbeat before he fired toward her. Bullets hit the column above her head, but otherwise caused no harm.

He managed to pull the trigger again, sending a swarm of bullets into the gift shop, shattering two large windows. She squeezed the trigger, this time killing the guard with a head shot.

"Get down! Get down," Danya shouted, from behind the column.

But it was too late. The second guard, having witnessed his friend being shot dead, swung his weapon in toward the barracks building. Uncertain where is enemy lay, he pulled the trigger before he had any clear target. Bullets ripped through the cluster of hostages.

Three of the children were hit and bleeding. Margaret lay on her back, her eyes closed. Her face looked serene, like she was peacefully asleep. For the briefest of moments, Toby thought she may have been unconscious from her head striking the ground. But then she saw the blood-soaked blouse, and knew the spunky grandmother was dead.

Toby grabbed the two closest kids and yanked them down by their arms. The rest, screaming at the sight of blood and gore, some of which had splashed onto their clothing, were still frozen in place. Toby launched toward them, her arms outstretched, and tackled them to the pavement.

A fusillade of bullets tore through the thin wall of the gift shop as the gunman sprayed the area with automatic fire. When his magazine emptied, he ejected it and rammed home a fresh one. Then he jerked back on the bolt and started hosing the area again. Danya knew from his action that he was shooting in panic, hoping for a lucky hit. An obvious amateur.

The red-dot optical sight on her weapon offered no magnification, but it wasn't essential in close-quarter combat. She placed the dot on the gunman's chest and fired twice—a double tap. The rounds hit his body with effect, but the bullet that struck the base of his neck is what killed him.

Staying low, she dashed away from the gift shop, toward the opposite end of the colonnade. Leonard caught her movement, despite the shadows, and snapped off a short burst.

As she neared the end of the arcade, the building housing the restrooms blocked any further gunfire. And it was then that she saw the line of seven drones.

"My God..."

She aimed the MP5 at the nearest drone and fired three shots. The third round blasted away fragments of plastic rotors. Then she methodically moved the red-dot sight to the next drone, and the next.

Sacheen locked her fist onto Flynn's windbreaker, her pistol jammed into his side.

"You double-crossing bastard. What did you do?"

"Nothing. It wasn't me. You got a bigger problem, sister."

Perhaps he was right. *Someone* had killed Charlie, and had taken his weapon. It had to be one of the tourists who'd arrived at Alcatraz that morning, before she and Leonard had taken control of the island.

The gunfire continued, although now it was from the opposite side of the restrooms. She realized what that meant, and turned around in time to see a drone shot to pieces. Even before the debris of the shattered remote-controlled aircraft landed on the pavement, the next one in line was suffering a similar fate.

Leonard had closed in tight with her, his MP5 pressed into his shoulder, and the muzzle going wherever his head swiveled.

"Back to the children." She held Flynn close. "They're our shield." Then she raised the radio to her lips. "Kyle, I need everyone from the cell house to immediately converge on the ferry landing. We are under attack, and taking causalities. I think the shooter is in the barracks building, but I can't confirm the exact location. Probably the portico. Move it! Now!"

"But what about the prisoners?" Kyle said. "Who's gonna keep an eye on them to make sure they don't escape?"

"Forget about the hostages, you moron. We're on an island. Where are they going to go? Get your ass down here. Now!"

Pushing the FBI man in the lead, she and Leonard noticed the shattered windows of the gift store. They kept a watchful eye on the colonnade, expecting *him* to pop into view around one of the columns. It never entered her mind that she might be battling another woman.

With their backs toward the bay, the trio edged closer and closer to Toby and the kids, all lying together on the pavement.

"Get up," Sacheen said.

The gunfire had ceased, and she didn't need to check the drones to know they'd all been destroyed by the shooter.

"No," Toby replied.

"Get up, or I'll shoot you one at a time."

"No. If we stand, we're all in danger of being killed in the crossfire."

Despite Toby's defiance, Sacheen knew she had the advantage.

"Listen to me!" she shouted to the unknown assailant. "Whoever you are. Show yourself, or I start executing the children."

Her challenge was met with silence, other than the whisper of a light breeze. She lowered her pistol, aiming at a small girl not more than ten years old. Her curly red hair partially hid her tear-streaked freckled face. She was sobbing, as were all the children

"Lower your weapon," Sacheen whispered to Leonard. "Aim at the children."

"What? I'm not taking my gun off this piece-of-shit federal agent."

"Do it," she snarled.

Reluctantly, Leonard lowered his submachine gun so the muzzle hovered over the children.

She called out again. "I mean it. I'm not bluffing."

Danya had reversed course and stalked back to a position where she could see the hostages, Sacheen, and the gunman. Hiding in the deep shadows, and using a concrete column for cover, her eyes burned with intensity as she watched the events unfolding less than fifty yards away. Her perfect ambush had fallen apart and was seconds away from an unqualified disaster, a complete fubar.

Her mind flashed back to the school bus filled with children, in the desert—the mission she'd led, and that had been a near-total failure. Again, she was facing failure.

"Not this time," she whispered.

Danya slowed her breathing, as she'd been trained, and relaxed her body. Adjusting her position, she took careful aim on Sacheen—placing the red dot of the holographic sight onto her head.

But Sacheen and Leonard weren't fools. They'd pulled in close behind the FBI agent. The best Danya could do was to aim for the half of her head that was exposed. If she pulled the trigger, she would kill the leader. Of that, she was certain. But it was likely she'd either kill or maim the FBI man with the same shot.

The life of an innocent for the life of a killer? It penciled out when she considered the children's lives hanging in the balance. Trouble was, there were two armed antagonists. And she could only kill one at a time, leaving the other one a full second, perhaps longer, to unleash deadly revenge on the assembled youth.

"Last warning!" Sacheen yelled.

Danya still hesitated to act, torn between what her training had taught her, and what her intellect told her. Her heartbeat was pounding in her ears like a drum, and it was becoming more and more difficult to regulate her breathing and keep a steady aim.

She moved the sight to the gunman. She'd seen him before, with Sacheen, and assumed he was also a leader of the group. But he offered no better opportunity for a clear shot.

"You think I'm bluffing? So be it." Sacheen casually pulled the trigger.

Boom!

CHAPTER 22

DANYA JUMPED AT THE PISTOL SHOT and swiveled the gunsight. The children were screaming, trying to move even closer together, some crawling on top of others.

Not again.

As she scrutinized the small bodies, all appeared to be alive and moving. Relief washed over her, and at least for the moment, lifted her guilt.

Sacheen still had her Beretta aimed down at her captives. She had just drilled a bullet into the pavement, and she adjusted her aim.

"The next shot will be into the chest of the little redhead. I don't think she's even in middle school yet. So much life ahead for her. A future filled with possibilities. And it will all end violently if you don't show yourself. Just think about it. *You* will be responsible for this little girl's death."

Danya's mind was racing. If she surrendered, it was likely Sacheen would kill her. But if she didn't give herself up, she believed at least some of the children would be killed.

She counted nine youths, plus Toby, and tried to complete the calculus: *I have to prioritize the man. He has the greater firepower. Take him out with a double tap. Sacheen will likely fire two shots into the children, maybe even a third, before I drill a round through her face. In all likelihood, the FBI agent will be killed, and two, maybe three children. But six of the hostages will survive. How many will live if I surrender?*

Taking no comfort in the decision she'd arrived at, and believing she was likely making a pact with the devil, she saw Sacheen adjust the aim of her pistol. Time had run out, and Danya had to act.

With the red dot placed where the torso of the male assailant was positioned partially behind the federal agent, she started to apply pressure. It was too risky aiming for his head. Better to place two quick shots into the center of mass—his chest.

In Hebrew, she murmured a short prayer she'd learned as a child, then took up the slack on the trigger. She excelled at delivering death. But too often, innocent lives were lost to the vagaries of battle.

Through extensive training, Danya had become intimately familiar with many weapons, including the MP5. Her finger had grown sensitive to the minute changes in the feel of the trigger as pressure was applied. In her mind, events had slowed, and her senses were acute. She felt the cessation of trigger movement, and knew she was microseconds away from sending the bullet downrange into the terrorist.

The silence within the portico was shattered by gunfire, and simultaneously, rounds ripped into the pillar just above her head. She rolled forward, seeking shelter from the barrage coming from the far end of the colonnade. More bullets pelted the concrete, chipping out large pieces of the aged material.

With no time to aim, she fired a quick burst to drive the shooters to cover. Then she was on her feet, dashing for the gift shop. Leonard snapped up his MP5 and fired at the fleeing figure, but his shots were trailing her, and none connected.

Reaching the relative safety of the store, Danya dove through the open doorway and slid to a stop behind shelves pilled with books and T-shirts.

"It's a woman!" Leonard said.

"Yes, I can see that," Sacheen replied. "But *who* is she, and how is it that she seems have caused so much trouble?"

"You've got no idea who you're up against," Toby said. "She's kicking your ass. And she'll keep at it until you're all dead."

Sacheen glowered at Toby. In less than ten minutes, her plan had unraveled. She still had the special agent in charge, to be used for leverage, but the drones were out of commission. Her threat would not be taken seriously unless she could place at least one more drone in the air.

All along, the plan had been to carry through with dispensing radioactive dust over the abandoned Alameda Naval Air Station. She and Leonard were certain that a demonstration would be necessary to prove their capabilities and determination. And by sending back Flynn—the top FBI agent from the San Francisco field office, who would certify the existence of numerous drones—all political opposition to their demands would be crushed.

Although she'd nearly achieved that goal, what they had done—delivering one drone with a radioactive payload—would be viewed as a bluff in a high-stakes poker game.

Sacheen still had an iron grip of Flynn's collar.

She told Leonard, "It's time we adapt to the changing battlefield."

Two gunmen advanced along the portico toward the gift shop. They clung to the sides of the arcade, closing the distance to where they'd seen Danya flee. The men handled their weapons like they'd had some training, but they were not skilled with firing under pressure.

She recognized their deficiencies and allowed them to approach closer and closer. She'd worked into a hidden location behind a product display consisting of a base cabinet topped with shelves. Sweatshirts of different sizes and colors we folded and stacked on the shelves. And resting stationary between two piles of garments was the barrel of her MP5.

Sacheen's voice carried over the distance. "Find her and kill her."

The men approached with weapons pointed, sweeping back and forth, searching for a target. Their faces were dappled with beads of perspiration despite the cool temperature, nerves tight as piano wire, wary of an ambush. Given the option, they'd have preferred to let someone else flush out the woman, but it wasn't a choice they could make. If they ignored Sacheen's order, they would forfeit their pay—more money than either would make in ten years cleaning hotel rooms and bussing tables at the casino. And that was the best-case scenario. Neither wanted to contemplate the worst-case possibility.

Danya willed them in, closer and closer. With her gaze on the tangos, she remained still, not even blinking. Any movement was likely to draw their attention. She remained hidden like a black widow, waiting and watching as her prey stumbled into her trap.

When they were twenty yards away, she pressed the trigger twice, sending two bullets into one of the tangos, hitting the middle of his chest. The other gunman squeezed off a volley of gunfire into the shop. But his finger pressure on the trigger ended a second later when she placed a single bullet between his eyes.

The echo of gunfire soon faded. She eased from her cover and returned her red dot optical sight to Sacheen. But the federal agent was still in the way.

"Drop your weapons!" Danya shouted across the courtyard.

Sacheen reached out and pulled Toby in next to Flynn.

"No," she said. "Not gonna happen. We're gonna get on that helicopter. Just the four of us. And you can wave goodbye as we fly away."

"The pilot's dead. How do you think you're going to leave?"

"You're not the only one with surprises."

Unseen by Danya, another pair of assailants emerged from the sally port, having taken the pathway down from the cell house. They were jogging toward the shouting and gunshots, and as soon as they set foot in the courtyard, they saw Danya and opened fire.

Rounds splintered wood from a display shelf she was leaning against, but she was unscathed. She snapped off a trio of shots toward them, and then dove deeper into the store for cover.

That was all the break Sacheen and Leonard needed. They shoved Toby and Flynn into the idling Eurocopter. Toby craned her head toward the children, shouting to be heard above the whine of the engine, her voice filled with angst.

"All of you. Into the restrooms. Go! Now!"

The small concrete building beside the courtyard appeared to be built like a bunker. It would be a safer location for the children if the shooting continued.

A short skinny boy wearing a Boy Scout uniform had removed his neckerchief and wrapped it around the leg of another child to staunch the flow of blood. A second child held a bloody hand against the side of her head, while a third had her arm cradled in a bulky sweatshirt.

Most of the kids moved toward the door, but then hesitated. With longing in their eyes, they watched as the door to the helicopter was closed.

Toby pressed a hand against the window and mouthed, *Go*.

Leonard kept his gun aimed at his two prisoners while Sacheen took hold of the controls. Increasing the turbine power, she soon had the aircraft rising straight up for fifty feet, and then dipped the nose and skimmed over the water. Leaving Alcatraz Island behind, the helicopter accelerated as it traveled east, and then turned north. Sacheen flew low and followed the contours of the land.

"You'll never get away," Flynn said, trying to sound more convincing than he felt.

"Looks to me like we're doing just that," Leonard replied.

"They'll track you by radar from the airports in San Francisco and Oakland. They'll know exactly where you land this bird. Local law enforcement will be on you before the rotors stop spinning."

Sacheen didn't bother with the pointless dialog, preferring to concentrate on her flying.

"You think we haven't thought this through, Mister FBI man?" Leonard said. "That we don't know what we're doing? No one will track this aircraft, because it's flying too low."

The helicopter skirted over the Richmond-San Rafael Bridge. The cars passing beneath were no more than fifteen feet below the skids. Just ahead and to the right were dozens of large cylindrical tanks for storing oil and petroleum products.

Sacheen nudged the cyclic, and the Eurocopter hugged the shoreline, flying between a point of land and a large tanker unloading its black gold at the end of a pier. She angled over San Pablo Bay, and then turned east. She was flying recklessly fast, and it was making Leonard nervous. He had flown with Sacheen countless times before, including in rotary wing aircraft. But never like this, where the water was close and there were obstructions—land, bridges, buildings—too close.

If Leonard was nervous, Flynn and Toby were terrified.

"You're going to get us all killed!" Toby had one hand in a death grip on a handle mounted to the sliding door.

Sacheen pulled back and to the left on the cyclic, causing the aircraft to slew north as the Carquinez Bridge loomed ever larger through the front plexiglass dome of the helicopter. The massive twin steel bridges—one a cantilever design, and the other a suspension bridge—presented a tight interlocking network of steel cables and I-beams, an impenetrable barrier for any aircraft.

On the left side of the helicopter, Flynn found himself looking down into muddy waters flowing out of the Carquinez Strait. Then they were flying level again, across the narrow Mare Island Strait. To both sides, Flynn and Toby watched as industrial facilities and ship docks passed by at a blistering pace. After covering a little more than a mile, the channel flared.

Sacheen followed the delta, hopping up to gain just enough elevation to clear the occasional bridge. As she continued flying on a northerly route, the shipping channels gave way to meandering streams. They were entering the California wine country.

Finally, Sacheen cut inland across broad marshlands and flat fields covered with wild grass. Two intersecting runways lay ahead—Napa County Airport.

CHAPTER 23

DANYA ROLLED BEHIND THE CHECKOUT COUNTER in the gift shop as bullets split the air above her. She was aware of the increased pitch from the turbine engine melding with the deeper whump of rotor blades biting into the air. The helicopter was leaving, and she was helpless to stop it.

She turned to her side and edged her head around the corner of the counter, only to be rewarded with another barrage of gunfire. Some of the bullets gouged chunks of wood from the cabinetry above her face.

The two terrorists split, one continuing on a direct path through the colonnade, while the second detoured past the shot-up drones on the far side of the restrooms, angling to flank their target. The small gift shop offered little protection from bullets, and the space was so confining she would be at a disadvantage if the two gunmen trapped her inside.

Time to move to a better position.

She looked over her shoulder, to the far side of the store, where another window was positioned. She nudged the barrel of her MP5 above the counter surface, rising to a knee to get a decent view through the optical sight. The register and other clutter on the counter broke up her profile just enough that she was able to get off two shots before being spotted. They were fired in haste, and missed, but had the desired effect of forcing the gunman to duck behind the first pillar at the arcade entrance.

She dashed across the store, zig-zagging between the assorted displays, shelving units, and clothing racks. Her shoes crunched on fragments of broken glass scattered across the floor. She didn't slow as she neared the far wall and launched herself through the window, tucking her head and driving her shoulder through first. Her velocity cleared her body of the frame, avoiding the largest of the falling dagger-like shards.

Her shoulder and back took the brunt of the impact as she rolled to a stop. The sting of skin abrading from her face where her cheek kissed the rough pavement momentarily overrode the ache in her shoulder. She brought her weapon up, aiming toward the boat dock, but there was no one in sight.

Although her tactical position was not ideal, at least she had room to move. Behind her, the courtyard extended to the slope rising up to the parade ground—to the right was the vertical edge of the pavement and the cold water of the bay. She stole a glance around the corner of the store.

The rapid flicker of motion caught her eye. The gunman was repeatedly poking his head past the restrooms. A bad tactic. His brief views limited his brain to capturing only a small portion of the field of view. Even worse, his rapid movements, somewhat akin to a woodpecker's bobbing head, was like waving a flag, announcing his presence.

She slowly pulled back from the corner to avoid sticking the MP5 barrel forward of the wall. She didn't have to wait long before the terrorist darted from his hiding spot. He was on a direct line for the portico where it joined to the gift shop. She tracked him, holding the red dot sight on the leading edge of his body until he was less than thirty yards away.

The first shot sent the gunman tumbling forward. His submachine gun slipped from his grip as he piled up just short of the arcade. When he reached for a holstered pistol, she fired twice more, ending his resistance.

The other tango responded with a full-auto burst in a vain attempt to save his partner. The first several rounds embedded in the corner of the store before the recoil raised the muzzle of his gun, sending the remaining shots harmless into the air. Then the gunfire ceased.

She gambled that the magazine was empty, judging that it would take a couple seconds for him to reload. She stepped into the open to have a clear angle of fire, and caught the man fumbling to get a fresh magazine inserted into his weapon.

"Drop it," she shouted, her ears ringing from the gunfire.

With her gun aimed at the terrorist, she closed the gap one step at a time, her gaze glued to the target.

The gunman glared back at her. He finished inserting the magazine and moved his hand to the charging handle.

"Don't do it. You can't cycle the bolt and raise your weapon fast enough. You'll be dead before you pull the trigger."

As she issued the warning, his lips retracted, exposing his teeth, yellowed from years of tobacco. Above his pockmarked cheeks, his eyes were narrowed with an intensity she had seen in other men when she worked for Mossad. Men whose misplaced hatred allowed them to be manipulated and twisted into mindless instruments of death. A certain part of her felt sorrow for them. To live their lives as they did, devoid of joy and love, was merely an existence, not a worthy or rewarding life.

As her heartbeat pounded loud in her ears, and time seemed to slow such that seconds were like minutes, she wondered about the man before her. *What set him on this path of destruction? Is he a victim of another's evil influences, or is his hatred the product of generations of racial mistreatment?*

The thoughts passed with another heartbeat, and she watched his hand retract the charging handle. As the bolt sprang forward, it shoved a 9mm round into the chamber. The gun was loaded and ready to fire.

"Just put it down. You don't have to die here."

The barrel began to rise, and it appeared to Danya as if everything was playing out in extreme slow motion.

"Don't!" she shouted, even though he was only yards away.

The muzzle continued to rise. He was going to kill her.

Boom!

The shot startled Danya. Her subconscious reflexes responded to training that had become part of her instinctive behavior.

The gunman's MP5 lowered a little as his nervous system responded to the shock of the bullet driving through the side of his chest. He appeared unsteady and took a half-step backwards, then seemed to channel his energy on raising his weapon. She fired again. The round blew out his heart and exited through his spine.

His body collapsed into a lifeless pile of flesh.

Such a waste.

Precious minutes had been lost in the firefight with the two gunmen, and the Eurocopter had a significant head start on her. Not that she had a clear plan of how to pursue them. Or to where.

First priority, though, was to get help. She approached the dead man and kicked away his gun. Placed a finger beside his neck—no pulse, as she expected. His radio was still clipped to his belt, and she removed it and turned up the volume. Just static. She listened for several seconds, expecting someone to check-in now that the gun battle was over. If any of the radicals remained, someone would want to touch base, circle up and regroup.

Nothing but static. Although she was listening intently, her gaze still swept her surroundings, ever wary of new threats.

A door behind her opened onto the arcade. She spun around, the MP5 moving as one with her body, ready to take down the assailant.

As she applied pressure on the trigger, she was greeted with the image of Sue Kincaid.

Danya relaxed and lowered her gun. "Do you have any idea how close you came to being shot?"

Sue's eyes bulged, and her mouth gaped. "I'm…I'm sorry."

"Forget it." Then Danya was running toward the three injured children who were still in the courtyard.

The Boy Scout had done an admirable job trying to stop the arterial bleeding from the leg wound. But pressure alone wasn't sufficient—a tourniquet was needed. She told the skinny boy to run back to the gift shop and return with a pen or something they could use to make a tourniquet.

He dashed off, and Danya examined the two wounded girls. A bullet had passed through the ear of one of the girls—painful, but not life threatening—and the other had suffered a nasty bullet wound to her forearm. It looked like either the ulna or radius had been shattered. White bone fragments were embedded within the mangled flesh. The girl was also suffering shock, as was the boy with the leg wound.

The Boy Scout returned with Sue right behind him. Without any words being spoken, Danya inserted an ink pen through the neckerchief and turned it to twist the scarf tight and close off blood flow to the leg. Fortunately, the young boy was already unconscious and he didn't have to bear the pain.

Next, she turned her attention to the arm wound. The immediate concern was blood loss. She removed a bandana from a pocket and pressed it against the wound, causing the girl to scream in pain. Then she, too, passed out. Danya secured the makeshift dressing with the web belt the Boy Scout had been wearing.

Sue took in the carnage—the three injured children and the dead grandmother—and felt sick. Abruptly, she turned, took two steps, and emptied her stomach. After retching for a half-minute, she wiped her mouth and faced Danya.

"Is it safe? We heard gunfire, and then it stopped." She glanced down to the children. "Are they all gone? The terrorists, I mean?"

Danya rubbed her hands over her face. They felt moist. She exhaled and raised her gaze to meet Sue's.

"In a manner of speaking, they're dead."

"All of them?"

"A couple escaped in a helicopter. They have one of my friends as a hostage, and an FBI agent. Since you're standing here, I assume there aren't any more guards inside?"

Sue shook her head.

"What about the cell house?" Danya said.

"What?"

"The prison, up on top of the hill. I heard them talking on the radio, and they have hostages up there. I think they called down the guards, but I'm not certain."

"I don't know."

Motion caught Sue's attention. A few people were creeping through the sally port.

She pointed. "There—more of the hostages."

Danya turned. "I guess that answers my question."

"What do we do now?" Sue said.

"Help me cover the injured children. They're in shock, and we have to help them stay warm. And we need to cover these bodies. No one should have to see them."

She led Sue into the gift shop, and together they stripped armloads of sweatshirts from the racks and shelves. After making the children as comfortable as possible, they covered Margaret's body, and then the dead assailants littering the courtyard.

When the task was done, Sue's face was streaked with tears.

"How could anyone do that?" She wiped her cheeks. "They were only children," she whispered.

Danya placed a hand on the teacher's shoulder.

"There is no answer. I'm sorry. But I need you to be strong—for the children."

Sue sniffled and nodded. "Okay. Okay." She dabbed a finger to the corner of an eye. "Now what? Are the police coming?"

"Soon. Are your students inside?"

Sue nodded. "They're with another group of kids. I told them to stay together while I checked outside."

"Good thinking. Now I need you to take charge of these people. They're frightened. They need leadership, someone to assure them help is on the way, and that they are safe until it arrives."

"I can't do that. I'm just a teacher."

"Yes, you can do it. You teach elementary school, right? Pretend all these people are students at your school, and you're trying to get everyone to settle down before an assembly."

"But—"

Danya raised a hand. "Believe me—getting adults to follow you is a lot easier than getting a bunch of rambunctious boys and girls to listen."

The restroom door opened, and a young boy meekly stuck his head out.

Seeing Danya and Sue, he said, "Is it okay to come out now?"

Sue stood with her arms outstretched, and the boy ran to her, followed by four other youths. The stream of people coming through the sally port was also growing, and they were all approaching Danya and Sue.

"Look," Danya said. "Organize several search parties to find the backpacks, cell phones, and wallets that were confiscated. They have to be around here somewhere. Maybe inside the barracks or cell house, in an office or closet. That will keep people busy."

"What are you going to do?" Sue said.

"I'm going to make sure help is on the way. Then I have a friend to rescue."

CHAPTER 24

DURING THE GRISLY CHORE of covering the bodies, an idea came to Danya. There were only two ways off the island, and flying was not an option. That left only one possibility—watercraft. She'd noticed the Jet Capsule bobbing alongside the floating dock. With luck, the ignition key would still be in place. And assuming it had a radio, she could call for help. Eventually, some of the tourists would recover their phones, confiscated when the terrorists seized the island. But that would take time.

She dashed across the courtyard, still carrying the submachine gun she'd taken. The floating dock was two feet below the level of the ferry landing. She jumped down and was at the Jet Capsule in four strides. The screech of fiberglass rubbing against the dock assaulted her ears with the same effect as grating fingernails across a chalkboard.

She untied the bow and stern lines, then entered through the aft bulkhead hatch and hurried to the instrument cluster and wheel. A polished chrome key was inserted into the panel. She lowered her weapon to the deck and took the solitary seat centered in front of the large bubble-like canopy. She turned the key, and the engine rumbled to life with a throaty growl. The instruments were basic. Gauges indicated engine temperature, oil pressure, and fuel level. Plus, there was a T-handle at the side that she assumed was the throttle. She pushed it forward and the craft began to accelerate, rubbing the dock as it moved. She turned the wheel to port, and the Jet Capsule moved in the same direction.

Once clear of the dock, and with the island receding behind, she turned on the in-dash radio. She knew the marine VHF international distress frequency was 156.8 MHz, more commonly known as channel 16. The Coast Guard constantly monitored channel 16, as did the San Francisco Police.

She pointed the small launch southwest, aiming straight for the middle of the San Francisco Bay Bridge, and ran up the throttle to the stop. With the water jet propelling the boat at its maximum speed of thirty-five knots, she keyed the radio and spoke into the microphone.

"Pan-pan. Pan-pan. Pan-pan. Coast Guard Station San Francisco."

She released the mic button, ready to repeat the call if it wasn't immediately answered. But it was.

"This is Coast Guard Station San Francisco. Over."

She keyed the mic. "Coast Guard, the hostage situation on Alcatraz is over. Hostages are free. I repeat. Hostages are free."

"This is Coast Guard. Who the hell is on this frequency? This is for emergencies only."

"The threat is clear, Coast Guard. Send in some boats. You have a couple hundred people who really want to go home."

"This is Coast Guard. Who's on this frequency? Over."

"A concerned citizen."

"Are you calling from Alcatraz? Are you one of the hostages?"

She paused to organize her thoughts. She was still figuring out her plan, trying to anticipate and stay ahead of the unfolding events.

Yes, this could work to my favor. "Yes. I'm one of the prisoners. I'm on the island."

"Are you okay? Is anyone harmed?"

"I don't…"

Images flashed in her mind of the three children in the courtyard, their tender bodies ripped by gunfire. Then she recalled other images, scenes of small bodies, burned and torn by a tremendous explosion. The burned-out hulk of a school bus.

"Yes. Some school children were shot by the terrorists. Also, an elderly woman. I don't know about anyone else."

"Roger that. Can you provide the location of the terrorists? Are they still armed?"

She knew that as long as the authorities believed the island was well-defended, they wouldn't approach directly. Eventually, they'd come up with a plan to insert a military special ops team, probably by submersible, and certainly at night. But it could take hours, maybe even a couple days to get the men and equipment together, and approval for the strike. The children needed medical help immediately. Maybe others, too.

"Listen, Coast Guard. The threat has been neutralized. The tangos have been eliminated. Hostages are free. Medical help is urgently needed. Over."

"This is Coast Guard. Message received. What is your name, ma'am? Are you military?"

"Never mind who I am. Just send help."

She turned off the radio. She had more important things to do, and she needed to focus.

The Bay Bridge was rapidly receding behind her, and the Oakland Inner Harbor opened up before her. The channel was about five-hundred-feet wide—plenty of room for passing ferries, blue-water freighters, and private yachts. The Alameda Main Street Ferry Terminal was about a quarter-mile ahead on the right. She angled in close to shore and eased back a little on the throttle.

Earlier in the day, she had parked her truck alongside Main Street, next to a dog park, since the terminal parking lot was full when she and Toby had boarded the ferry for San Francisco. Now, she was grateful for that stroke of luck.

She pointed the launch directly to the bank. Maintaining full engine throttle, the fiberglass hull shot up onto the shallow, rocky bank before coming to rest. After turning off the engine, she looped the sling of the MP5 over her shoulder and departed through the stern hatch, traversing to the bow, and then hopped onto dry land. A hundred feet across a vacant lot was her pickup, and she covered that distance in record time. She didn't know if law enforcement had spotted the Jet Capsule leaving Alcatraz. But if they had, it would be easy to follow it.

The traffic flowing by on Main Street was light, and no one seemed to notice her weapon. She unlocked the extended-cab truck and stashed the submachine gun behind the rear seat next to her combat tomahawk and SIG Sauer P226 pistol. The extra MP5 magazines were secured in a pouch on the seatback.

She took a deep breath as she sat behind the wheel. She wasn't free and clear yet, and she needed to quickly melt away into the traffic. If a drone or manned aircraft was overhead surveilling her, she could still be cornered by police cars.

Fighting the temptation to floor the gas pedal and get away as fast as possible, she instead eased onto Main Street and merged in with the flow of traffic. The GPS app on her phone was set to guide her back to Hatfield, on the Oregon-California border. Although that wasn't her immediate destination, it would suffice to get her out of the Bay Area. Once on the interstate, she could think and refine her plan—which wasn't much of a plan at all.

She focused on being anonymous, blending in with the other drivers as she followed the GPS directions. From Main Street, she turned left onto Ralph M. Appezzato Memorial Parkway. She was frequently checking the rearview mirror, but so far, she'd not seen a single police car. The parkway was a major thoroughfare, with two lanes in each direction and few traffic lights, and she made good time. The GPS chimed, and a feminine voice instructed her to turn left onto Webster, a quarter-mile ahead.

Just as she made the turn, her pulse quickened. A police roadblock was set up ahead, and both lanes of traffic were being directed into a turnout normally designated for buses. If she did a U-turn, her red truck would certainly draw unwanted attention.

With no good alternative, she stayed the course and followed the cars in front of her. Hopefully, the traffic cops would be operating with little specific information about who they were looking for. Maybe the action didn't even have anything to do with finding her—the suspected driver of the launch. She decided to play it cool, willing her body to calm and her pulse to slow. She could talk her way out if the cops were suspicious.

The line of cars crept forward, merging to a single queue on the right. Ahead, she watched as a uniformed police officer questioned each driver, checking ID and vehicle registration. A second cop on the right side of the cars peered in through the windows. The process was only taking a minute or so for each vehicle.

In front of her was a top-of-the-line Mercedes sedan, and the officer waved it through. *Apparently, luxury cars don't fit the profile.*

The officer held up his hand, and she slowed to a stop before shifting the transmission into park. The policeman had short brown hair and a boyish face. She estimated he was in his late twenties, probably only a few years on the force. The shoulder patch on his uniform indicated he worked for the Alameda Police Department.

She lowered her window and smiled. "Hello."

The officer nodded once. "Driver's license and vehicle registration, please." He sounded uncertain, maybe even nervous.

She kept her left hand on the steering wheel while reaching to open the glove box. Through her peripheral vision, she noticed the other cop was peering in the passenger window, checking the contents of the glove box. His right hand was obscured from her view, and she imagined it was resting on his service weapon.

She handed over the registration and insurance documents.

"My ID is in my pack." She indicated the passenger seat.

Although it was forged with one of her many aliases, she was confident it would pass the scrutiny of a traffic cop.

"Is it okay if I get it out?" she said.

He nodded again, staring as she unzipped a front pouch and produced the license.

"You're from Oregon?" he said.

"Yes. I'm visiting a friend. Well, really, my niece."

A careless slipup. She hoped he didn't notice.

"Just a minute." He walked around the truck to his partner, and then radioed in her license and vehicle plates.

The two cops exchange words, but she wasn't able to overhear them.

Stay calm. Just relax.

After a long two minutes, the officer returned to her window.

"Does your niece live in Alameda?"

"No. She's a student at UC Berkeley. But I wanted to visit the old naval air station. I'm a big fan of the original *Myth Busters* TV show. You know, they filmed a lot of the episodes there."

A quick lie. But like all good deceits, it was built on elements of truth.

"What happened to your face? Did someone assault you?"

She touched her fingers to the scrape on her cheek. It stung.

"Oh, this. No. I slipped and fell down a short flight of stairs. Wrenched my shoulder at the same time." She grimaced and rubbed her hand over the injury.

Truth was, it did ache. When she got further up the highway, she planned to take three or four ibuprofens before the shoulder stiffened up too much. There was still a long way to drive before she could rest.

The officer nodded, but he looked skeptical.

"You sure a boyfriend, or maybe your husband, didn't hit you?"

"I'm not married. And no, I wasn't assaulted. Just clumsy." She flashed a quick smile.

He'd already noted she wasn't wearing a wedding band. Still, he narrowed his eyes, searching her countenance for an unspoken message, an indication she wasn't being completely forthcoming. But all he saw as an attractive smiling face.

"You headed back to Berkeley?" he said.

"Yes, tonight. But first, I'm meeting my sister and niece at Trader Vic's in Emeryville."

"Were you on the ferry today?"

"No. I don't understand. What's this about?"

"Security cameras showed a red pickup leaving the Alameda Ferry Terminal. The driver may be a person of interest."

She raised her eyebrows. "Oh, my. What did he do?"

It was a subtle ploy, but often a successful one. Usually, one thought of the male gender as the perpetrator of violent crimes, unless there was direct evidence indicating otherwise, such as an eyewitness or video. She was gambling that any eyewitness reports from the hostages on Alcatraz had not filtered down yet to patrol-cop level.

Still, for the police to be searching for vehicles that had recently left the ferry terminal meant that the launch must have been discovered, and someone was piecing together the clues, and quickly. She doubted that was the local police. More likely, the FBI. They would be in charge of the operation. All the more reason to put distance between herself and the Bay Area.

The cop ignored the question and returned her documents.

"Have a safe trip. The traffic can be pretty bad this time of day."

"Yeah, I don't know how people deal with it every day." She shifted into drive and eased forward, then merged back onto the parkway.

The young patrol cop said to his partner, "I thought that might be the one. But dispatch said everything checked. No warrants."

"Come on." His partner scoffed. "She looked more like a soccer mom than a terrorist."

CHAPTER 25

Napa, California
May 22

THE EUROCOPTER BLED OFF FORWARD SPEED and landed beside a taxiway. It was a large, paved area intended for parked aircraft. Presently, a half-dozen private airplanes were tethered there, ranging from single-engine aircraft to corporate jets.

As the rotors were winding down to a stop, a man exited the airport terminal, which housed flight operations and a small restaurant. He was obviously agitated, and strode the short distance from the terminal build to the parked helicopter, leaving him winded and with ruddy cheeks. His blonde hair was thin on top, which he tried to disguise with an obvious combover. Judging by his slacks and gray sport jacket over a white dress shirt and loose tie, he probably worked in management.

He labored at catching his breath while waiting for Sacheen to exit. She'd had the foresight to tuck her Beretta Model 92 pistol inside her waistband at the small of her back, where it was hidden by her shirt tails.

"Are you deaf?" the man shouted.

"What?" Sacheen replied.

"You ignored all radio communications, and didn't have clearance to land."

Sacheen opened her hands and shrugged. "Sorry. Who are you?"

"Bryce Washburn. I'm the manager. Do you have any idea how many regulations you violated?"

"I have eyes, and I could see that there were no aircraft in the area, or moving on the ground."

"That's bullshit. What kind of pilot are you?"

Leonard emerged from the far side of the helicopter, a step behind Toby and Agent Flynn. He was pushing his gun into Flynn's back, blocked from Washburn's view.

Sacheen was still feeling the adrenaline rush from the high-speed, nap-of-the-earth flight.

"A damn good one," she replied.

"I want your license. I'm going to report—"

"No, you're not, Mister Washburn. Are any of those planes for rent?" Sacheen pointed toward the parked fixed-wing airplanes.

"Excuse me? You really think I'd rent any of our aircraft to you after that stunt?"

"Hey, she asked a simple question," Leonard said, still standing behind Toby and Flynn. "Are any of those planes for rent?"

He faced Leonard for the first time. "Well..."

"Mister Washburn. Yes or no?"

"Yes, but—"

"Thank you," Leonard said.

Sacheen was already moving toward a sleek piston-engine aircraft, with a single propeller at the front of a long nose.

"Tell me about this one," Sacheen called back.

Washburn hurried to catch up. Leonard and the hostages followed some distance behind him.

"That's a Malibu Mirage," Washburn said.

"And?" Sacheen replied.

"It will carry five passengers. Range is about fifteen hundred miles, and top cruising speed is about two hundred fifty miles per hour."

"Good. That will work."

"Now wait a minute. Not that fast. I have to check your pilot's license and insurance. Where are you planning to go, and when will you return? I have to make sure the aircraft isn't already booked."

"Why is the hatch open?"

"It was detailed this morning. Our policy is to air-out the cabin for several hours. Some people don't like the smell of the cleaning supplies."

"Is it fully fueled?"

"Yes. But—"

"Good. I'll take it. Leonard, let's go."

Washburn hurried to block Sacheen from climbing the steps into the cabin. She sighed dramatically, reached behind her back and pulled her pistol. She placed the muzzled inches from Washburn's nose.

"I'm sorry, Mister Washburn. But you leave me with no choice."

"You can't steal this plane. It's worth almost a million dollars."

Leonard produced his MP5 while holding Flynn by the collar.

"Let's not argue," he said. "Okay?"

"Please just stand aside," Flynn told Washburn.

Exasperated and terrified, Washburn stood aside as the entourage boarded and shut the cabin door. Sacheen eased behind the controls and worked through the checklist, then started the engine. It turned over a couple times, before roaring to life.

Leonard took the rearward-facing passenger seat directly behind the co-pilot's station, and directed Toby and Flynn to sit opposite him. The ever-present submachine gun was nestled in his lap.

Washburn stood on the tarmac with his mouth agape as Sacheen taxied the high-performance plane onto the runway and accelerated into the pale blue sky.

Leonard and Sacheen both wore headsets with intercom to communicate over the roar of the engine.

"What's your plan?" he said.

The Malibu had climbed to three thousand feet, and was flying due west.

"We'll cross over Point Reyes and continue due west for fifty miles," she said. "We should be off radar by then. But to be certain

I'll descend to one hundred feet. After the descent, I'll turn off the transponder."

Leonard grinned. Having outwitted the female shooter on Alcatraz, followed by the adrenaline-charged helicopter flight to the Napa Airport, both he and Sacheen were feeling giddy.

"I like it," he said. "The officials will think we plunged into the ocean, and they will begin searching. But we won't be there, right?"

"No. I'll turn north and skim the waves for about three hundred miles, then turn east. We'll cross land north of Crescent City, and then fly low, under radar, paralleling the California-Oregon border until we're over Nevada. It's so desolate out there that the last few hundred miles to the reservation will be easy."

"You can put this plane down on that crappy 'ol dirt airstrip?"

"Leonard." She twisted her mouth into a pout. "I'm hurt that you have to ask. I learned to fly in the back country of Western Canada and Alaska. That *crappy 'ol dirt airstrip*, as you put it, is a piece of cake. I landed the de Havilland on that strip, didn't I?"

Leonard glanced over his shoulder at Sacheen.

"Yes, you did," he said. "But that plane is a workhorse. And this one is a racehorse. A bit more delicate, if you ask me."

"Piece of cake. Just sit back and enjoy the ride."

"You and me, baby. We are an awesome pair."

After a moment, Sacheen's thoughts returned to her passengers, raising a new concern.

"Well, we still got a problem to solve," she said. "What are we going to do with those two?"

Toby and Flynn were looking out the side windows, seemingly lost in thought. The drone of the powerful Lycoming engine rendered them deaf to the conversation between Leonard and Sacheen.

"You leave that to me," he rumbled.

"You think the woman can be useful?"

He looked at Toby. She seemed to be in a trance, her gaze fixed upon the water below.

"I do," he said. "It just takes time, and the right environment."

"Yeah, right. And the FBI man?"

"We'll see if he has any value once we're back on the reservation."

"And if not?"

"Like I said, you leave that to me."

CHAPTER 26

Alcatraz Island, San Francisco Bay
May 22

THE SUN WAS RESTING LOW on the western horizon when the first Coast Guard vessel circled Alcatraz, joined by an orbiting California Highway Patrol helicopter. Failing to draw any gunfire, the assistant special agent in charge—the number two man at the FBI San Francisco Field Office while Special Agent in Charge Flynn was unaccounted for—directed the *USCGC Tern* to deliver a security detail to sweep the island.

Scores of civilians—men, women, and children—occupied the courtyard. But their meanderings stayed clear of an imaginary perimeter around Margaret's body. One adult, holding his little girl, sat with the corpse. Both wept.

The three wounded children had been moved inside the barracks building, where they were watched over by anxious parents, hoping and praying for help to arrive soon. One of the hostages—a nurse—had helped provide first aid to check the bleeding. But between blood loss and shock, medical care was urgently needed if the children were to survive.

About two dozen Coast Guardsmen disembarked from the cutter. They all wore the standard dark-blue operational dress uniform, topped with a blue ball cap. All were brandishing MK18 Carbines, backed up by a SIG P229R pistol secured in a tactical holster strapped mid-thigh. Three took up strategic positions beside the restrooms, while others dispersed—some to the barracks building, others took the trail up to the cell house. A small group even fanned out and crested the rise from the courtyard to the parade ground, securing the rocket launcher that had attacked their sister ship, the *Pike*.

A half-dozen Guardsmen addressed the growing crowd of civilians.

"Everyone, please stay where you are."

The crowd was beginning to press toward the ship at the edge of the landing.

Two more Coast Guardsmen stepped off the vessel, carrying what looked to be several orange tarps. They went to the body of the old woman.

The base health services technician directed several Coasties to follow her to the barracks building. Although she didn't normally join missions, given the nature of this action and the casualties, the base commander made certain she was among the first to arrive. The wounded children were placed on stretchers and rushed to the cutter for immediate aid. Later, they would be transferred to civilian hospitals.

Sue Kincaid stepped up to the petty officer. Above the right breast pocket, his nametag read *York*.

She said, "Everyone is frightened, and just wants to go home."

"I understand, ma'am. The ferry will be dispatched to take everyone back to San Francisco as soon as we can establish a secure perimeter."

"What can I do to help?"

As the crowd was organizing and pushing toward the cutter, the engines revved and the *Tern* separated from the dock. It would take up position, circling the island from a safe distance.

A chorus of calls rose from the disgruntled civilians.

"Hey, you can't do that," someone nearby cried.

"What's your name, ma'am?" York said.

"Sue Kincaid. These are my students." She indicated a group of school children gathered at her side.

"Okay, Miss Kincaid. You can help by working through the crowd. Everyone needs to calm down before someone gets hurt. Tell everyone that the ferry is coming to take them home." Then York turned his attention to several other adults within earshot. "All of you people. Spread the word. The ferry is coming soon. Just stay here and remain calm. You'll be off the island soon."

York stood next to Margaret's covered body. Although he'd joined the Coast Guard to save lives, not take them, at this moment he wished nothing more than to shoot dead the villains responsible for this murder and the injured children.

York unrolled an orange fabric bundle that appeared to be a tarp, but was a human-remains body bag. He laid it out next to the body and began to lift the lifeless form, only to be stopped by a burly man with a shaved head and a long beard. Tattoos decorated his neck and arms, and his chest and shoulders were beefy. The man looked like he could bench two hundred pounds. He nudged the Coast Guardsman aside. Then he reverently cradled the body of his mother and laid her on the orange plastic. He leaned forward and kissed her forehead, then closed the zipper.

He raised his face to York. His eyes were red, and wet streaks disappeared into his beard.

"I made her life hell as a boy, always gettin' into trouble. But she never gave up on me. She was always there to get me back on track, steer me in the right direction. She never hurt no one."

Speechless, York looked the man in the eye and shared his pain.

"Make them sons-a-bitches pay. You hear me, mister? Make them pay for what they did to my mother."

York was overcome with grief, but he managed to find enough composure to give the man a sharp nod.

The Malibu Mirage was racing north over the Pacific Ocean, paralleling the California coast. Sacheen flew the aircraft level and low to stay below any coastal radar they might pass. She spoke to Leonard over the intercom, believing her two passengers would not be able to hear through the roar of the powerful engine.

"Lewis Blackhawk won't be pleased."

Sitting directly across from Toby and Special Agent in Charge Flynn, Leonard brought a hand to his mouth before replying so his lips couldn't be read.

"He knows plans don't always work out."

"Listen, everyone cares when it's their money. Excuses are just that. We won't get any more funding to back the Movement."

"Sure we will. We just have to ask politely."

"Get serious, Leonard. We need another plan."

"Remember, you're the brains."

Toby had mostly been watching the blue waves race by not far below. But once Leonard began talking, she paid attention, straining to make out his words through the constant drone of the engine. She didn't get everything, but enough to piece together the gist of the conversation.

"What's wrong?" She faced Leonard. "Worried you're going to be in trouble with whoever financed your operation?"

"You should be more concerned with your own safety, and less concerned about my business."

"If you ask me, I'd guess millions were invested in your little operation. Whoever put up that money probably expected positive results. I think you're going to have to tell your benefactor that you were outsmarted and outgunned by a woman. Don't imagine that'll go over so well, do you?"

Leonard produced a switchblade and flicked open the cutting edge. He leaned across the gap and pressed the blade against Toby's thigh.

"I can slice your femoral artery faster than you can blink those pretty eyelashes. Wanna see?"

Flynn said, "It's okay. Just take it easy. We're not going to cause any problems."

"Yeah? Well, you should coach her to keep her mouth shut." Leonard leaned back in his seat and folded the blade back into the handle.

Toby smiled, happy she'd been able to goad him. Then she turned her gaze back to the side window.

CHAPTER 27

NORTHERN CALIFORNIA
MAY 22

AS THE SUN DIPPED BELOW THE HORIZON, Danya turned on her headlights, still mindful to avoid any traffic violations which might attract unwanted attention from the CHP. An hour ago, she'd gassed up at Fairfield before pressing eastward along Interstate 80.

She was sipping cold coffee from a paper cup. On the seat was a half-eaten bag of chili corn chips and some beef jerky. Referring to the GPS app on her phone, she still had a long way to drive. At least on the California interstate, moving with the traffic, she would make good time. Still, it would be early morning when she arrived at her destination. Based on bits and pieces of information Toby had shared from her conversations with Sacheen and Leonard, Danya formulated a hunch as to where Sacheen had fled with her boyfriend and two hostages.

As darkness set in, boredom and fatigue would soon become a challenge, made all the worse by lights from oncoming cars. She settled the radio channel on a particularly obnoxious talk show. Whenever she found her eyelids getting heavy and her concentration waning, she'd grab a of stick of jerky and spend the next ten minutes grinding pieces between her teeth.

The traffic was steady up the western slope of the Sierra Nevada, and not until she'd passed through Reno did it begin to thin. As the highway snaked east into the Nevada desert, population centers were smaller and fewer. And the speed limit was faster. A little over three hours after leaving Reno, she was entering Elko.

With sunrise still hours away, she exited onto the Mountain City Highway, more officially known as State Route 225. Her destination was Owyhee, but first she needed some sleep. She'd been going hard for almost twenty-four hours, and the long drive, combined with monotony, made pressing onward reckless.

She pulled into a small rest area and parked as far away from the restroom as possible. Knowing that remote rest areas often attracted criminal behavior, she placed her SIG Sauer pistol between her back and the seat, and shut her eyes. Soon, she was fast asleep.

After turning east over the Pacific, Sacheen chose to cross over land just south of Brookings, Oregon. Once she cleared the coast range, skimming the rough terrain, she climbed to ten thousand feet. With the transponder still off, it was unlikely any air traffic control would pick her up. Even if they did, they wouldn't be able to identify the flight.

The Malibu Mirage streaked across the desert sky. She navigated by the in-dash GPS system, flying a direct route to Owyhee in northern Nevada. At a hundred miles out, she transmitted a message to one of their accomplices, a young woman with the passion of an activist. Even though it was the middle of the night, she had been instructed to have the VHF radio on. In fact, it was to be on at all times in case of emergency transmissions.

"This is Sacheen calling for Anna Banks. Over."

Only static.

"This is Sacheen Crow Dog calling for Anna Banks."

Nothing.

She waited a minute, closing the distance and giving Anna time to rise if she'd been asleep. Sacheen glanced at the time—12:41 a.m. *Yeah, she must be sleeping.*

Anna was in her mid-twenties. She was both African American

and Native American, and was decidedly attractive. The young woman had a keen mind, which she applied to her work as an IT consultant. Her job seldom required she leave her home. She usually worked from an office-converted bedroom, the only interface to her clients being conference calls and emails. Although it seemed she lived a lonely existence, it worked for her.

Sacheen capitalized on the young woman's self-doubt and insecurity. She found it easy to befriend Anna, initially sharing conversation over coffee or lunch, and later extending the show of friendship by inviting Anna to Leonard's house for dinner, and then streaming a movie. It was never a sexual relationship. But Sacheen and Leonard manipulated her emotions, nonetheless, and over the course of months, recruited her to support the movement.

"Sacheen calling Anna. Over."

She was about to key the mic again, when a groggy voice replied to her hailing.

"This is Anna. Receiving you clearly. What's going on? It's the middle of the frigging night."

"Anna, I'm flying in tonight, and I'm just under a hundred miles out. I'll be landing in a half-hour, and I need you to turn on the runway lights."

"You've got to be kidding me."

"I'm dead serious, Anna. You must turn on the lights. I can't see the runway and make the approach if the lights are out."

She thought she heard a stifled yawn over the speaker.

"Okay," Anna replied. "Give me five minutes to get dressed. Then another twenty minutes to the runway."

"Thank you, Anna. You're the best friend anyone could have."

"Yeah, sure. But you owe me."

The Mirage flew on in silence. Toby and Flynn appeared to be asleep. But not Leonard. He was alert and ready with the MP5 in case the FBI agent made any threatening moves.

Sacheen enjoyed the silence, the solitude. It freed her mind to think. The nuggets of a plan were coming together, but there were still details that she had to work through, contingencies to plan. Once on the ground, and with a few hours rest, she would finalize the strategy with Leonard.

Although many of the particulars were lacking, she knew with certainty that she would deliver a stunning blow to the US Government. One that would dwarf 9/11 in severity and long-term impact. She would rock America to its foundation, and never again would American Natives be an overlooked minority, a people without a contemporary voice. Retribution would be hers. And it would be sweet. Very sweet.

The aircraft banked and circled above the GPS coordinates for the runway. After the third circuit, tiny lights appeared in two parallel lines. She lined up the Mirage and began her approach. Without an instrument landing system, she had to judge the approach visually. The night sky was clear, but the starlight did little to illuminate the ground five thousand feet below her aircraft.

In line with the runway, and descending, she lined up with the parallel strips of illumination. That the lights were exactly in front of her was a good sign there was no crosswind. She checked her angle of descent—also good—and maintained her heading. Her tension was mounting, but it wasn't apparent to anyone in the cabin. She kept a firm grip on the yoke, pulled back on the throttle to reduce airspeed, nudged the flaps and made final adjustments to the direction of the plane. Then, with a hard bump, followed by a brief bounce—during which Toby let out a truncated scream—the Malibu Mirage was on the ground.

Sacheen slowed, and at the end of the runway turned the aircraft to taxi back to the hangar. A thin line of radiance appeared on the front of the hangar. It grew in thickness as the large door opened. Anna was standing by the side, her form flooded in the light. The de Havilland DHC-2 Beaver was still parked there, to the side, leaving just enough room for the second plane.

Once the Malibu was inside the large building, Anna lowered the main door. Sacheen allowed the Mirage engine to idle for a couple minutes to cool the engine. Then she killed the power.

"Be quiet," Leonard said to his captives.

Sacheen exited the pilot chair and worked past Leonard to open the cabin door. As she exited, the other three remained behind.

"Is everything all right?" Anna said, as Sacheen strode up to her.

She stopped a couple feet away and yawned.

"Yeah. Just tired. I'm ready for a good rest in a real bed."

"What happened? I heard the news. Was that our people who took over Alcatraz?"

Sacheen could only guess as to what had been broadcast. She'd not had an opportunity to tune into the major news channels.

"Everything's fine. Just some negative press, that's all."

"Negative press? Are you crazy? They say that armed terrorists took everyone hostage on Alcatraz, and fired upon a police boat and Coast Guard cutter."

"It's nothing to worry about, Anna. Go on home and back to bed. Thanks for getting up to turn on the lights for me."

The young woman's jaw hung open and she raised an eyebrow, but decided not to ask any more questions. In time, if she wanted to, Sacheen would share the whole story.

Anna exited the passage door beside the closed main hangar door. The cavernous space was well-lit. Steel trusses supported the peaked roof above a smooth concrete slab floor. White-painted walls fifteen-feet high—even higher at the tip of the gabled ends—help create a bright and cheerful atmosphere. Five drums of high-octane aviation fuel were arranged in a line, side-by-side, near the entrance. On a shelf above the fuel barrels were a dozen quarts of synthetic oil. A black four-foot-high metal tool chest on casters was nearby.

Another doorway connected to an adjoining office.

Sacheen called through the open hatch. "Take them to the office."

Toby and Flynn climbed down the stairs, followed closely by Leonard.

"To the right. Over there." Leonard motioned with his free hand without lowering the MP5 barrel.

Flynn pretended to comply. But as he placed one foot forward, he spun and reached out for the gun. Had the FBI man been decades younger, he might have succeeded. But he'd been behind a desk too long, and his reflexes were slow, his movements awkward. As soon as Flynn began to turn, Leonard swung the stock up in a sweep arc and clipped Flynn across the side of his head. He stumbled and fell to concrete, one hand over his ear and jaw. He was still conscious, but barely.

"Try that again, and I'll kill you," Leonard said.

Toby helped Flynn to his feet, and they continued the short walk.

Inside the office, Sacheen had them place their hands behind their backs. Then she wrapped heavy-duty tape around their wrists. All the while, Leonard remained vigilant with his submachine gun pointed at them. Next, she had them sit on the floor, and she repeated the process, binding their ankles together. As a final measure, she stripped their shoelaces and tied them around their hands and feet. Satisfied, she motioned to Leonard, and the two returned to the parked Mirage.

Believing they were far enough from the open office door that their conversation wouldn't be overheard, Leonard said, "We have to do something to strike a blow against the government."

"Yes, I know. And I have an idea."

"I'm listening."

"We still have some of the radioactive powder. I made sure we had a surplus of strontium-90 and cobalt-60 when I acquired it from my sources."

Leonard nodded. "Yes. It's stored within lead boxes in the workshop at my house. But the drones were all destroyed. We'd have to purchase more, and that will take time and money. Money we don't have."

"Don't worry. If my plan works, we'll have plenty of financial support."

"You think you can salvage this mess and satiate Blackhawk?"

"He invested his money to get results. It doesn't matter what the target is, so long as it's significant. One that will impact the populace psychologically, and have a huge financial cost to the government."

"Sure. That's why we selected the Bay Area. But that target is now off the list. It'll be well-protected, and we won't be able to get within striking distance. What city do you have in mind?"

She wore a wicked smile. "How about Sin City?"

Leonard grinned. "See, that's why I love you. You are so smart."

"Bullshit. You love me for my other attributes."

Still grinning, he reached around Sacheen and placed a hand on her derrière. He squeezed and drew her closer until their lips joined in a passionate kiss.

After a lingering moment, she pushed him away.

"Later, my love. Right now, we have work to do."

Leonard frowned, but his eyes were bright.

It was widely known by those working within the IPM that he and Sacheen were lovers. Not surprising—both were attractive and around the same age. Both had aggressive, take-charge personalities. But it was more than just a physical attraction. Leonard looked forward to the time when he and Sacheen could step away from the Movement and start a family. He believed that once they succeeded in their struggle against the federal government, money would flow to all Native Americans, relieving the crushing poverty and substance abuse on the reservations.

Once his people were given equal access to the nation's resources, the opportunities to earn an honest living, enough to support a family, would multiply many times.

But more than anything, he was weary of the struggle. It seemed that was all he lived for, day in and day out. He wanted to have a normal life—a steady job, a loving wife, and a family.

Soon. He released Sacheen. *Soon, we will begin our lives anew, together.*

CHAPTER 28

Duck Valley Reservation, Nevada
May 23

AFTER A COUPLE HOURS' TIME, during which she didn't stir once, Danya awoke refreshed and ready to drive. The eastern horizon was a shade of gray, signaling that sunrise was not long off. She had less than sixty miles to cover. Her destination was the small town of Owyhee on the Duck Valley Reservation. With a population of about one thousand residents, it was the largest community on the Paiute-Shoshone Reservation. She figured that someone there must know Leonard Cloud. Maybe Sacheen Crow Dog as well.

As small towns go, Owyhee wasn't much to write home about. Many of the commercial buildings were vacant and in need of repair. The town was also emblematic of reservation life, with a third of the population at or below the poverty level.

She cruised along the main street, which was a continuation of State Route 225. Her stomach rumbled. The chili corn chips and jerky she'd consumed the prior night had long since been exhausted. She passed a few other vehicles on the road, mostly old pickups in need of body work. The sun had risen, and she'd expected more traffic. *Maybe most people are late risers.*

After passing through what appeared to be the epicenter of Owyhee, and thinking the view of the town was about to be relegated to her rearview mirror, she spotted a diner. The sign fixed to the cement block building said, *Taste of Heaven Kountry Kitchen*. She didn't understand why the owners chose to spell country with a K. The parking lot was only half-full, and finding a spot where she could keep an eye on her truck wasn't a problem.

A bell rang as she pushed to door open.

From behind the counter, a waitress said, "Take a seat anywhere you like."

Danya scanned the medium-sized room. Vinyl-covered pedestal stools were fastened to the floor in a row along the counter, behind which was the kitchen. Several booths—the bench seats sporting the same red vinyl as the stools—wrapped around the front and side wall of the diner.

She selected a booth at a window overlooking the parking lot and the main street. Without saying a word, the waitress turned over a mug and filled it with steaming coffee. Then she stood there, pen and pad in hand, as if she had no other chore at that time. She was wearing a white shirt and apron, and her nametag said *Alice*.

"Thank you," Danya replied.

She had just opened the menu. The breakfast options were limited, but promised to be the best food in Owyhee. At least, that's what it said in bold italics across the top of the menu. *Probably true, given this is the only restaurant I've seen.*

Alice stood at the end of the booth, pen gripped tight, shifting her weight from side to side.

Danya made a quick decision. "I'll try the south-of-the-border omelet with bacon on the side."

Alice scratched something on her pad and retreated to the kitchen.

While Danya sipped her coffee, she gazed surreptitiously across the other faces and realized she was the only white face in the diner. Everyone else appeared to be either American Indian or Hispanic. Most of the patrons were middle-aged men. There were no children present, and only a few women. Flannel shirts and blue jeans with cowboy boots seemed to be the dress code, making her feel even more conspicuous wearing athletic sneakers and a sweatshirt.

The cafe was filled with the murmur of many voices, but no

one was boisterous. To the extent that she could make out what was being said, conversation seemed to be centered on ranching, leaving her with the distinct impression these people had important local issues to focus on, rather than international affairs or national politics.

Even though she stood out from the locals, no one paid her much attention.

Her meal arrived and lived up to the boast on the menu. She cleaned her plate, expecting it might be the last hot meal for the foreseeable future.

Which brought her back to the business at hand.

When Alice brought the check, Danya said, "Hey, you wouldn't happen to know where Leonard Cloud lives, would you? He was with a client on a project I worked a few years ago. Thought I might say hello since I'm passing through."

"Nope," the waitress replied, but her eyes said otherwise.

"Oh. I was really hoping I could buy him lunch or dinner. I used to be an advocate with the ACLU."

Alice looked squarely at her. "Figured you for a big-city lady. You're obviously not a rancher. I thought maybe a nurse or doctor. Never would have guessed you're a lawyer."

Danya gave a sheepish smile. "Well, I'm really not a lawyer. But I've done paralegal work for various nonprofits over the years. I met Leonard doing pro bono work on tribal rights."

"I don't know you'll find many clients in Owyhee. Not that the folks here couldn't use some legal help. Just that no one can afford to hire a lawyer."

"I'm just passing through on my way to Seattle."

Alice smiled. "If you're headed for Seattle, you're quite a ways off course."

"I'm taking the scenic route. Kinda between jobs right now, and decided to go on a road trip. I've seen a lot of the US, but never this part. Not much out here, but the land sure is beautiful."

"Owyhee is the biggest town between Elko to the south, and Mountain Home up north in Idaho. Make sure you have a full tank of gas when you leave."

“Thanks. But I think I’ll hang around. At least for a few days. Count on seeing me back here. The food is delicious. Besides, I didn’t see many dining options.”

“There’s a motel up the road, near the hospital. But they don’t always have rooms available.”

Danya waved off the suggestion. “I’m more inclined to camp over by Sheep Creek Reservoir. A guy at a gas station down in Elko said it’s a popular spot for boaters, and the bass fishing is pretty good. I checked it out on Google Maps. Looks like there are some good camping spots near the water.”

Alice nodded.

At the end of the small talk, and feeling like she’d broken the ice with Alice, Danya decided to try one more time.

“I’d really like to connect again with Leonard while I’m here. Any idea how I might find him?”

Alice narrowed her eyes. “If you worked with Leonard, how come you don’t know how to reach him?”

Danya had been hoping for this type of response. It meant Alice was lying previously when she said she didn’t know him.

Danya smiled. “It was the strict policy of the office I worked in—in Phoenix—that everything about a client be treated as confidential. I’d imagine that’s true at every law firm. There were some exceptions, naturally, but only if the client approved in advance and in writing. And when I resigned, of course those files stayed with the Phoenix office.”

“Like I already said, I don’t know anyone named Leonard Cloud.”

“That’s okay. It was worth a try. Hey, is there anyone you could direct me to who might be able to help me?”

“Nope.”

Alice was about to walk away from the table, but hesitated. She leaned a little closer and lowered her voice.

“You seem like a nice lady. But you know, this is a small town. Most people have lived here all their lives, and they don’t trust outsiders. Especially pale-skinned outsiders from big cities. It makes them nervous.”

Danya understood the message clearly. The sentiment was rooted in generations of bad history between indigenous peoples and the American government. And she also knew from talking with Toby that the prejudices against America Indians still ran deep. The signs were there before the world to see—except no one was looking. No one wanted to see.

She knew the same story played out daily in the Middle East, only the cast of characters was different. In her homeland, it was Jews versus Palestinians and Syrians. As a child and young adult, she'd been indoctrinated in the mandate that Israel was entitled to a security buffer around the homeland. That security buffer consisted of the lands seized by the victorious Israelis during the 1967 Six Day War—East Jerusalem, the Golan Heights, and the West Bank. Only as an adult did she come to appreciate the singularity of this pivotal decision on events that came to pass in the decades following Israel's stunning triumph. She sometimes wondered how history would be different if the conquered lands had been returned following the war, or if the war had never happened.

She thought about what little she knew of the history of relations between American Indians, white settlers, and the federal government. She admitted her knowledge was pretty close to zero before she'd shared a long car trip with Toby. Still, the parallels were inescapable.

"Thanks for the tip." Danya passed a twenty-dollar note to Alice. "Keep the change. Maybe I'll see you tonight."

She smiled inwardly as she sat behind the wheel and slowly backed the red pickup out of the parking spot. She deliberately took her time shifting from reverse into drive. When she looked at the rearview mirror, she was certain she saw Alice gazing at her through the large picture window.

CHAPTER 29

ZOOMING IN ON THE SATELLITE MAP IMAGE showed several promising camping spots surrounding Sheep Creek Reservoir. Almost too many. *What if Leonard can't find me*?

Danya dismissed the thought. After all, she was driving a red pickup, and she'd given Alice plenty of time to record the license plate. And it was an Oregon license plate—not all that common on the reservation.

The satellite image showed dirt roads wrapping around the lake. She decided to follow the road on the east side of the reservoir, hoping to find an isolated spot that was still easily visible to a passing driver.

She turned off Owyhee Road and was chased by a dust cloud as she paralleled the lake, frequently glancing out the driver's window at the blue water. It looked inviting, but she wasn't here for the recreation.

After she'd covered about a half-mile, the land poked out into the reservoir. The peninsula was too narrow for a boat launch, and seemed to be overlooked as a campground. Around the shore, for a distance of about twenty feet, where the ground was reliably moist from the lake water, shrub willows created a thick hedge row. She steered off the dirt road and blazed a path well onto the finger of land. Tactically, it was a great location, as an adversary could only approach from one direction, the path she'd taken. Unless they planned an amphibious assault—possible, but unlikely. Besides, a motorboat would be heard hundreds of yards away. Even a rowboat could be heard at considerable distance—the distinctive clank and squeak of wood in the oarlocks carrying across the water.

She parked her truck sideways across the neck of land. A quick escape was not part of her plan. Then she completed a quick inventory of her arsenal—one MP5 with spare magazines, one SIG Sauer pistol, one combat axe, and one Condor Kukri machete. With an approving nod, she was ready to take on whoever came for her.

Since it was still early morning, and assuming it would take some time for word to reach Leonard, she decided to catch up on much needed sleep. Rather than remaining behind the wheel, where her silhouette would be visible from a distance, she opted to stretch out in the shade of the truck, on the far side from the road. Trusting her sixth sense to rouse her if danger was approaching, she placed the submachine gun just inside the truck door, easily accessed on a moment's notice.

But she wouldn't rest if unarmed, and she strapped the SIG to her thigh, secure in a tactical holster. The Kukri was nestled within a full length wrap, high and at the center of her back. Preparations completed, she placed a rolled-up blanket on the ground as a pillow. She laid on the cool earth, wiggling her shoulder to push out a slight depression in the sandy soil. The tomahawk was at her fingertips. Laying on her side, she could view beneath the truck, toward the dirt road.

She closed her eyes and dozed off into a light sleep.

Some hours later, Danya woke with a start, the alarm having signaled in her subconscious mind. Something was amiss. Searching forward, completely still, she listened intently for clues. Soon she heard an approaching vehicle, but it wasn't in sight yet.

She rose to her knees and rammed the axe handle beneath her belt, at her back. Peering through the truck windows, she saw a dust cloud, and then an older pickup. Most of the body was pale blue, but the left front fender and hood were primer gray. The vehicle bounced along the bumpy road, bottoming out with a clang in the deeper depressions.

As it neared, the beater truck slowed, and then stopped. In contrast to the neglected appearance of the body, the engine purred whisper smooth. The window was rolled down, and the driver was facing her direction. She could hear him clearly.

"Think that's the right truck?"

Another man in the passenger seat craned his head, trying to see the red pickup from a different angle.

"Maybe," he said. "We should check it out to be sure."

She noticed that the passenger remained inside the cab while the driver exited. As he approached, Danya stepped from behind her vehicle and into view.

"Good morning," she said.

He stopped, returning her stare. Like the patrons in the diner where she'd eaten breakfast, he was also dressed in boots, with worn and faded blue jeans. His plaid shirt, cut in a classic western style, was untucked. Atop his head was a black cowboy hat. He seemed to notice her pistol, his gaze darting to the holster on her right thigh.

"We're not lookin' for no trouble," he said.

"Neither am I." Her arms hung at her side, leaving her fingertips to brush against the grip of her sidearm. "Sorry, but this spot is already taken. There's bound to be more campsites farther down the road. Looks like a big lake to me. Plenty of room to have some space. If you know what I mean."

The driver splayed his hands, palms up. "Sure thing, lady. We'll be on our way."

He turned back toward his rig and faced the other man, who was now standing beside hood. The driver nodded, almost imperceptibly.

Almost.

The driver dove to the ground as his partner raised a scoped rifle and snapped off a quick shot. But Danya's pistol had already cleared her holster, and she'd taken several steps to the side, simultaneously firing three shots in rapid succession. The bullets all impacted the front fender, no doubt stopped by the engine block. But the rounds forced the rifleman down.

She continued her movement sideways, both to confuse the shooter and to flank him. He popped up, leveled the rifle across the hood, and fired. The SIG Sauer barked in return, but he was already behind cover. Even though she'd only had a glimpse of the weapon, she recognized it as a bolt-action hunting rifle—deadly at a distance if cradled in trained hands, but a supremely lousy choice for close encounters.

The driver pushed off the ground and was halfway to his knees when she said, "Stay on the ground! Hands where I can see 'em."

He hesitated, holding his position.

"On the ground!"

This time, he complied and pressed the side of his face into the dirt.

She continued circling, pistol raised and tracking wherever her gaze pointed. It was almost certain the sporting rifle did not have a detachable magazine. Reloading would be slow. And she was counting. *That's two. Only one or two more shots before he has to reload.*

The gunman rose again to fire, sweeping the muzzle as he tried to get sighted on his target. She had moved considerably toward the rear of the old truck. When he fired, the bullet smashed through the windshield. From the resulting hole, a spiderweb of cracks and fissures spread across the safety glass.

She returned fire, both bullets passing through the fractured windshield. With her ears ringing from the gunfire, she couldn't hear if the rifle bolt had been cycled or not.

She edged around the rear of the vehicle. The gunman was on one knee, fumbling to stuff cartridges into the magazine.

"Stop! Drop the rifle."

He hesitated and locked his gaze with hers. It was a look she knew too well. If you fought long enough, eventually you'd run into someone who truly believed they could take you, even in an untenable situation. Certain people just wouldn't accept they'd been beaten. They believed that somehow, by shear malevolent will, they could emerge victorious.

That wasn't going to happen today. She fired, placing the round into the earth inches from his boot.

"Next one kills you. Understand? Now drop it."

He held fast to the rifle, sneering. Danya applied pressure to the trigger.

"That's enough, lady. Drop your gun."

Any thoughts she had of resisting evaporated with the sound of a hammer cocking at the back of her head. She raised her left hand and slowly lowered the pistol to the ground.

The driver strode in front of her. He was holding a short-barrel revolver, his shirt hung up on a black hip holster where the gun had no doubt been concealed. His partner rammed the rifle bolt home, chambering another round.

Staring into the muzzles of two guns, Danya had no choice. She raised her hands in surrender.

CHAPTER 30

THE INSIDE OF THE OLD BLUE TRUCK was vintage 1980s. The upholstery was held together with so much cloth tape that only the sides revealed the original blue vinyl. Both windows were rolled down, and they'd kicked out the windshield since the maze of cracks made it near to impossible to see through the glass.

Danya sat between the two men, hands on her lap and secured at the wrists with a couple wraps of gray duct tape. They bounced along secondary roads for about three quarters of an hour, she estimated, before stopping at a lone ranch house. It was the first building she'd seen since leaving the dirt road that encircled Sheep Creek Reservoir.

The house had a couple front-facing windows to the left of the entry door. Draperies covered the windows, blocking any view inside. Cement blocks, with paint peeling from years of neglect, formed the lower three feet of the exterior walls. The roof was clad in decades-old, weathered asphalt shingles curling along the exposed edges. A compacted gravel driveway led up to the double-car garage.

Inside, Leonard was standing before a beat-up old cast-iron wood stove. He was holding a photo of his mother and father, but his thoughts were elsewhere, imagining a newborn swaddled in a soft blanket and cradled in his arms. He longed for a family with Sacheen, but he had no time for such indulgences. He was at war.

Later, he told himself. When the fighting was over.

His mind was drawn back to the present by the sound of crunching gravel. The pickup parked beside two rusted sedans, both with flat tires and sun-faded paint.

"Let's get her inside," the driver said. "Leonard wants to talk to her."

"What about?" his partner said.

"Hell if I know. You know, sometimes you ask too many questions."

The driver got out and strode toward the house, while the other man held the door open so Danya could slide across the seat and exit. She dangled her feet out the opening, but the truck was too high, and her feet wouldn't reach the ground.

She rolled her eyes. "A little help…"

He reached forward, squeezing her bicep in a tight grip, and steadied her while she dropped a couple inches and planted her feet, legs slightly bent at the knees. As soon as he released his grip, she uppercut him in the chin with both fists. His head snapped back, and his teeth crunched together. Before he could stagger backwards and away, she thrust her knee into his groin. He doubled over, and she yanked her pistol from his lower back where he'd tucked it inside his belt, figuring to sell the gun later for a few hundred dollars.

She landed a brutal kick that whipped his head to the side, knocking him out. It all happened within the span of three heartbeats—too fast for the driver to realize the gravitas of the situation.

Gripping the SIG with both hands, she spun sideways and brought her sights to bear on the driver. The sound of the scuffle had drawn his attention, but too late.

"Drop the gun," she said.

"Okay, okay." He slowly removed the revolver from his holster.

The front door flew open, and a shotgun blast split the air. Danya dropped behind the front wheel. She needed to get her hands free.

She fired two shots around the front grill and then darted alongside the body of the truck, angling toward the back and a rusted corner of steel bumper. The ragged metal wasn't exactly sharp, but it didn't need to be. She rubbed the edge of the binding against the bottom of the bumper. As soon as a nick was formed in the tape, it rapidly spread, and she separated her wrists. Hands free, she made herself small behind the rear wheel.

The shotgun roared again, sending a cluster of buckshot through both rear fenders, narrowly missing her. Then the driver fired, sending a bullet through the body of the truck above her head. She lowered her face, and peering underneath the vehicle, spotted a pair of legs only a few yards away. It was the driver, and he was searching above the pickup, not under it.

She squeezed off a trio of shots. The rounds smashed through both legs below the knees. He fell forward, writhing in agony on the gravel. She fired once more into his prone body, the bullet entering his shoulder and tearing a massive wound cavity down through his chest, and eventually stopped at his pelvis. His death was quick, if not painless.

The shotgun fired again, but as before, the load of shot was placed too high. She had glimpsed a figure within the entryway, lost in shadows. She fired at the doorway, attempting to drive the shooter deeper into the house.

Hopping to her feet, she reached into the cargo bed to retrieve her tomahawk and the machete, which she returned to the sheath on her back. Ducking again, she dashed to the far side of the nearest derelict automobile. It was a Cadillac, and in its day was the epitome of American luxury. Now, with the peeling vinyl roof and oxidized bronze paint, it was a shadow of its former glory. Still, it was a massive chunk of steel, affording her precious moments to consider her options.

The metal hulks would give her reasonable cover to skirt around the garage and angle for an opening at the back of the house. *Will the gunman be expecting that, and be lying in wait? And where are they holding Toby?*

From her position, she still had an angle on the front windows, albeit an obtuse angle. Maybe she could set up a diversion of sorts.

She aimed over the trunk of the Cadillac and rapidly fired the remainder of her rounds into the windows, shattering the glass into thousands of fragments, and certainly drawing the attention of the gunman. She ran around the garage, even as the empty magazine fell to the dirt.

With a full mag inserted, and round chambered, she reached the back of the garage. The rear wall went straight from the back of the garage all the way to the end of the structure. She stuck her head and neck out further to take in the details, and saw two doors. One was nearby, and she reasoned it entered the garage. The farther one probably connected to a dining room or laundry room. Beyond the second door were a couple large picture windows.

She stalked forward, passing the garage door, weapon raised and ready to fire. Upon reaching the second door, she gently tested the latch. Locked.

Although her shoulder still ached from the tumble the previous day, she barely felt any discomfort—a welcomed side-effect of being jacked up on adrenalin. The pain would come later, and so would the meds.

She threw her shoulder into the door and crashed inside with barely any resistance. Her forward progress was arrested by a washing machine. Another closed door was to her left.

Knowing she'd announced her presence, Danya didn't waste any time. Standing to the side, she threw open the door and then waited for the count of two before passing through.

Of all the varied types of combat she'd trained for, house-to-house—or in this case, room-to-room within a house—was the most nerve-racking. The confrontation distance was short, and almost always the first to shoot was the victor. Although the walls looked solid, modern framing and sheetrock were no match for bullets.

A table with two chairs was pressed against the far wall, separated by a counter from the galley kitchen. She edged forward. Once in the kitchen, she noticed another door to the right. *Probably goes to the garage.*

The sound strategy was to clear the building, room by room. That meant she had to either clear the garage or secure the door so that if the shooter was in the garage, he couldn't sneak up behind her. She chose the latter and wedged a chair underneath the door handle.

The front door was ajar to her right, adding some natural light to the illumination from two table lamps ahead in the living room. She continued her cautious advance. A hallway extended toward the far end of the house, which now seemed much larger than it appeared from the exterior. The musty smell was pervasive, but she was happy to have the lime-green shag carpet underfoot to soften her steps.

Every two steps, she paused, straining her ears for any sound that might betray the position of her adversary.

There were two doors ahead in the hallway. *One must connect to the bedroom, and the other to the bathroom*. Both doors were closed.

She continued to edge forward, and then stopped four feet short of the first door. Shifting her grip on the pistol to one hand, she used the other to draw the Kukri from its sheath across her back. Then, her arm stretched to its full length, she rattled the doorknob with the tip of the machete.

A blast of shot blew a ragged hole in the center of the door, followed by a second load of buckshot blasting through the door and frame just above the latch.

Danya imagined the shooter sitting in a corner of the room opposite the door. She returned fire through the walls, hoping for a lucky hit. But her shots also hinted at her position.

The scatter gun roared again. This time, the shot was close enough to spray white gypsum powder from the drywall onto her clothing. She fired back, again and again, making minute adjustments to the bullet's trajectory, until the slide stopped open.

Her gun was empty, and she had no more reloads. She dropped to her belly and crawled along the rank carpet for the deep shadows at the end of the hallway farthest from the living room. There, she waited with the Kukri in hand, her legs coiled, ready to spring forward.

After a long minute, the door swung open and Leonard emerged with the shotgun cradled in his hands—a twelve-gauge riot gun.

She had wagered that his tactics would be crude and undisciplined. And she was right.

He turned to the stretch of hall leading to the living room, never considering the threat that was right next to him.

She sprang to her feet, thrusting forward with the curved blade. At the last second, Leonard swiveled and blocked the knife with the barrel of the shotgun. Although he held a far more powerful weapon, the hallway was too confining for him to effectively bring it to bear.

He was backpedaling rapidly. Danya kept pressing her attack—thrusting and slashing, forcing Leonard to parry her attacks rather than aim his weapon.

He'd made it to the open space of the living room. Emerging from the hall only feet from Leonard, she slashed downward. The hardened steel blade bit into the blued barrel, generating a cascade of orange sparks, before sliding forward and into Leonard's fingers. He cried in pain and released his grip. The muzzle of the riot gun drooped, and he drew his injured hand to his chest. With several fingers nearly severed, he was bleeding profusely.

Both warriors stood facing the other, sizing up the opponent, seeking vulnerabilities.

"You," Leonard said. "You attacked my men on Alcatraz. How did you know to find me here?"

"Wasn't hard to piece together. You talked a lot. Told Toby about your home here, your connection to family that lived here."

"The FBI ordered the murder of my aunt and her children at their home only a mile from here. They burned them alive."

"Your allegations are just that. The investigation—"

"The investigation was a joke. A coverup."

"It was a tragedy. And you let it consume you with anger and hatred, like a cancer. This sciamachy you've been waging against imagined conspirators has led you to ruins."

"I'll kill you!" he screamed, and raised the shotgun barrel, one-handed.

But not fast enough. Danya seized her advantage and whipped the machete downward. The Kukri, designed as a combat knife, performed as expected. The steel bit into his shoulder, just missing his collar bone. It slashed diagonally across his chest, leaving an eighteen-inch laceration down to the ribs.

In an agonized scream, he pulled the trigger, even though he knew the shot wouldn't connect. He staggered, but stayed on his feet. His eyes burned with hatred.

"Where is she?" Danya said.

Leonard laughed. "You're too late."

"Where is she? Or I'll cut you up piece by piece until you tell me."

A spasm of pain choked off his amusement, rendering his countenance a grimace.

"Not here," he said.

"Where?"

"Gone. Poof."

"Drop the gun."

"This?" He summoned the strength to raise the barrel and grasp the foregrip with his bloody hand. "No." He jerked back the foregrip to chamber a shell.

She swung the blade horizontally, which cut deep into his arm and knocked the gun aside. She pivoted. A glint of light flashed off the polished blade just before it sliced through his neck. With wide eyes, Leonard stared back at her. As the blood drained from his carotid arteries, he collapsed to the shag carpet and bled out in seconds.

CHAPTER 31

LOOKING DOWN ON LEONARD'S LIFELESS BODY, Danya picked up the shotgun. It had a shell in the chamber, but the tubular magazine was empty. Still, even one shot was better than nothing if she encountered other associates of Leonard's.

She proceeded to finish clearing the house, room by room. It didn't take long. After checking the bathroom and closet, she passed back through the front of the house and stopped in the kitchen. Before her was the door to the garage.

Leading with the twelve-gauge, she kicked the chair aside, freeing the door, and yanked it open. Although she'd hoped to find Toby confined there, the garage was empty, other than an assortment of tools and equipment.

A bank of overhead lights illuminated the windowless space as if it were open in broad daylight. Even better, the lights were arranged so the rays didn't cast any shadows. The walls were clad in galvanized corrugated sheet steel, the reflective surface adding to the brightness of the large room.

Curious, she rapped her knuckles against one of the rippled metal sheets. She expected it to flex where it spanned the space between studs. Surprisingly, the sheet felt rigid. She ran her fingernail over the edge and examined it. She discovered that multiple sheets were overlaid and fastened securely to the wall. *That's odd.*

Continuing her inspection, she was drawn to a metal overhead hood—like the type used in residential kitchens to draw smoke and hot air from above a cooking range—suspended in a rear corner of the garage. A blower was fixed to the ceiling above the hood to assist with drawing air up and discharging it outside, above the roof. Beneath the hood was a brick furnace, open at the top. Propane tanks fed gas to two torches inserted in opposite sides of the masonry cube. And suspended within the open top was a large ceramic crucible. By all appearances, it seemed Leonard was operating a small foundry. But absent were foundry sand and flasks for making molds.

What were you up to, Leonard?

In another corner, she discovered a pile of black plastic husks from old car batteries. And nearby were two metal buckets. One was empty, but the other was a quarter-full of lead wheel weights. Hanging on the wall behind the buckets were several rectangular metal frames. They'd been fabricated from steel bar stock, and welded at the four corners. Each frame was about twelve-by-six inches, and an inch deep.

A well-used workbench was against the wall, cobbled together from scraps of mismatched plywood and dimensioned lumber. Scattered across the surface of the bench was a collection of hand tools, most marred by rust. A cheap MIG welding machine sat underneath the bench. In contrast to the other tools, it appeared to be in new condition.

As she took it all in, understanding dawned on her. *This is where they prepared the cannisters of radioactive material.* She tapped the steel-clad wall again. *Of course. The steel sheets would attenuate the radiation, confining it more or less within the garage. And the old car batteries—they stripped the lead sheets out and melted them down with the wheel weights. Then cast sheets within the steel frames.*

She gazed upon the concrete floor, searching for proof of her theory. And there it was—two markings identifiable because of their slight discoloration, a gray-brown appearance. Easy to miss.

She grabbed one of the frames from the wall hanger and laid it down—a perfect fit to the rectangular mark, the concrete having been scorched when the molten lead was cast into each frame.

It all made sense. The furnace in the corner for melting the scrap lead, which was then cast into thick sheets. It was easy to imagine the lead shapes being screwed to a steel frame, no doubt assembled using the welding machine. The resulting lead box would be ideal for transporting the radioactive dust.

It would have been dangerous, of course, for whoever had to place the deadly cargo inside the home-built containers. Then it dawned on her. The suit she'd seen the day before on Alcatraz, near the drones. Looked like a chemical protection suit. No, more like a firefighter's flame-retardant suit, complete with full head cover and bottled air. *That must have been a lead suit to shield whoever placed the payload onto the drones.*

She turned a full circle, searching for a similar suit now. But there wasn't one.

A new fear began to grow, threatening to overtake her concern for Toby.

Is there more radioactive powder? If so, where is it now?

She hurried out of the garage, then circled back to the man she'd knock out and left beside the old pickup truck. With the shotgun slung over her shoulder, she knelt to the ground and grabbed him by the collar, then shook him.

"Wake up, you son of a bitch."

He murmured, then barely opened his eyes.

"Where is she?" Danya shouted in his face.

"Who?"

"Sacheen and her prisoners."

"I don't know."

"Liar. Where is she?"

"I'm telling you the truth. I don't know. Leonard sent me and Clyde out to the lake to search for your red truck. Someone at the diner—a waitress, I think—told him that's where you'd be. Sacheen and the other two were still here when me and Clyde left. That's all I know."

"The other two—you mean a man and a woman?"

He nodded. "The guy was older, middle-age. The woman was

Indian. Young, attractive. She had fire in her eyes."

"Where did Sacheen take them?"

"I'm telling you. I don't know."

Danya pushed him back to the gravel, then rose and placed a foot on his right forearm. His hand was laid open by his side. She removed the combat axe and hefted it to admire the steel blade.

"What's your name?"

He replied with a murderous glare.

She shifted weight onto her foot, pressing his arm into the gravel.

"Come on. It's an easy question. They'll get harder in a moment. So now's not the time to be stubborn. What's your name?"

"Clint," he said, through gritted teeth.

"Good. See, that was easy." She eyed the hardened steel weapon. "You know, I can remove two fingers with a single blow. Should I start now?"

"No, please."

"Where did Sacheen go?"

"I don't know. You gotta believe me."

"Does she have relatives here? Friends she might hang out with?"

"No. No one. Only Leonard. She's from the Tlingit tribe, up north."

Danya spun the tomahawk in her hand, then made several showy slashing motions in the air.

"So if she doesn't have friends or relatives here, where would she go? Why leave the house, when that's where Leonard was? There has to be a reason. A *good* reason."

"Maybe to get food or something. How should I know?"

Swoosh! The blade buried two-inches deep in the gravel, so close to Clint's fingertips that they rubbed the gleaming side of the axe blade.

"I won't miss next time."

"Please…"

"She wouldn't take the hostages to the store. You think I'm an idiot?"

Silence.

Danya raised the tomahawk and swung it down in a mighty arc.

"Okay!"

Smack! Gravel shot out as the blade buried deep. A trickle of red appeared at the end of his middle finger where the very tip was shaved off.

"You have any idea how close you came to losing two or three fingers there?"

"Damn, lady. I said okay." Clint caught his breath. "All right. Maybe she took them to the airstrip. That's the only place I can think of where she might go. That's all I know."

Keeping her foot on his forearm, Danya bent down until her face was less than two feet from his. She pressed the blade of the tomahawk against his open palm.

"What airstrip? The Owyhee Airport?"

"I don't—"

She pressed the razor-sharp edge into his palm, lacerating the flesh to produce a crimson line where blood oozed to the surface.

"No. No," he said. "There's a primitive dirt airstrip about a mile from here. That's where she and Leonard fly in and out of. They don't use the public airport."

"Now see? You could have saved yourself some trauma by being reasonable from the beginning."

With Clint laying on the ground, she slipped the axe beneath her belt and then reached over her shoulder. When her hand came back into sight, it held the Kukri machete. She placed the tip of the blade against Clint's belly.

"I don't like you much, Clint. And I'd just as soon run this blade through you, as not. So don't give me a reason, and we'll probably finish out the day with you in one piece. Mostly, anyway." She backed away two steps. "On your feet, and lace your fingers behind your head."

Clint did as ordered, the blood already beginning to coagulate at the tip of his finger. It seemed the fight in him had evaporated.

"Walk on over to your partner. Clyde. Is that his name?"

"Yeah." Clint shuffled to the dead body, never once loosening the grip between his hands, or making any threatening move, the tip of the Kukri tickling his back.

"Stop right there. On your knees."

After he dropped down, Danya picked up the revolver, only inches from Clyde's lifeless fingers. She pressed the cylinder release, allowing the richly blued six-shot cylinder to roll open. As suspected, it held five live rounds.

She let out a low whistle. "Colt Python, four-inch barrel. They called this finish royal blue. Did you know that? They don't make these anymore. Worth a lot of money if it's in good condition. You know, I didn't care much for Clyde, either. But I have to give him credit for having good taste in firearms." She examined the rub marks on the bluing along the side of the barrel. "This piece has been carried a lot in a holster. If I had to guess, I'd say this fine specimen was likely the sidearm of a law enforcement officer. I wonder how your partner came to own it?"

She looked at Clint, but he only returned a blank stare.

"No matter. I think I'll borrow it. Doubt that Clyde will mind one bit."

Clint returned a sneer. His hands were bloodied, and his head probably ached from the blow she had delivered. But he was a hell of a lot better off than his partner—or Leonard.

"What do you say we go for a drive. You can show me this dirt runway."

After securing Clint's hands behind his back with the roll of duct tape from the truck, Danya forced him into the passenger side of the cab. She cranked over the motor. After a couple tries, the ignition caught and the engine sputtered to life, belching out a cloud of blue smoke through the exhaust.

She hoped it would make it the short distance she expected to drive. No telling what damage the lead shot had delivered to the mechanicals of the old truck.

CHAPTER 32

CLINT WAS RIGHT. The primitive runway was only a little more than a mile from the house. Close enough that the gun shots, albeit faint, were certainly heard by anyone there.

Danya stopped a couple hundred yards from a simple steel building big enough to house two private planes. And none too soon as steam billowed from the radiator.

An SUV and another pickup truck were parked in front of the building and to the side, to allow ample room for the aircraft to taxi out without fear of a wingtip striking a vehicle. The hangar door was open. Inside was a white Malibu Mirage single-engine aircraft and a de Havilland Beaver. A man was working to fuel the Mirage, cranking a hand-operated pump to transfer aviation fuel from barrels into the fuel tank. Two others were shuttling small, heavy boxes and placing them within the open cabin door.

Two of the men glanced at the pickup when it stopped, recognizing it as Clyde's old truck. The driver's face wasn't familiar, but they saw Clint in the passenger seat and went back to their chores.

Danya opened the driver's door, which was on the far side of the vehicle from the hangar, and stepped out. She had the Colt Python tucked under her belt, and Leonard's shotgun pinched under her left arm. Then she grabbed the scoped Winchester rifle resting on the gun rack mounted against the rear window. The same bolt-action rifle Clint had used to try to kill her.

The Winchester was chambered in .30-06—a historic, but now obsolete, military cartridge. A popular and powerful round for hunting, it was lethal for all North American big game, including elk, moose, and bison. Even used for taking black bear, although experienced hunters preferred a larger caliber with greater one-shot stopping power for grizzly and brown bear.

She pulled the bolt back, confirming the magazine was loaded.

With the rifle slung over her shoulder, she waited until the men were focused on their activities, then she dashed for the side of the hangar.

Clint wasted no time and called out to the men in the hangar. But between the distance and whatever noise there was inside, they didn't hear his calls. He tried to squirm sideways in the seat so he could reach the door latch, but he just couldn't get the right angle. In frustration, he wormed out over the dash, where the windshield used to be, and rolled off the hood, onto the dirt. He gained his feet and ran for the open door.

Danya was already off to the side of the structure, where she couldn't be observed by anyone inside.

Clint's effort to raise the alarm actually worked to her benefit. Three men left the hangar, running out to meet their colleague. One of the men produced a knife and cut the tape, freeing Clint's hands. An effective distraction which allowed her to slip inside the hangar.

A quick survey revealed the space was empty. She glanced over her shoulder. The four men were a hundred yards away and huddled in conversation, reminding her of a consultation on the pitcher's mound during a baseball game.

She crossed in front of the aircraft to the office door. Opened it and nearly ran into Sacheen, who was about to exit. Both women were frozen in surprise.

Danya punched her in the face. Her head snapped back, and she fell to the floor, unconscious.

"Who are you?" Flynn said.

The side of his face was reddish purple where he'd been struck by Leonard.

"She's my friend," Toby replied.

Danya produced a short drop point knife, and with a flick of her wrist, cut through the shoelaces and tape, freeing Toby and then Flynn.

"Are you okay?" Danya said.

"Yes, I'm fine," Toby replied. "Boy, am I glad to see you."

"I'm Agent Flynn. Special agent in charge of the San Francisco office."

Danya nodded. "I saw you at the helicopter with Toby."

Flynn tipped his head and pinched his eyebrows.

"You were there?" he said. "On Alcatraz?"

"I was."

"But how—"

"Long story. And we don't have time now."

Toby reached out for her hand. "How do we get out of here?"

"There's a couple vehicles out front. The one I arrived in is shot up. It's leaking coolant, and not going anywhere. We'll have to use one of the other vehicles."

A commotion on the taxiway leading to the hangar was getting closer. Clint and the three other men, no doubt all briefed by now on Danya's presence, were converging on the open hangar. She drew the Python from her belt.

"I'll attract their attention and keep them occupied. SAC Flynn. You need to commandeer a car. Hopefully they left the keys in the ignition. If not, we're screwed." She handed Leonard's shotgun to Flynn. "It only has one shell, and it's chambered."

Flynn grasped the weapon and locked his gaze on Danya's. Somehow he sensed that she was a dangerous woman.

"I'll go with you," Toby said.

"No," Flynn replied. "Stay here, out of the way. Assuming I can get a vehicle running, when it's clear—and only then—run for the open door and pile in. Got it?"

Toby nodded.

Danya cocked the hammer and moved to the opening furthest from the parked vehicles. She dropped to a knee and took aim. At seventy-five yards, she fired the first round. The revolver bucked in her grip. Flynn ducked out the hangar doorway in a crouch and hurried to the nearest pickup.

She cocked the hammer and fired again. This time, one of the men pitched forward like a crash test dummy. He tumbled on the dirt and lay there motionless.

Clint shouted to his friends. "She's shooting Clyde's pistol and only has three shots left. We should rush her. She can't get all of us."

Danya would have preferred to wait until they were closer, and ambush the men. But she needed to keep them focused on her actions so Flynn could search the vehicles, and with a little luck, find the keys in one. The short four-inch barrel was a significant handicap at this extended distance, but she had no choice.

The roar from the revolver was wicked, as was the muzzle blast and recoil which pushed the gun high. The shot missed, kicking up dust about five yards behind Clint. She rolled her head, feeling tension relieved from her neck.

The three men spread apart, preparing to charge the hangar. She aimed, gently applying pressure to the trigger. The gun's mechanism was well-crafted, and she felt no creep at all until the trigger broke and released the hammer. *Boom!*

Clint missed a step and leaned to the side. He reached a hand down to his hip and grimaced in pain at the grazing wound, but continued forward.

Down to the last bullet, she lined up on the nearest man. He was a beefy man, broad across the chest, with muscular shoulders and arms the size of tree limbs.

"All the more to aim at," she whispered for no one to hear.

Boom! The round smacked high on his torso. Still, he kept moving forward, having only momentarily registered the bullet impact. The revolver was now empty, and useless. She tossed it to the side, then pulled her Kukri from its sheath.

Despite his wound, the barrel-chested man was the first to arrive at the hangar. With a bestial roar, he charged Danya. An ill-conceived charge, pointless. He stretched his arms out, apparently to wrap her in a bear hug. But she ducked and pivoted, slipping under his grasp. At the same time, she slashed the large-curved blade. It bit deep into the man's abdomen. His momentum carried him forward several more steps before he stopped, covering his belly with both hands. Blood flowed between his fingers as he attempted to keep his guts within his body. He dropped to his knees, then to his back. Shock and blood loss overwhelmed his adrenaline-fueled rage.

Danya never saw his arms fall limp to the side. She was already back in the battle. She had just recovered from her parry when Clint and the other man were on her, moving fast. Clint was unarmed, but the other man had a twelve-inch Bowie in his grip.

A glint of polished steel raced toward her. She blocked with her Kukri, catching the Bowie at the large brass guard, and halted the thrust only inches from her chest. With the crossed blades locked, she planted her foot in his groin. He stepped backwards, grunting. Now free, she retreated farther into the hangar, drawing in her pursuers. They couldn't be allowed to glimpse Flynn as he searched the parked vehicles.

But where was the FBI man? She had yet to see him since he'd left the hangar.

Clint and the other man separated some. Clint was still unarmed, and he moved well despite the superficial wound.

The knifeman lunged for her. With a clang of steel, she swatted the Bowie to the side, and with her free hand, grasped her tomahawk.

The two men hesitated and then exchanged a concerned glance. The knifeman charged again and swung his blade at her face. An easy move to block with the combat tomahawk. The knife blade struck and sparked as it slid along the forged steel handle, and then hooked into the axe head. He twisted inward, closing the gap between them, and swung a left hook.

She ducked, feeling a swoosh of air over her head. At the same time, she swung the Kukri low. It sliced deep into his calf muscle, halfway between knee and ankle. A gasp of agony escaped his lips. But the wound only seemed to enrage him, and he drew his arm back at the same time he shoved the tomahawk to the side.

A massive blow landed on the side of Danya's head. She staggered to the side, but didn't let go of her weapons. After stumbling several steps, she shook off the blow and regained her fighting stance.

The knifeman moved in, slower this time, and favoring his sliced leg. Clint was circling, but keeping well-beyond her reach. She was slowly retreating, turning her head side to side to keep an eye on both attackers. If she could retreat to a corner, the two assailants wouldn't be able to flank her or approach from behind.

She dared to steal a glance over her shoulder to make sure the path she was backpedaling was clear. An opening the knifeman had been looking for.

Through her peripheral vision, she saw the Bowie slicing toward her. She raised the axe to block his attack, and thrust the machete, but he clamped his hand onto her wrist, halting the forward movement of the curved blade. She slammed her forehead into the knifeman's nose. The snapping sound of crushed cartilage was joined by a stream of red blood flowing from his broken nose. The explosion of pain blasting through his face and head forced him to slacken his grip on her wrist.

Anticipating an attack from Clint, she yanked her arm free from the knifeman and side-stepped inside of Clint's swing, such that only his forearm connected with her head.

With instincts bred from battle, Danya knew she was a second away from being overwhelmed by the two men. She rotated her wrist, reversing the Kukri blade, and delivered a reverse slash across the knifeman's abdomen, cutting through muscle and into his stomach. As blood poured from the twelve-inch gash, he doubled over, but somehow stayed on his feet. He still grasped the big knife as he staggered backwards in a daze.

Clint seized the opportunity and latched onto the tomahawk and Danya's arm with both his hands. But his position could hardly have been any worse. She glared into his eyes and gripped the handle of the axe while keeping Clint focused on acquiring it.

She brought the Kukri forward, stabbing Clint. He never saw it coming. The steel lacerated deep into his side just below his rib cage. His eyes opened wide, and his jaw dropped. His hold on her arm relaxed. She thrust the blade deeper and then withdrew it in a vicious slash that nearly severed his torso. His mouth moved, but no sound escaped. And then he collapsed in a growing pool of blood, the two halves of his body held together by only his spine and some thin strips of muscle.

The knifeman had witnessed the final gruesome battle from twenty feet away.

"No. No!" he rasped, in agony.

She took a deep breath and faced the man. He still brandished his knife. The cut across his stomach was deep, but not fatal if the blood loss was staunched.

"Drop the weapon," she said.

"No. He was my friend!" His tone gathered ire when he said *friend*.

"Your buddies kidnapped my friends and attacked me, remember? Drop the knife." She placed the blade on the concrete floor, trying to de-escalate the showdown. "We don't have to do this. You need medical help."

"You butchered him."

"I was defending myself. Drop the knife."

He took a step forward. His stare bore into her, his brows pinched together. She saw him adjust his grip on the knife—his forearm muscles contracted as he squeezed the handle.

Then he let out a banshee scream. "Ahhhh!"

With his legs pumping, he accelerated like a Mack Truck, oblivious to the pain of his wounds. After two powerful strides, he was at full speed.

The tomahawk cartwheeled through the air, having just slid free of her fingertips. The light alternately reflected off the cutting edge and the polished spike at the opposite side of the head, creating a kaleidoscopic display.

The knifeman's rush and the velocity of the axe combined with grisly effect. The spike pierced through his sternum, the tip impaling his heart. The Bowie knife fell from his hand, and his limbs seemed to stiffen as they were rocked with spasms. His body contracted in sharp pain, his heart unable to rhythmically pump blood. His subconscious mind was in survival mode, firing impulses through his nervous system. The pain radiating from the center of his chest forced neighboring muscles in his abdomen and back, including his diaphragm, to constrict, choking off his ability to breathe.

He stood there for ten seconds, wavering on his feet, barely able to maintain balance, hanging in limbo between life and death. Then he fell forward, driving the point of the axe head out of his back.

CHAPTER 33

THE HANGAR WAS DEATHLY SILENT. The only sound was Danya taking deep breaths and exhaling. Sweat beaded on her forehead and traced rivulets down the side of her face. Her head throbbed from the blow she'd suffered.

Why? She didn't come here to kill these men. They'd attacked her. *What were they protecting? What was so important?*

Now, only one person had those answers.

Sacheen.

Her thoughts were interrupted by a familiar voice.

"Danya. Are you okay?"

Toby stood and pushed away the black tool chest she'd been hiding behind.

Danya belayed the grisly chore of extracting her combat tomahawk from the deceased knifeman. She approached Toby, and they shared an embrace. Toby teared up.

"Are we safe now?"

"For now. We still have to get out of here."

"I was so scared. They said they wanted me to help them. To support their cause. Sacheen and Leonard. They're the leaders."

"Sacheen…I better check on our Sleeping Beauty."

An acquainted voice came from behind Danya. Toby's eyes were wide in fear.

"Thank you for your concern," Sacheen said. "I'm doing just fine."

Danya rotated and found herself staring across the open room at her nemesis. With 9mm pistol in hand, Sacheen strode toward the two women. When she'd decreased the separation by half, she stopped.

"Where is the man? The FBI agent?"

Danya made a show of looking around the space.

"I don't know. Seems he left. Probably far away by now. I was a little...*preoccupied* with your guards to pay any attention."

"You are a very dangerous woman. First, you attacked and killed many of my warriors on Alcatraz. And now this." Sacheen motioned with one hand, the other maintaining a steady aim with the pistol.

"I do my best," Danya replied.

"I never imagined a woman could have skills such as you have demonstrated. A pity. You would have been a great asset to our cause."

"You're delusional. I'd never sign on with a bunch of terrorists."

"So you say." Sacheen took one step forward and stared into Danya's eyes. "Who taught you to fight? The military? Maybe the CIA?"

With no weapons in hand, Danya was defenseless. The bolt-action rifle strapped across her back might as well have been ten feet away. She could never unlimber it, aim, and fire before being shot dead by Sacheen. But she still had time.

Danya smiled. "Yes."

"Ah. The CIA, I think."

"I'm not an American citizen."

Sacheen shrugged. "It makes no difference. Maybe you worked for MI6, or Mossad. Or some other foreign agency. You were a tool. A blunt implement of the government to carry out state-sponsored terrorism. Am I right?"

Danya's brow rimpled. The accusation hit too close to home.

"So I am right," Sacheen said.

"What I did is none of your concern."

"Oh, my. We are just a bit defensive, aren't we. I must have touched a nerve."

She had. Danya's service with Mossad was a part of her history that pained her. She began every day with the goal of doing more good than harm, of trying to atone for past sins. In her mind, she had been a tool of her government—sometimes completing missions involving heinous violence. Supposedly necessary to protect innocent civilians. But not always. She was expected to act without question. To follow orders without subjecting those orders to moral scrutiny. As she recounted every mission, she could not say her track record was perfect. That those less guilty, or even totally innocent, were not dispatched by her hands.

"These men didn't have to die," she said. "What were they protecting?"

Sacheen tilted her head, and her mouth turned downward in a frown.

"The mission we set out to complete yesterday was interrupted. By you. Had you not interfered, we would have succeeded. All the hostages, everyone, would have been released by now. Unharmed. No one had to die. There, or here."

"You planned to sprinkle radioactive pixie dust all over the Bay Area. Thousands would have died slow, lingering deaths."

"No. My plan was to *threaten* to do just that. We delivered a drone with a sample of the powder. And I brought the FBI's top man to Alcatraz to witness our fleet of drones. Within hours, they would have conceded to our demands. But *you* interfered. *You* started shooting my warriors."

"Don't pretend to be innocent. Your men opened fire on the police boat and the Coast Guard cutter. I saw it. You drew first blood, not them."

Sacheen pulled her shoulders back and worked her jaw. She returned Danya's glare for several seconds.

"It was necessary," she said. "They would have tried to place soldiers on the island."

"Save it." Danya held up a hand, palm out. "The ends don't justify the means. They never do."

For a moment, the fire appeared to leave Sacheen's eyes, and they looked like black, innocuous marbles. But after she blinked, the blaze had regained strength.

What is she hiding?

Sacheen said, "Spoken like someone who knows from experience."

"I won't deny it."

Sacheen twisted her wrist and checked the time.

Danya said, "Anxious about something? Someone to meet, maybe?"

"Leonard will be here soon. Then we will complete our mission. You've only caused some minor delays, that's all."

"I don't think so. In fact, I'm certain of the contrary."

Sacheen's eyes conveyed a mix of curiosity and concern.

"You've only caused us to change our target. But the plan remains. We will achieve our goals and see our rights as Native Americans restored."

"Leonard won't meet you here, or anywhere. He's dead."

This news hit Sacheen like a sucker punch. Her legs buckled, and her grip on the weapon slackened. One hand dropped to her belly, where she seemed to intuit something unseen by Danya and Toby.

A mother's sense? Is that her secret?

Sacheen's eyes glistened as tears welled up. Danya saw her opening and took a step forward.

"Stop." Sacheen had regained her composure, and with it a firm hold on the pistol.

Her brows were pinched, and etched across her face Danya saw both sadness and remorse—feelings she knew all too well.

"You're pregnant, aren't you," she said.

Sacheen drew in a sharp breath. "Yes. We were going to have a family once this was over."

"I'm sorry."

There was more she could have said—how the path she and Leonard had chosen was incompatible with raising a family. But there was no point in lecturing the obvious. Oddly, she felt sorrow for Sacheen, knowing she'd sacrificed her future to realize a lofty goal, a greater good. The tragedy was the abominable method employed by Leonard and her. Their tactics had doomed not only their future together, but also would forever overshadow the objective of equal rights for indigenous people, as well as reparations for past treaties that were broken and lands that were illegally taken.

Instead, she offered the only hope Sacheen had left.

"Put the gun down. You can still walk away."

"Walk away?" Anger had replaced remorse. "To what? To live in poverty? To raise my child in a society that will fail to recognize him or her on an equal basis? A society that will fail to provide access to a decent education? Is that what you think I should do?"

"I know something of what you feel. What you are fighting for. Millenia ago, my tribal ancestors were embroiled in warfare with neighboring tribes. That history has locked us into constant internecine conflict. I know the face of desperation, of hopelessness."

Sacheen nodded as if in response to an unspoken thought.

"You are Hebrew?"

"I am."

"Then you know the bitter heartache of persecution, as my people do."

"What I know is that violence won't solve the problem."

"Really?" Sacheen said. "The Israeli government has never shied from use of violence to enforce its will, or to retain an iron grip on conquered lands."

There was nothing more Danya could say. She recognized the truth in the accusation. But even more, she knew very well the sense of hopelessness that had driven Sacheen and Leonard to do the unthinkable. As a Mossad agent, she'd witnessed it firsthand. She'd fought against dozens of young Palestinians turned into martyrs by injustice, poverty, and despair.

Sacheen pointed at Danya. "The rifle. Slide it off your shoulder. One hand only. The other one in the air. Lay it gently on the floor and slide it over to me. Use your foot."

Danya did as she was told. Then Sacheen ordered both women to lay on the concrete, face down and arms behind their backs. With little choice, Danya and Toby complied.

Both the Kukri machete and the combat axe were out of reach and of no concern. Sacheen grabbed the rifle, one-handed, and placed it on the workbench, keeping the pistol aimed at her prostrate prisoners. On the bench, she laid her hand on a spool of wire and a pair of cutters.

After returning to Danya, she pressed her knee into Danya's back and then wrapped wire around her wrists before cutting and twisting it off. It was snug, but not so tight as to cut the flesh. She bound Toby's hands in a similar fashion.

"Now stay there." She returned the cutters and wire to the bench.

"Or what?" Danya said. "You're going to kill us anyway."

Sacheen stood over the two women and aimed her Beretta. Toby's eyes were wide. Danya knew what was coming. Knew that any second now, there would be a deafening gunshot that she would never hear, and the world would forever go black.

After several uneventful seconds, she heard Sacheen, her voice measured.

"Your battle is finished." Another pause. "Let it go."

"Easy enough for you to say," Danya replied. "What's the plan now? Pick another metropolis and kill thousands of innocent civilians?"

"I didn't start this war."

"Too much blood has been shed already. There are other ways. Think about your child."

"My people—my sisters and brothers—have always been called upon to sacrifice. Why should I be any different?"

"Whatever historical justification you conjure up, it won't change anything. You'll still be judged a terrorist, a mass murderer."

Sacheen looked back over her shoulder. "In an hour, I'll make a call. The tribal police will cruise by and free you."

After kicking aside the wheel chocks, she planted her feet and pushed the Malibu Mirage out of the open hangar door. Once free of the steel building, she climbed into the cabin, took her seat behind the controls, and started the engine.

CHAPTER 34

THE HANGAR WAS LOCATED AT THE MIDPOINT of the runway, and the Mirage would have to taxi to one end before starting its takeoff roll. Once the plane was out of the hangar and rolling toward the end of the runway, Agent Flynn gunned the ancient Ford Explorer he'd confiscated, and skidded to a stop in front of the open doorway.

Danya was already on her feet, her back against the workbench, and her fingers fumbling across the surface for the wire cutters. Flynn jumped out and darted to the workbench. He grabbed the cutters and snipped the wire binding her hands.

"Go." She snatched the tool from his hands. "Stop that aircraft before it takes off."

"Why? She can't hide for long. Agents will find her and pick her up within a few days. A week, at the most."

Danya rolled her eyes at the boast. She'd managed to elude the FBI and Mossad for nearly two years. And even now, the SAC had no idea he was face to face with a wanted fugitive.

"She's planning an attack on another city. You have to stop her. Now, go!"

Flynn dashed back to the vehicle and stomped the accelerator, sending gravel flying as he raced toward the Mirage while it taxied toward the end of the dirt strip.

She freed Toby of her bindings and helped her up.

"Las Vegas," Toby said. "She's going to attack Las Vegas."

"How do you know?"

"I overheard them talking when they left us in the office. Their voices were faint, and I didn't get all the details. I don't think Flynn got it. Leonard hit him pretty hard."

"But they lost all their drones on Alcatraz. I shot them up myself, and there aren't any more here."

"No, not drones. She's going to fly there. That's why they were filling up the airplane with aviation fuel."

"But what can she hope to do? Fly the plane into a casino? How is that going to help their cause? They left the radioactive material on the drones I destroyed. They didn't have time to remove the capsules before they flew off with you and Flynn in the helicopter."

Toby stared back with a blank expression.

"Unless…" Danya thought of what she'd found in the garage at Leonard's house. "They were making small lead sheets."

Realization dawned on Toby. "And we saw two of the men loading small, heavy boxes onto the plane."

Danya's eyes opened wide. "She's going to irradiate The Strip."

"But how? Someone has to fly the plane."

"I imagine the original plan was just that. Sacheen would fly the aircraft, while Leonard would dispense the powder. But one person can still do it. Sacheen can fly low and slow, and then turn on the autopilot. That will free her to open the hatch and drop the radioactive dust over the city."

"We have to stop her," Toby said, but Danya was already sprinting for the hangar entrance.

As she watched the Explorer race down the dirt strip, a new plan was coalescing in her mind.

Flynn was closing on the Malibu Mirage, the SUV nearly obscured behind a dust cloud. The prop wash was also kicking up a dense fog of sand and dust. As Flynn got closer, he found it hard to see exactly where he was speeding. He was closing quickly on the slower aircraft. The tail was even with his windshield. When he judged that he was just about to ram into the rear of the plane, he cut the wheel to the right, trying clip the rudder. But his aim was off, and the edge of the roof just grazed the tail, not sufficient to cause any problem with flying the airplane.

Now, Flynn found himself racing toward the edge of the runway. Beyond, lay sage brush, rocks, and mounds of soft sand. Not the terrain he should be entering at a high rate of speed. He slammed on the brakes and cut the wheel to the left, slewing the heavy Ford into a sideways skid.

Meanwhile, Sacheen reached the end of the runway. Knowing that she was being pursued, she spun the aircraft, pointing the nose down the strip. She pushed the engine to maximum power, and the Lycoming engine responded with a throaty roar as the Mirage accelerated. A little over a thousand feet is what she needed to become airborne, and the sporty airplane would cover that quickly.

The SUV halted as the rear wheel skidded sideways into a mound of sage. Flynn stomped on the gas, but only succeeded in launching a rooster tail of dirt and gravel as the rear wheel burrowed into the soft earth. He let up on the accelerator and allowed the engine to drop to idle before shifting into four-wheel drive. After easing the vehicle forward until he was on solid ground again, he jammed the pedal to the floor and took off in pursuit once more.

Sacheen had a good head start. At first, the SUV was gaining. But then the Mirage started to pull away. Flynn's hope sank with the realization that he would not catch her before the plane lifted off.

Danya didn't wait to see how the high-speed chase was going to end.

"Stay here," she told Toby, and then hurried back to the workbench and grabbed the rifle.

Even as she dashed out of the hangar, she opened the bolt just enough to ensure a round was chambered. Then she locked the bolt down and proceeded to the center of the runway.

The Explorer was off to the side, apparently stuck. And then she saw that Flynn had the presence of mind to feather the gas pedal and maneuver the vehicle back onto firm soil rather than continue to sink the rear wheel.

As the SUV renewed its pursuit of the Mirage, now under full throttle and accelerating rapidly, she knew it was too late for Flynn to intercept the plane.

She dropped to a prone firing position, her side and shoulder aching in protest, and pulled the sporting rifle in tight against her shoulder. The airplane bounced around, light on its landing gear. In the magnified image offered by the scope, the plane jittered left, right, up, and down. As she worked to center the crosshairs on the nose, she hoped the .30-06 rounds were loaded with heavy bullets and not varmint loads. The latter were designed to fragment quickly on small animals, rather than to hold together and penetrate deeply. If she was really lucky, she'd be firing 180 grain jacketed bullets into the engine. At fifty yards, those rounds would penetrate a half-inch of stainless steel—on an unprotected engine, they'd deliver some serious damage.

As she concentrated on the image in the scope, the fast-approaching plane was close enough that she could discern Sacheen's face. She focused on her eyes, and it seemed Sacheen was staring back. But more likely, she was merely concentrating on keeping the plane pointed straight forward and gaining speed.

When Danya judged the distance to be under two hundred yards, she fired the first shot. Although she was certain she hit the nose of the plane, there was no evidence of a strike. No puff of smoke or sound of the engine faltering. She turned the bolt handle, extracted the spent brass cartridge, and rammed home the next round.

She fired again, continuing to aim for the engine, rather than risk firing at the much smaller pilot. If she missed Sacheen, the bullets would not strike any vital machinery.

The butt stock pressed into her shoulder simultaneous with the report. Rather than wasting time assessing damage, she reloaded and fired again.

The roar of the engine was almost loader than the blast of the rifle. The Mirage was barreling down on her. She saw the cockpit lift slightly, weight being removed from the undercarriage. Any second now, the craft would take to the air. Whether it ran over the top of her body first was anyone's guess.

Down to her last round, she aimed just below the hub of the prop, and fired.

With a woosh and roar, the plane cleared Danya by a few feet. Her clothing was flapping wildly, threatening to be ripped from her body by the hurricane wash of the propeller as the performance aircraft scooted over her and clawed for altitude. She'd dropped the rifle and covered her head—not that it would have made any difference if the wheels were two feet lower.

With the overwhelming fatigue that comes with failure, she rolled over and gazed at the receding plane. As she watched Sacheen angle the aircraft ever higher, her frustration mounted.

And then the plane seemed to level off. Danya blinked, thinking it an optical illusion. She didn't notice the SUV stop off to her side. Flynn hopped out and shaded his eyes. He, too, stared at the aircraft making its escape, the drone of the engine steady, but diminishing in intensity.

While she watched, the plane made a turn to the left, and Danya thought she saw a plume of gray smoke trailing. Seconds later, the engine drone stuttered.

And then the Malibu Mirage dipped, angling toward the desert a few thousand feet below.

By now, Toby had joined Danya.

"I think you hit the engine," she said.

They all watched as the plane continued its descent at an ever-steeper angle.

Sacheen knew she was in a race for her life. Her turn at the end of the runway had been reckless. She was moving too fast and nearly overshot the edge of the prepared surface. If she'd misjudged the turn, the tires would have been stuck in the soft earth for certain.

Her piloting skills prevailed, and she swung the nose around just in time, then throttled up and raced forward, urging more speed from the Lycoming engine. As the plane accelerated, each bump came closer and closer to tossing the aircraft into the air, as if it had been bounced on a trampoline.

Ahead, Danya appeared out of the hangar and positioned herself in the middle of the runway. She saw the rifle Danya was cradling, and cursed for not having rendered the weapon useless. Now, all she could do was hold the yoke firmly and guide the plane straight forward.

The first round struck somewhere in the engine compartment. At first, she wondered why it had hit so low. It wasn't even close to her. Then Sacheen realized that *she* was not the target.

Come on! She encouraged the plane to go faster.

The airspeed indicator showed that she was close to minimum takeoff speed. She resisted the urge to pull back on the yoke, and kept the nose down, concentrating on keeping the plane straight. It was as if she was looking through Danya, rather than at her.

The *ping* of additional rounds hitting metal carried over the roar of the engine, but she ignored them. A quick scan of her instrumentation indicated everything was normal. She pulled back on the yoke, and the nose lifted first. Then the rest of the plane followed. She was airborne.

She kept the engine at full throttle, and the aircraft continued to gain speed, leaving the hangar and dirt runway behind. Images of Leonard flooded her mind. His masculinity. His gentle touch. She longingly recalled their last tender embrace, and how she felt anything was possible when wrapped in his arms.

She steeled herself, forcing back tears, longing for his strength to give her the fortitude she needed to carry through with the mission.

The engine stuttered, drawing her attention back to the cockpit. A quick scan of the instrument panel showed the engine coolant temperature was rising into the red, and the oil pressure was falling quickly. The engine coughed and missed. The plane seemed to buck as engine power alternately fell off, then came back online again, only to fail completely. With a grinding of metal on metal, the engine seized, the result of overheating and loss of lubrication.

She hadn't quite reached three thousand feet. Now, without power, she was forced to glide to a landing. But where? She swiveled her head, but for as far as she could see, the terrain was a mix of hills and valleys dotted with sage brush and rocks. Not good for a landing.

Air drag was reducing her speed, and with it came a reduction in altitude. The ground was approaching quickly. No time to be choosy—not enough speed and altitude to keep flying in hopes of finding a more suitable place to put down. She crossed a hill, barely clearing the top, and turned the yoke to line up with the valley and avoid flying into the side of the next rise.

Her thoughts turned to her unborn child. She knew the date that the conception had occurred, two months earlier. She could almost feel Leonard's strong but soothing caress again. His musky scent seemed to pervade the cockpit. Time seemed to slow—a gift—as once more she placed her hand on her belly, certain she could feel the tiny fetus growing inside her. In only moments, two lives would be lost. One guilty of the most horrible of crimes, while the other was perfectly innocent. Polar opposites—yin and yang.

With that realization, Sacheen wished she could turn back time and choose a different path. Now, all she wanted was to give life to her child, to hold and nurture the newborn. It was a vain wish, one born of desperation and regret.

As tears ran down her cheeks, she gripped the yoke and flared, trying to soften the landing. Maybe, with luck she didn't deserve, she could still live and become the mother she so desperately yearned to be.

The wheels hit harder than she'd wanted. Following a brief bounce, the Mirage was still speeding forward. A waste-high clump of sage took out the front landing gear, and the nose slammed down. The propeller and front of the aircraft dug into the soft dirt, while momentum flipped the tail of the aircraft over. The fuselage slid forward until a wing tip also snagged on the ground. With a terrifying rent of metal, the wing snapped off.

High-octane aviation fuel dripped from a ruptured fuel line onto the hot exhaust manifold, creating an invisible cloud of flammable vapors. A spark ignited those vapors even before the wreckage stopped moving, and a fireball engulfed the cockpit.

Sacheen never felt the flesh burn from her bones. She was already dead from head trauma, the result of the initial impact. In her final thoughts, she pictured being held in Leonard's arms while she nursed a swaddled infant.

CHAPTER 35

BLACK SMOKE BILLOWED into the clear sky, marking the crash location.

Flynn frowned. He'd wanted to capture and question Sacheen, not kill her.

"One of you two had better fill me in. Attack on what city? And how?"

Danya opened her mouth to speak, but Toby cut her off.

"I overheard them—Sacheen and Leonard. After he hit you." She told Flynn the details of their plan to dust the Las Vegas Strip with radioactive powder.

Flynn said, "Mary, mother of Jesus. If that was for real, we just avoided a major disaster."

"Twice in two days," Danya said.

"Yeah, well, my office is going to be buried in paperwork for weeks. I have to get agents in here ASAP. If there's dangerous material at that crash site, we've got to get it secured." He looked at Danya. "Don't suppose you have a cell phone? Mine and hers," he indicated Toby, "were on that plane."

"Nope. Confiscated when Leonard's men picked me up."

Flynn nodded. "There's a radio in one of those pickups." He pointed over his shoulder, where two other vehicles were parked beside the hangar. "I'll see if I can raise some help."

He trotted off, leaving Danya and Toby in the middle of the dirt runway.

After a long silence, Toby said, "I thought we were dead. Why didn't she kill us back there, in the hangar?"

"I don't know. Maybe she finally realized it was wrong."

"Really? That simple?"

Danya shrugged. "It was for me."

"What now?"

"I'm going back to Sheep Creek Reservoir. That's where I left my truck. Then I'm going to do what I always do."

Toby cocked her head. "What do you mean?"

"I have this thing with government officials. Especially law enforcement. I avoid them. It's better for everyone that way."

"Will I see you again?"

"I don't think so, Toby." Danya's face reflected the sadness she felt.

Being on the run carried many burdens, including not having regular contact with friends and family.

"I'll retrieve my trailer from your barn before you get home. The FBI will take you to their office in Reno or Las Vegas, for questioning. Do you have money to get home after they're done?"

Toby nodded. "Still have most of the cash you gave me. It's enough for a bus ticket."

Danya turned and took a step toward the SUV, but stopped midstride when Toby said, "Thank you."

Danya looked over her shoulder and nodded.

"Sure thing." She turned fully and squared her shoulders to her friend. "You opened my eyes to an injustice I never thought could exist in this country. Not at this time. Take care of yourself, okay?"

In silence, she strode to the Ford Explorer and plopped behind the wheel. She was fairly certain she could navigate back to the lake. Worst case, she'd find her way back to Owyhee and…

"Crap. Where the hell did he put the keys?"

"You looking for these?" Flynn held a set of keys at eye level, and had a pistol in his other hand. "No one is going anywhere."

Danya sighed. "Where'd you get the gun?"

"Under the seat in the pickup. Found it when I sent out an emergency call on the citizen's band radio. And before you go getting any crazy ideas, I want you to know it's loaded. One in the chamber, and a full magazine. I've been in the Bureau for almost thirty years, and I didn't get this far by being stupid."

"The thought never crossed my mind."

"Uh-huh. Anyway, good news. That airplane that crashed had a GPS tracking device. Standard precaution against theft. Suspected as much when Sacheen and Leonard stole it. To tell you the truth, I was surprised they didn't think to disable it."

"Lucky for us," Danya said.

"Anyway, a team from the FBI office in Las Vegas is already en route, and should be here in a few minutes. Would've been here sooner, but it took some time for the plane theft report to work through the bureaucracy."

Toby had come forward, uncertain why the FBI agent seemed to be threatening Danya.

"What does any of that have to do with us?" she said.

"For starters, I need statements from both of you."

"Sure. No problem," Toby replied.

"I'm happy to comply as well. But I'd like to retrieve my truck before someone vandalizes or steals it. You know, we," Danya pointed between Toby and herself, "were both victims here. I was kidnapped this morning by men working for Sacheen and Leonard."

"That's a good point," Flynn said. "Where is Leonard?"

Danya rolled her eyes, sensing where this was going.

"He's, um…he's at his house. Dead."

She noticed Flynn's grip tighten on the pistol, and he edged back a half-step, opening up more space between the two of them. A wise defensive move.

As the tension escalated, the sound of helicopter rotors beating the dry air drew everyone's attention. The helicopter cut a tight circle around the hangar and then settled down in the middle of the runway. The rotor wash bathed Toby, Flynn, and Danya in dust and grit.

Four men sporting aviator sunglasses disembarked as the

engine spun down. They spread apart, each armed with an M4 Carbine, and approached the trio. In Toby's opinion, they could have been extras from *The Matrix* trilogy. Except, instead of being clad in ankle-length leather dusters, they were wearing dark-blue nylon windbreakers emblazoned with the letters FBI—just like the one Flynn was wearing.

"Hands up!" the nearest shouted. "Drop the weapon."

They all complied. Flynn tossed the pistol to the side and then shouted back to be heard over the idling helicopter.

"My name is Andrew Flynn. Special agent in charge out of the San Francisco office. It was my team that tipped you off on the stolen Malibu Mirage."

"Got any ID?"

"Inside my jacket." He kept his hands elevated.

Staring into the business end of the military rifles was unnerving, to say the least.

"Left hand. Nice and slow. Take it out and toss it over here."

Flynn followed the directions with meticulous care, and plopped the leather ID wallet in the dirt only a couple feet from the lead agent, who reached down and retrieved the wallet without lowering his weapon.

After examination, he said to Flynn, "Sorry, sir. I'm agent Harrison." He extended the ID in his free hand.

Flynn lowered his hands and approached the agent. Toby and Danya interpreted the greeting as a thawing of tension, and lowered their hands, too, but remained in place. The other three FBI men kept their guns trained on the women.

"I don't think there are any more threats here," Flynn said to Harrison. "We need an army of technicians to scour this site for evidence. And a hazmat team out at the crash site. Probable radioactive material. Make sure they know so they take the proper precautions in securing the site once the fire is out."

Harrison turned. "Did you get that, Davidson? You'll need to call it in from the radio. No cell coverage here. While you're at it, you and Kolinsky have the pilot fly out to the wreckage. Do a few circles and report on the situation. Especially if you see any survivors." Then he turned back to the SAC. "How many were on that plane?"

"Only one. A woman. Sacheen Crow Dog. She was one of the leaders of the terrorist group that took over Alcatraz yesterday."

Davidson and Kolinsky had climbed aboard the helicopter. As the engine powered up, Harrison issued another order.

"Sweeny. Check out the hangar, just in case the SAC missed any threats." Harrison returned a lopsided smirk to Flynn.

Flynn ignored the good-natured jab. He was relieved to still be alive, and free of his captors. He'd been involved in several kidnapping cases during his multi-decade career with the Bureau. The victim was usually a child or a young woman. Less than half of those cases had a positive outcome. He'd always thought he could relate to the relief and joy the victims experienced upon being rescued. Only now did he truly understand.

"What's the status on Alcatraz?" Flynn said. "I've been cutoff ever since they took me and Toby Riddle."

Harrison looked past the SAC, to the vehicle.

"Which one is Riddle?"

"I am." Toby raised her hand, earning a nod from the FBI agent.

He returned his attention to the senior agent.

"You missed the good news, then. Two hundred and seven civilians rescued. Only one was killed—an elderly woman. Shot by the terrorists. After you and Miss Riddle were taken away in the helicopter, someone cleaned house. The Coast Guard went in first, ready to kick some serious ass. But all the terrorists were dead. Don't know who the shooter was, but some of the hostages reported it was a woman. Can you believe that? I mean, a woman? Really?"

"Yeah, I believe it. If I'm not mistaken, she's sitting over there." Flynn pointed toward the Explorer.

"Are you shitting me?"

"Nope. We've got a lot of work to do, Agent Harrison. You've got two witnesses here to get statements from—"

"Hangar is clear," Sweeny called from the open hangar door. "Got a lot of bodies, though. Some of it's pretty messy. Like a goddam butcher's shop."

Danya knew that every minute she remained here was placing her freedom at ever greater risk. If she allowed herself to be taken in for questioning, they'd surely figure out she was wanted on suspicion of terrorism, and murder of an Oregon State Police officer.

She leaned out the open driver's door. "Hey, guys. If it's all the same to you, I'd really like to go get my truck."

Flynn's professional instincts told him there was something peculiar about this woman. *Ex-military?*

"Not so fast." He closed the distance to the SUV, picking up the pistol he'd tossed on the ground.

He shoved it in his pocket, the weight causing the jacket to hang unevenly off his shoulders.

Good. Keep coming closer. Danya was betting that the years he'd spent in an office had dulled his reflexes.

Flynn stopped a few feet from the open door, looking down at Danya.

"I suppose I should thank you for saving me and your friend. And for shooting down the airplane. You know, I didn't get your name."

"That's because I didn't give it to you." She stepped out of the vehicle.

Although he hadn't worked field operations in years, the SAC's brain was still sharp. As she squared off before him, the alarms began blaring in his head. He placed a hand in the pocket with the gun.

She was the same height as Flynn, but he outweighed her by at least eighty pounds, giving rise to a false sense of confidence. His hubris turned out to be his downfall. It was too late when he saw the punch coming.

A fist caught him at the base of his throat. Not wanting to kill him, she had checked her swing at the last millisecond to avoid crushing his windpipe.

His eyes bulged, and he threw a hand to his neck as he gasped for air. His mouth was open and his chest heaving, reminiscent of a fish out of water, struggling to breathe.

She grabbed his collar and yanked him closer, even as Harrison and Sweeny raised their M4 Carbines. With Flynn's pudgy bulk as a shield, she spun him around so he was facing Harrison. Then she reached into his jacket and extracted the pistol to jam the barrel into his back. In the other pocket, she found the keys.

"You." She locked her gaze with Harrison's. "Throw the rifle to the side. Tell your partner to do the same."

At first, neither Harrison nor Sweeny retreated, opting to keep their weapons trained on Danya. This necessarily meant they were also aiming at SAC Andrew Flynn. The only shot either agent could make would have to be through the senior agent.

"Tell them to stand down, or I'll blow your spine in half."

"If you kill me, they kill you."

Toby was standing to the side, clear of impending gunfire, but she didn't retreat.

"No!" she yelled. "Please. Stop!"

Danya said, "No one else needs to die. We can both walk away. Now tell your men to stand down."

After a moment of hesitation, Flynn nodded toward Harrison.

"Do it," he said.

Harrison and Sweeny tossed their carbines aside and raised their hands.

"Now the sidearms," she said.

Flynn nodded again, and both agents obliged the order.

"Tell your men to stay where they are and keep their hands up. I'm going to drive away, and no one gets hurt." She leaned in close to Flynn's ear, her raspy voice a menacing whisper. "You've seen my abilities. Trust me, you don't want to engage me. You'll lose. Am I clear?"

He nodded.

After releasing her human shield, she got behind the wheel, cranked over the engine, and gunned the accelerator. The four wheels spun, throwing back volumes of gravel and dirt. She cranked the wheel and pointed the vehicle away from the hangar, expecting to receive a barrage of bullets.

Harrison was the first to his weapon. He shouldered the carbine and snapped off a shot without taking the time to properly aim. The bullet went wide.

Toby screamed. "No!"

She threw herself in the line of fire, forcing Harrison to jerk the rifle to the side. His second shot also missed.

Sweeny had joined the fight, and given his angle, he had an unobstructed line of sight on the speeding SUV. He squeezed off shot after shot after shot. Bullets riddled the Explorer, but all impacted just behind the driver.

"Cease fire, dammit! Cease fire." Flynn waved his arms frantically.

Toby was on her knees, a hand over her mouth, sobbing.

Sweeny fired twice more before the order registered in his mind. The Ford swerved following the last shot, then straightened and raced out of sight.

Biting back his anger, Harrison said, "We could've had her. Why'd you let her go?"

Flynn shook his head. "I didn't let anyone go."

"What do you call what just happened! Sir."

Toby still had her face buried in her hands, and Flynn helped her to her feet.

"It's okay," he said, his voice soothing.

She opened her eyes, gazing at the dissipating dust cloud. The SUV was gone.

"She made it?"

Flynn nodded. "Yeah, I suspect she made it just fine." Then he faced Harrison. "In case you haven't figured it out yet, *Agent* Harrison, that woman saved my life today, and the life of Miss Riddle. She stopped a likely terrorist attack that, if successful, would have made nine-eleven look like an opening act. And furthermore, when the forensics is completed on Alcatraz, I strongly believe we will know that she singlehandedly thwarted the threatened attack on the San Francisco Bay Area, and saved more than two hundred hostages."

"With all due respect, sir—"

"Save it," Flynn said. "Inside the hangar, you'll find her prints on several weapons. The techs may be lucky enough to extract viable DNA as well. The Bureau will find her."

EPILOGUE

BY THE TIME DANYA MADE IT BACK TO HER TRUCK, her shirt was soaked in blood. The bullet had grazed her right side after running the entire length of the Ford Explorer—passing first through the tailgate, then two seat backs, and finally the dash.

Her spare key was still secure under the rear wheel well. Fortunately, no one had vandalized her pickup. Even the MP5 submachine gun was still in the cab of the truck, exactly where she'd left it.

She retrieved the first aid kit from behind the seat. It contained adequate sterile gauze bandages, tape, and antibiotic to dress the wound. Even more important was the QuikClot® powder, which she applied to staunch the bleeding.

She removed her blood-soaked top and put on a clean sweatshirt fished out of the small duffle bag she'd prepared for what she expected to be a two- or three-day trip with Toby. Next, from beneath the seat, she removed a military surplus bayonet originally made to fit the first-generation M16. It was a thick blade that came to a spear-like point.

With the bloody shirt in one hand, and knife in the other, she returned to the Ford SUV and punctured the gas tank with three thrusts of the bayonet. Gasoline poured out onto the parched dirt. She captured enough of it on the soiled shirt to saturate it, then placed it over her blood stains on the seat. She tossed a lit match into the cab, and a second one onto the expanding pool of gas beneath the Ford. The expanding fire quickly engulfed the vehicle, ensuring there would be no fingerprints or DNA to be recovered by forensics.

By the time the FBI helicopter returned to the dirt airstrip, and Flynn conferred with the pilot and the rest of the team, she was several miles from the burning vehicle. She cruised back through Owyhee, and on to Elko, where she stopped to top up with fuel and fill up on fast food. She made good time on her drive back to Toby's home near Hatfield, on the Oregon-California border, and arrived late at night. After dousing the headlights so as not to startle Toby's mother if she was home, Danya drove into the barn and hitched up her trailer. A quick check indicated that her possessions—including many firearms—had not been touched.

She opened a safe hidden inside the trailer beneath a floor panel. Inside was the cash she'd taken from the gun deal in Idaho. She removed a dozen bundles of hundred-dollar bills, $120,000 in total, which she stacked inside a brown paper bag as if she were packing groceries. Using a black felt-tip marker, she wrote a note to Toby on the Kraft paper.

> Channel your drive and passion. You have the ability, intelligence, and charisma to advance the cause for Native American rights. Maybe this will help.
> —D

After locking the trailer door, she placed the bag on the gravel floor of the barn and settled behind the steering wheel of her red pickup. Once she left the driveway, she pulled to the side of the rural road, next to the mailboxes, where she jotted down Toby's address, planning to send a postcard every now and then.

She drove north for a couple hours, until she found a secluded and unmarked dirt road not far from the Steens Mountains. It was about a mile to the end of the road, and that's where she parked on a level plot of ground. Overcome with exhaustion, and feeling the effects of the bullet graze to her side, she decided not to prepare a cooked meal. Instead, she popped some more ibuprofen and antibiotic, changed her dressing, and climbed into bed. With shotgun and pistol within easy reach, she fell asleep.

In the morning, over a cup of coffee, or maybe two, she'd decide where to go.

Hundreds of miles to the south, two FBI offices were working overtime to process four crime scenes—three on the Duck Valley Reservation, and one on the entire island of Alcatraz.

The San Francisco FBI office, under the direction of Special Agent in Charge Andrew Flynn, ordered Alcatraz closed for weeks, while they completed their investigation. A mountain of evidence was collected, labeled, and cataloged.

It took several days to repair the gift shop, where much of the fighting had occurred. And the park service did their best to spot and fill the hundreds of bullet holes. But a few would escape discovery and become the focus of gawking visitors when the former prison was reopened for tours.

At the same time, the Las Vegas office was doing similar work on the Duck Valley Reservation. Officially, they were treating three locations as crime scenes—Leonard's house, the hangar, and the plane crash site. They also investigated the burned-out Ford Explorer on the shore of Sheep Creek Reservoir. The tribal police had received a report of the abandoned and burned vehicle three days after Danya had fled. It had taken another four days for the report to reach the right person within the FBI's Las Vegas office. It was easy to connect the dots—SUV with bullet holes certainly pointed to this being the escape vehicle. But without any useful forensics concerning the driver, this thread was soon dropped.

The hazmat crew arrived by helicopter shortly after the fire had consumed every flammable material on the crashed Malibu Mirage. Not surprisingly, the aircraft was a total loss. No less than six lead-lined metal boxes were recovered, thrown free of the cabin. Fortunately, none had split open on impact. Dressed in protective suits, the hazmat team secured the deadly cargo in additional radiation shielding. Only then were they transported away by helicopter.

Later analysis would reveal that the boxes contained enough enriched strontium-90 and cobalt-60, in the form of fine oxide powder, to have contaminated downtown Las Vegas for at least a century. Privately, the FBI breathed a sigh of relief, knowing how close they'd come to a disaster of unprecedented impact on property and lives. No one understood this better than Flynn, who buried the evidence on the mysterious woman, his savior, and reduced the priority of investigating her to close to zero. The more he wondered who she was, the more he began to suspect that she played on both sides of the law. At least this time, she had been playing for the right team.

After a day of questioning by the FBI, the trip home for Toby was long—a bus to Klamath Falls, where her aunt picked her up and drove her home to Hatfield. She'd hoped Danya's trailer would still be parked in the barn, but knew that was wishful thinking. Still, the first thing she did was to check the barn. She found it empty, except for a brown paper bag.

The long trip home from the FBI office in Las Vegas gave Toby ample time to think and reflect on what had happened, her life in general, and what she wanted to do with her future. She returned with a new purpose. Her conversations with Leonard Cloud and Sacheen Crow Dog, despite their violent intentions, had fueled her interest in activism for the rights of all indigenous people. She took heart in the minor concessions coming from a few state governments to rename Columbus Day to Indigenous Peoples' Day. She told herself that it demonstrated a growing recognition of, and willingness to right, past wrongs. A small step forward. But a step, nonetheless.

And as odd as it seemed to Toby, the news that had followed the story of the Alcatraz takeover, and of the life-and-death struggle on the Duck Valley Reservation, had added considerably to public awareness of the plight of the nations. Especially the story of Sacheen and Leonard, and their doomed love affair, which captivated the media and public attention. For weeks, the story dominated the twenty-four-hour news channels, with the reporters always citing unnamed sources when mentioning the unborn child that had perished with Sacheen.

Toby suspected the fire that had engulfed the plane wreckage must have cremated Sacheen and her fetus, which meant no one in the FBI would have known she was pregnant. She concluded the unnamed source was Danya, but it was only an educated guess. And if it was Danya, Toby could only speculate as to why her mysterious friend would risk contacting the media. *Maybe she's trying to help raise awareness of our plight, and the desperate measures some members of the tribes are driven to undertake*?

The next morning, Toby called Clyde Means. It hadn't been too difficult to track down his phone number. After twenty minutes of conversation, mostly about the American Indian Movement, she volunteered to work for the cause. The money she'd received from Danya allowed her to quit her job at the gas station and split her time between caring for her mother and advocating for compensation from the federal government for the dozens of broken treaties.

For the first time, Toby felt she was doing something meaningful, and she learned how to effectively deal with lawmakers and their staffers, who often couldn't care less about the rights of American Indians. Toby used the news media—which appeared ever-eager to fan the smoldering flames of bigotry and discrimination—to her advantage, appearing often on radio and television. Within months, she'd become a national celebrity who was being sought for speaking engagements at a range of public and private events.

Donations to the American Indian Movement surged. The once all-volunteer organization had the means to hire a professional PR firm and rent a modest office space. The publicity elevated national awareness of the injustice indigenous people had been suffering since the arrival of European settlers. Politicians were reaching out to Toby for input on drafting new legislation that would include reparations, and return of some tribal lands.

"It's just the beginning," Toby had told her mother. "I hope and dream we can finally see this through."

"You can't trust the government," her mother had replied. "You should know that from history."

Toby smiled. "As a wise friend once told me, it doesn't have to be that way forever. History cannot be changed. But together, we can change the future."

AUTHOR'S POSTSCRIPT

IN THE AUTHOR'S NOTES AT THE BEGINNING of this work, I addressed much of the technical background underpinning the plot. Another facet of the story that deserves serious treatment relates to the American Indian Movement, and the historical notes from the 60s and 70s, when Native Americans were protesting for recognition of their civil rights.

For most of my life, I've held an intense interest in American Indian culture and history, which is grim indeed. Partly by design, ever since the landing of Europeans in the Americas, disease and warfare have claimed an untallied number of Indigenous Peoples' lives. The original inhabitants of the Americas lacked antibodies to many deadly diseases, including smallpox, influenza, measles, and typhoid fever, leading to catastrophic epidemics.

According to Guenter Lewy, writing in History News Network (Columbian College of Arts and Sciences, The George Washington University), there were an estimated twelve million indigenous people occupying North America in 1500, and only 237,000 by the end of the nineteenth century.[1]

Relations between native tribes of North America, and the invading colonial powers, is marked by a string of broken

1 Guenter, Lewy, "Were American Indians the Victims of Genocide?", History News Network, September 2004, https://historynewsnetwork.org/article/7302.

treaties. Following independence from England, the United States government continued this practice. The result was that the native people were constantly being forced off their land and onto reservations.

President Andrew Jackson's Indian Removal Policy opened the South for American settlers to take land belonging to five tribes. The policy was the beginning of three decades of forceful evictions of Native Americans westward, beyond the Mississippi River.[2] In 1838, more than fifteen thousand Cherokee were compelled to march the Trail of Tears, to present-day Oklahoma. Nearly four thousand perished under the brutal conditions of the forced march.

During the second term of Ulysses S. Grant, his peace policy with the indigenous tribes was abandoned when settlers, seeking gold, began to covet the Black Hills. Grant secretly precipitated war with the Sioux, in violation of the Treaty of 1868, which granted the Black Hills to the Sioux people in perpetuity.

Gold also sparked another disgraceful chapter in American history, this time in California. In the twenty years following California's admission into the Union, 80 percent of the state's indigenous population was wiped out in what has been called California's little-known genocide.[3] During the first session of the state legislature, laws were passed, allowing whites to enslave indigenous children. Backed by the power of the legislature, Peter Hardeman Burnett, first governor of California, began to arm militias and citizens alike, and pay a bounty for scalps. It was the beginning of more than two decades of terror, the goal of which was the extermination of California's native inhabitants.

The latter half of the nineteenth century was marked by numerous massacres of Native Americans, usually women,

---

2 Robert McNamara, "Indian Removal and the Trail of Tears", Thought Company, December 12, 2019, https://www.thoughtco.com/the-trail-of-tears-1773597.

3 Erin Blakemore, "California's Little-Known Genocide," History Stories, first published November 16, 2017, updated July 1, 2019, https://www.history.com/news/californias-little-known-genocide.

children, and elderly. The last major defeat of Native Americans in armed conflict occurred in 1890, at the Battle of Wounded Knee. Far from a battle, it was another massacre of unarmed women, children, and elders.

The American Indian Movement (AIM) is factually accurate as portrayed in this story, as is the history of the Modoc War, which straddled President Grant's first and second terms. I find it remarkable that so little is heard of the AIM these days.

Two of our bank notes carry the portraits of Grant and Jackson, both notorious for deceitful and treacherous treatment of American Indians. And then there is Mount Rushmore. Construction began in 1927, on sacred land illegally taken from the Lakota Sioux. Carved into the granite are the sculptures of four white presidents of the United States, a government with a notorious history of breaking treaties with the native tribes, forcibly evicting them onto reservations. Such a monument could not be more insulting and hurtful to all Native Americans.

We would do well as a nation to reflect on our treatment of the American Indian Nations, and seek to right our historical wrongs.

—DE

ABOUT THE AUTHOR

DAVE EDLUND IS THE USA TODAY BESTSELLING author of the award-winning *Peter Savage* novels, and a graduate of the University of Oregon, with a doctoral degree in chemistry. He resides in Bend, Oregon, with his wife, son, and three dogs—Lucy Liu, Dude, and Tenshi.

Raised in the California Central Valley, Dave completed his undergraduate studies at California State University, Sacramento. In addition to authoring several technical articles and books on alternative energy, he is an inventor on 114 US patents.

An avid outdoorsman and shooter, Edlund has hunted North America for big game, ranging from wild boar to moose to bear. He has traveled extensively throughout China, Japan, Europe, and North America.

www.PeterSavageNovels.com

THE PETER SAVAGE SERIES

BY DAVE EDLUND

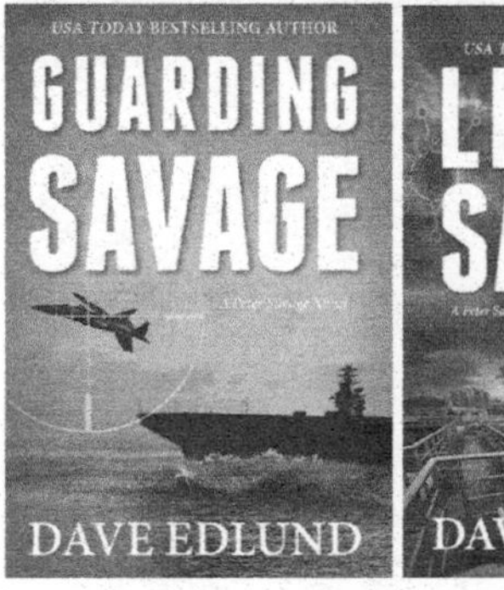